The Elevator

by

David E. Burnell

RoseDog ❧ Books

PITTSBURGH, PENNSYLVANIA 15222

For information or to order additional books, please write:
RoseDog Books
701 Smithfield Street, Third Floor
Pittsburgh, Pennsylvania 15222
U.S.A.
1-800-834-1803

Or visit our website and online catalogue at www.rosedogbookstore.com

For my loving wife, Pamela.
And with grateful acknowledgement
to our dear sister-in-law, Marion,
who helped so much with my first
writing venture.

Prologue

My name is Robert McLeod and if you are reading this, then I am dead. I am, or was, the President and Chief Executive Officer of McLeod, Gilbert Systems Ltd., which I can say without boast is the largest plant systems and production software company in the world. James Gilbert and I started the company in the mid sixties. He did the selling and I wrote the software. In 1971, when my story starts, we were very small, less than two-dozen employees, but we were becoming noticed. Our systems were already firmly established in a few of the larger plants in North America, and their production efficiency had jumped beyond all expectations. Foreign companies were becoming interested and suddenly Gilbert and I had to go to West Germany.

My story starts on that trip to West Germany. The story never came out in the press, not fully anyhow. It was covered up. Almost all affected by it are dead, so publishing it did not seem important at the time. I am a computer systems analyst by trade and my whole working life has been based on math and cold logic, one and one make two and nothing else. Therefore, I am not given to flights of fancy. But I witnessed events and happenings in Germany that were beyond my comprehension, events that did not just give me a belief in a life after death, but rather a sure and certain knowledge of it. I want the story to be told because it happened, but I have a position to uphold in my business and social life, and that is why I prefer not to publish the story while I am still living.

I did not choose to become a part of this story, and as must be apparent to the reader, I survived the events in this book. I look back now and wonder at the workings beyond the grave, and as you are reading this, then I have, in all probability, discovered them for myself.

Robert McLeod, August, 1993

Publisher's note: Robert McLeod passed away in his sleep on the 12th of October, 1998.

Chapter 1

They showed me into a small office somewhere on the second floor of the Israeli Consulate in Bonn. The man behind the desk stood up as I entered and held out his hand in greeting, though he did not smile. A print of Rembrandt's *Moses Smashing the Ten Commandments* hung on the wall behind his desk, and I caught sight of my reflection in the glass as I crossed the office. No wonder he did not smile. I looked worse than a tramp. My badly bruised face, my disheveled hair, my filthy suit with the torn and blood stained trousers did nothing to enhance my appearance. I shook his hand and he motioned me to sit in the chair in front of his desk. He was not a tall man, probably almost five feet ten inches, and his dark hair cut short and parted to one side, a neat, precise man, a man of total contrast to how I looked and felt at that moment. His eyes were deep blue and he looked at me questioningly. "My name is Karl Levin. How can I be of service?"

Another man sat in an easy chair in the corner of the room, a much older man, wearing a rumpled, navy blue suit. His hands rested in his lap while he watched me through wire frame spectacles. I could not see his features clearly as the overhead light shone directly above the desk, leaving the rest of the room in shadow. I did not like speaking in front of the stranger and it showed.

Levin, noting my hesitation, said, "Anything you say in this room will remain in the strictest confidence." But he did not introduce the other man.

The room seemed intolerably hot, the windows being closed. I wondered if that was deliberate to make me feel uncomfortable. It must have been after eight in the evening, for it was getting dark outside. I did not know the time for sure as my watch had been ripped from my wrist. To add to my discomfort, I stank. The heat of the room and my own nervous sweat made it worse, but I could smell the stale urine and the vomit emanating from my suit.

The stranger made me even more uncomfortable. Could he have been from the German police? They must be looking for me everywhere. Perhaps he would

1

listen to what I had to say then arrest me for murder. I started to babble somewhat nervously. "I am a Canadian citizen and partner in a computer software development company. Our business has been quite successful. Our sales this past year have exceeded twenty five million US dollars. So you see I am not the type to make up strange stories, or hand out false accusations."

Levin, if that really was his name, looked impatient. "We know who you are, Mr. McLeod. Perhaps if you start from the beginning."

The beginning? That was more than thirty years ago? No. That was not where I entered the story.

"We, that is my company, McLeod Gilbert Production Systems, have developed a computer software that is revolutionizing the manufacturing industry. Fundamentally, the system handles parts ordering, inventory control, that sort of thing." I realized I sounded as if I was launching into a sales pitch, but I had to start somewhere.

Levin nodded. He looked bored.

"Well," I continued, "After a good start in North America, we began to get inquiries from Europe. One of those inquiries came from Mannhauser, here in Germany. As you know, Mannhauser is a huge company and the possibility of selling our software to them was extremely attractive. An order for their German operation alone would be many millions of dollars, and if they were to decide to equip world wide, our fortunes would be made. So important then was this enquiry from Mannhauser, that both James Gilbert, my partner, and I decided to come to their headquarters in Munich and try and make the sale. We received the initial contact in December of last year, 1970, and we arrived in Munich on Sunday January 10th, just six months ago."

.   .   .   .   .

Quite arbitrarily, or by some strange twist of fate that would defy the imagination, we selected to stay in the Marrianne Hotel. The Marrianne is not a large or fancy hotel by any means, but rather one of the older buildings in town, a square block, four floors tall, squeezed in between two larger buildings. The hotel is centrally located, not far from downtown, near the Marien Platz. Gilbert and I had a room each on the fourth floor. Again, as fate would have it, I drew room number 405

The Mannhauser plant and head office are located to the north of the city, by the Olympic Stadium, about fifteen to twenty minutes drive from downtown. Gilbert arranged a car, for we needed to be at the plant before nine on the Monday morning, as a meeting was set up in one of their conference rooms.

Mannhauser considered the meeting so important that it was to be chaired by the Company Secretary and Director of Manufacturing, Rudolph Kruger, the second most powerful man in the Mannhauser organization. The meeting went well. Kruger was interested in the concepts we explained. Apparently, it was Kruger who had read about the installation of our software in North America, and he was enthusiastic to have it installed in a pilot plant in Germany.

Both Gilbert and I were jubilant when we returned to the hotel that night. It looked as if we had the contract in the bag. We were sure that once they had our software in a pilot plant, they would want it throughout their organization. We had supper in the hotel, and I, still suffering jet lag from the flight of the previous day, went to bed early, leaving Gilbert to his own devices. I needed to be on good form the next day as we were to demonstrate the software to the top executives of Mannhauser.

I went to sleep more or less as soon as my head touched the pillow, but by midnight any semblance of sleep had left me and I lay wide awake. I suppose I had been thinking about how to clinch the deal, what incentives we could offer them, but suddenly sleep was very far away. I got out of bed and dressed. The bar downstairs would still be open, and perhaps a nightcap would help me get back to sleep.

With my hair tussled, and my shirt and trousers pulled on roughly, I made my way down the short passageway to the elevator. Imagination can be a strange thing; the feeling of being watched followed me down the silent corridor. I turned quickly, but, in spite of my feelings, I was quite alone; the passageway lay silent and empty. I pressed the button and waited for the car to come up from the ground floor. The elevator, though in good working condition, was old and not very fast. Eventually, the car arrived, and I opened the two gates and entered a small, gilded cage, made of something like wrought iron, with about enough room for six persons standing shoulder to shoulder. After pressing the button for the ground floor, I waited while the relays clicked that would make the circuit to start the car downward through the shaft.

The cables and machinery creaked as the car moved downward, and I suppose I listened for the sake of having nothing else to listen to. The creaking of the wire seemed to become more of a singing noise as the car moved nearer to the bottom; and then, even above the noise of the cable, I heard another sound, a strange, almost human sound, the sound of people crying, screaming even. But though it grew louder as I drew nearer the ground floor, it remained very faint.

Obviously, the antiquated machinery must have made the sounds that I had heard, but all the same, when I alighted from the car, a strange feeling hovered in the pit of my stomach. One or two couples were still drinking and I sat on a stool at the bar and ordered a whiskey and soda. "What time do you close?" I asked conversationally.

The barman, an older man with thinning hair, graying around the temples, and dressed smartly in the uniform of the hotel, spoke almost perfect English. "One o'clock, sir."

I glanced at my watch. Twelve forty. "Don't worry. I won't keep you up."

He returned my smile. "That's all right, sir. If you don't, it will be someone else."

I nodded towards the elevator. "Creaks a bit. Is it safe?"

"Oh, quite safe, sir." He looked surprise that I should ask. "It is inspected regularly by the authorities."

I shook my head. "Only asking. How old is it, anyway?"

"I suppose it must be around twenty years now. They put it in just after the war."

Surprise showed on my face. "I thought it much older than that. It certainly sounds much older."

His interest seemed to be waning, so I pointed to my whiskey. "Can I buy you a drink?"

"Indeed, sir. That is very kind of you."

While he poured himself a whiskey, I pondered my recent ride in the elevator. For what ever reason good or bad, my interest had been piqued and I felt a need to know more about the hotel. "What about the building? How old is that?"

"That's a difficult one, sir. The hotel as it stands, dates from the late forties. But there was a hotel here before that. The original was bombed, but not as badly as many of the other buildings around here. I believe they re-built the building using much of the existing structure. Many of the furniture and fittings are from the original hotel."

I thought back to my room. "There is a picture hanging in my room, by the door, an old photograph of Munich Town hall, the Rathaus. I guess that is from the original building?"

"Undoubtedly, sir. There are many such pictures in the hotel."

"Was Munich badly bombed?"

The barman sighed. "What kind of bombing isn't bad?"

I was about to interject, but he went on, "Munich was virtually destroyed. However, we, that is, the people of Munich, decided to re-build the city as it was before the war. We tried to preserve the city. It is part of our heritage."

My mind wandered - part of a darker heritage: Munich being synonymous with the rise of the Nazis.

"Munich is the capitol of Bavaria," he went on as if reading my mind. "There is much history here. Much happened before the Nazis came."

I may have been smarting from his quick retort to my bombing remark, so I think I pushed him too far. "Wasn't the Brown House located here, the original headquarters of Hitler's Nazis?"

"Yes," he said quietly. "I think it may have been."

He took his drink and went to the other end of the bar to clean some glasses. I sipped my whiskey and glanced around. There were two couples and both were in deep and private conversation, and certainly not needing my company. I did not know whether I was tired enough to sleep or not, but there was nothing else I could do other than to return to my room. I drank the remains of my drink and turned towards the elevator.

The elevator waited for me, just as I had left it. Nobody else had used it since I came down. I opened the outer door, slid back the gate and stepped inside. The sounds were there again, almost as soon as I pushed the button for the top floor. Above the noise of the cable, I heard the sounds of human screaming, of people cast suddenly into a state of mortal terror. My imagination ran wild for a moment, and it was as if the elevator shaft was a portal to hell, and the sounds of torment were traveling up from the fires below. The sounds grew fainter as I ascended, and

4

by the time I reached my floor, I strained to hear them above the creaking cable. I went back to bed, with sleep still very far away. I lay for what seemed like hours and I began to worry: I had to be on top form in the morning. But every time I laid my head back and closed my eyes, I heard those dreadful distant screams.

I arose soon after dawn, and even after I showered, shaved and changed into fresh clothes, I still felt like hell. A dark veil of tiredness covered eyes, and my head hummed with a dull ache. I must have slept some of the time, for I had the most vivid dream. The dream stayed with me and I remembered it still. I was at a farmhouse in the country. The white stucco walls and bright red tile roof contrasted sharply with the green fields all around. White-railed horse paddocks separated the fields and a long barn stood off to the side of the house. It was nothing out of the ordinary, and yet as I looked upon it, a feeling of dread possessed me. The windows were dark, the house deserted and I felt as if I was looking upon a place of unspeakable evil.

I had arranged to meet Gilbert in the dining room at seven-thirty, and at seven-twenty eight I left my room and walked down the passage to the elevator. The car stood on my floor, seemingly waiting for me. I slowed my pace as I approached. Imagination or not, I did not want to hear those sounds again. At the last minute, I dived through the door and took the emergency stairs. It was all down hill, and four floors wasn't so much. All the same, by the time I reached the ground floor, I could feel it in my hip joints. Gilbert, having arrived before me, had already secured a table for us in the dining room.

"I didn't see you come down in the elevator," he said.

"I used the stairs."

"Why on earth?" He looked at me, the question written all over his face.

"I need the exercise." I patted my spreading waistline.

"You?" he said.

Not feeling in the best of humour, I walked over to a table in the corner of the room and grabbed a couple of bread rolls, some jam and some coffee.

"Continental breakfasts," I muttered to Gilbert upon my return. "Whatever happened to good old bacon, eggs and hash browns?"

"I thought you had a sudden concern over your waist line." He grinned at me.

I didn't dignify his remark with an answer, and started into my bread roll.

"How did you sleep?" he asked.

"Lousy," I said, without looking up. I had a rotten night. What about you?"

"Slept like a top."

Good old Gilbert. Nothing phased him. "You would," I said resentfully.

"Kruger phoned this morning."

I looked up at Gilbert, all interest in my roll forgotten. "He did? What did he want?"

"It seems," said Gilbert, dragging it out because he knew he had my interest, "That the big boss of Mannhauser will be at the demo this morning."

"Big boss?" I said. "Who is he?"

"His name is Fredrick Stanholt. He is getting on a bit, about seventy, I think."

5

"What else do we know about him?" This could be vital. Such a man could make or break the project.

"Not much." Gilbert scratched his earlobe, as I had seen him do before when he was worried. "Only what I was able to get out of Kruger. It seems that Stanholt is a bit of a recluse these days, made a fortune, millions by the sound of it, and now keeps a low profile. But for some reason, he has taken an interest in this project."

"Is that good or bad?" I said.

"Don't know. Only time will tell. But one thing is for sure. Stanholt will be the one we have to convince."

"High pressure day," I said. "You'd better do most of the talking. I'll answer the technical questions, but you give the spiel. I feel like shit."

I did not feel like eating anymore. "Let's go," I said to Gilbert. "We don't want to be late."

I followed Gilbert to the elevator, for we had to return to our rooms for our things. I reluctantly stepped inside, all the time knowing that this would not do. If we were to make this sale, I had to beat whatever was causing this. I clung onto the gate until my knuckles were almost white, sweat beading on my forehead, as Gilbert pressed the button to take us to the top floor. The car began to move. The wire creaked and the old metal work groaned, but there were no underlying human sounds. I looked at Gilbert, my ears and every sense in my body straining to detect anything abnormal.

Gilbert looked at me, a puzzled expression on his face. "It's old, but I think it's safe."

Damn, I thought. He must have seen the concern in my eyes. Concern? No. What he saw was naked fear. I tried to smile and shaking my head, I said, "I must be developing claustrophobia in my old age."

"You've been working too hard," he said. "When we get back to Canada, you'd better take a couple of weeks off."

"Time off? What's that?"

But he had set my mind thinking. Could that be all that was wrong with me? It had been so long since I had taken time off even my children were forgetting what I looked like. I would take him up on it. A vacation would be nice.

After I had retrieved my briefcase from my room, I arrived first at the elevator, but I prudently waited for Gilbert before entering the car. We returned to the ground floor without incident, and by then I was convinced that Gilbert's explanation was the truth. I had been working too hard and it was beginning to affect my nerves.

The demo went off fairly successfully. We had an overhead projector and a computer terminal laid on. With a demonstration package loaded on the computer, I sat at the terminal and pressed the keys to make it happen. Gilbert worked the overhead projector and gave the spiel. Kruger and about half a dozen senior executives of the company were in the room. One man, somewhat older than the rest, sat alone towards the back of the room. I felt sure he was Stanholt, but we were not introduced. He was quite tall, but very thin. He had tight wavy hair that had gone completely white and he wore a black patch over his left eye. Gilbert, too, guessed that this was Stanholt, and centered his sales pitch in his direction. But the man asked no questions; he simply sat in silence watching everything we did and listening to everything we said, until at last the demonstration was over. And then, without saying a word, he rose from his chair and left the room.

The others began to leave and Kruger walked over towards us. "Thank you, Gentlemen. Most impressive."

"Thank you," I said. "What about the chairman of the company?" I nodded towards the door by which the man had left. "Was he impressed?"

Kruger grinned. "Only time will tell. We see him very rarely these days. You should be pleased that he is interested enough in your system to make the effort to come here."

"Doesn't he take much interest in the running of the company now?" asked Gilbert.

Kruger was not a tall man, perhaps 5'-9"and very fit, though his full head of iron gray hair placed his age at somewhere around fifty. His back was ramrod straight and his suits were a perfect fit, obviously made to measure. He was a man that cared about his appearance. "He still holds the purse strings," he said. "Without his signature, your bird won't fly."

I quickly asked Kruger to join us for lunch, being as he was our strongest ally, and I wanted to find out more about Herr Stanholt. He accepted and we were soon seated in one of the fine beer garden restaurants that flourish in Munich.

We each drank a stein of lager and discussed our families and the more subtle differences between Germany and Canada, when I raised the subject of Stanholt. "Your boss didn't ask any questions this morning. If he needs any further information, we are available to meet him anywhere at his convenience."

Kruger grinned. "If he needs you, he will ask."

"What kind of a man is he to work for?" asked Gilbert.

Kruger thought for a moment. "He's tough," he said. "I've known him for a long time. He is a German Jew, you know. Any Jew that survived Germany during the war has to be tough. He spent three years in Dachau."

"Good, God," I breathed. "And he built up Mannhauser from scratch since then?"

Kruger's steely grin became broader and he said, "Get the picture."

"As far as getting our software into Mannhauser's," said Gilbert, changing the subject. "Where do we go from here?"

"There is a meeting of the directors tomorrow," said Kruger. "I will propose that we install the software in a pilot plant. We will discuss it and vote on it. The minutes of that meeting will be sent to Stanholt. He will make the final decision."

"What do you think our chances are?" asked Gilbert.

"Good," replied Kruger. "There is some resistance, but then there is always resistance to change. Some of our quite senior people do not believe in the computer."

"What about us?" I said. "If there is nothing else for us to do, we could return to Vancouver."

"True." Kruger looked doubtful. "But if I were you, I would wait a couple of days. What do you have to lose? Enjoy our beautiful city. You never know. There may be more questions. If you are on hand, they can be answered quickly and easily."

So it was decided: We would wait for the initial reaction from Stanholt before returning home. That would not come for at least three days.

After lunch I didn't see Gilbert again that day. I spent the time buying a few gifts to take home to the family. I had arranged to meet Gilbert for breakfast the next day, and at seven thirty next morning, I made my way again down the emergency stairs. Upon entering the dining room, I saw that Gilbert had company, a blond woman sharing his table. My first thoughts were that Gilbert was up to his old tricks again. It would not be the first time that he had combined business with this sort of pleasure. I would probably be in the way, but after I had collected my continental breakfast from the side table, I would go over and find out what was going on.

As I approached the table, I could see the woman more clearly. With the aid of make-up, she looked about forty, though I would guess she was probably older. Her platinum hair matched her very fair complexion and her slim and striking figure told me that the years had been kind to her. They both looked up as I drew near.

"Mind if I sit down." I smiled dryly at Gilbert.

"Oh, please, don't mind me," she said softly. Her accent told me she was an American.

"Good morning," I said, sitting down.

"Heidi Mortimer meet Bob McLeod. Bob meet Heidi." Gilbert made the introductions.

"Please to meet you," I said doubtfully.

"Likewise." She looked at me strangely. Perhaps my thoughts were becoming transparent since I had been in this place. I sipped my coffee.

"Jim tells me that you are here on business," she said. "Have you ever been to Munich before?"

"No," I replied. "This is the first time I have ever been to Germany."

"What do you think of it?"

I shrugged my shoulders. "Nice place, but I won't be sorry to get back to Canada. I have things to do."

"Busy man. You have to relax sometimes." I wondered for a moment if she was being sarcastic, but I wasn't sure.

"That's what I have been telling him," Gilbert said, before I had a chance to reply. "He should take a vacation when he gets home."

I started into my bread roll, and the table lapsed into a moment of silence. I looked up and they both seemed to be watching me. "Am I holding you up from doing anything?" I said. "Don't wait for me if you want to be off."

"Not me," said Gilbert, shaking his head. "I'm planning to ride the eleven o'clock plane to Frankfurt. I've been talking to a company there. Never know, might be able to stir up a bit more business."

Knowing Gilbert, he probably already had something lined up in Frankfurt, which may or may not have anything to do with business. "Want me along?" I said.

"No, Bob, no. Just trying to make some initial contacts."

Judging by his quick reaction, what he had lined up in Frankfurt probably had nothing to do with business. But in that case, where did the woman, Heidi, come into the picture?

"What are your plans today?" Gilbert asked me the question to deflect the subject from his forthcoming trip.

I shrugged. "I thought I might try and pick up one of those sight seeing tours. Go out to the mountains, or something."

"That is exactly what I am going to do," said the woman. "But I have a car. Would you like to join me?"

"Oh, thanks all the same," I said. "But I wouldn't want to impose. I'll be quite alright on the bus."

Gilbert looked at his watch. "You'll never make the bus; they leave the town center at eight thirty and it's almost eight now."

I looked at Gilbert, consternation written all over my face. What was he trying to do?

"Then you have no choice," said Heidi. "We will take a drive and I will show you some of the best of Bavarian countryside."

"Sounds nice," I said with more than a touch of resignation. "Thanks very much."

After breakfast we returned to our rooms to freshen up. I had arranged to meet Heidi in the hotel lobby at nine o'clock. I traveled the elevator with Gilbert, with no reoccurrence of the mystery sounds. As soon as we were alone I went for Gilbert "What are you trying to do: fixing me up with a strange woman?"

"Your face." He laughed. "Get a chance to spend the day with a good looking blond, and you look as if someone's hit you with a sledge hammer. Make the most of it. The change will do you good."

"Where did she come from, anyway?"

"Not me, honest," said Gilbert. "She appeared from nowhere. Introduced herself and asked if she could share our breakfast table."

"Oh boy," I grimaced. "I don't know what's going on, but I smell a rat. Woman aren't in the habit of forcing themselves on me for no reason."

I said good-bye to Gilbert. He checked out of the hotel, but promised to keep in touch from Frankfurt. If I needed him, he would return straight away.

"And don't do anything I wouldn't do," he said facetiously, as he went out to his cab.

"Don't do anything you would do, you mean," I called back.

I checked with the hotel clerk and made sure he would take messages, for I intended to phone in periodically throughout the day. I met Heidi exactly at nine o'clock. She smiled sweetly as I approached.

For a moment I pondered Gilbert's words: Most men in my position would grab at a chance to escort such a beautiful woman for the day. She stood about five

9

feet six and her blond hair was tied into a bun. She wore a white pleated skirt with a navy sailor's jacket. "Hi," I said. "You look lovely."

"Thank you." Her smile broadened.

I took her arm and I said, "It's a nice day out there; let's go and make the most of it." And we crossed the road to where her Mercedes sports car was parked.

"Do you want to drive?" she asked, as we approached the vehicle.

"Not particularly," I replied. "I'm not overly fond of driving in strange cities."

She smiled. "Not the adventurous type then."

"I suppose not. I'm just a run of the mill computer type, introverted and rather boring."

"I doubt that's true on any one of those counts," she said. "But we shall see."

She accelerated away and we headed through town to pick up the autobahn. It soon became apparent that Heidi was an accomplished driver, and I felt relieved I had not accepted her invitation to drive.

"Are you over here on vacation?" I asked, suddenly realizing I knew almost nothing about her.

"Sort of," she said. "About ninety percent vacation and about ten percent research."

"Research? Now you intrigue me."

"Oh, it is nothing to be intrigued about. I lost my husband a few months ago, and I found myself left alone in the world. All my relatives in the States are gone. At one time, I had relatives here in Germany, but we lost touch during the war. When the war ended, I tried to find out what happened to them. But it is difficult to do that from the States, and I never found time to come here before."

"Had any luck?"

She shrugged. "At this moment, I am not sure."

"What do you mean?"

"I do not know whether I should tell you this."

I looked at her from across the seat. He face looked strained, as if the subject we had broached had suddenly become painful. "Please yourself," I said.

"I believe I have found my uncle," she went on. "But he won't see me. I have called him and written to him, but he wants nothing to do with me. I don't understand."

"Why don't you go and see him without his permission. Maybe he is getting on a bit and he doesn't remember you."

"He is getting on a bit, but I am quite sure all his faculties are in order. If you knew him, you would agree. And it is not so easy to go and see him unannounced."

The subject did not seem worth pursuing, so I turned to look out of the window. The car sped south along the autobahn, in the general direction of the mountains and the Austrian border. We were moving fast, confidently passing other vehicles on the road. I thought again about the woman who drove. After a while, we turned off the autobahn and seemed to be heading deeper into the country.

"Where are we going?" I asked suddenly.

She laughed. "I wondered when you were going to ask."

"There, I am a trusting soul. I haven't a clue where I am and I am completely in your hands."

"I am going to take you first to Oberammergau. You know, where they hold the passion play."

"Oh, that will be nice," I said automatically, not wanting to show my ignorance. I realized then, not for the first time, that my world consisted mainly of a desk and a computer terminal. I knew so little about anything else. I need not have worried, for she gave me a short history lesson. She told me of the Black Death in the sixteenth century, and the play that the villagers of Oberammergua put on every ten years since then to give thanks for being spared. We spent some time in the village, mainly in the souvenir shops. I bought a few more gifts for home, and telephoned the hotel. There were no messages for me.

We left the village, heading in the same general direction, towards the mountains. I passed the time either chatting with Heidi, or watching the scenery slip by. I began to feel hungry and a quick glance at my watch told me that it was nearly lunchtime.

"We are almost there. We shall stop for lunch shortly." She seemed to be reading my mind.

"Fine," I said. A good lunch is what I need."

We arrived in Neuschwanstein, in the shadow of King Ludwig's famous castle. "Walt Disney?" I said, looking up at the shining towers with their red tiled turrets.

"It is a bit, isn't it? We'll go up there after lunch and see if we can find Snow White."

We stopped outside a quaint but busy hotel and managed to get a couple of seats in the restaurant, near a window. The waitress came to our table with menus and I ordered a stein of lager for each of us. Heidi spoke to the waitress in fluent German, and I realized once again that I was completely outclassed.

"You'd better order," I said, after the waitress had left. "I didn't know you were so comfortable with the language."

She laughed. "I was born near Vienna."

"How come you let me struggle in that souvenir shop?" I reproached her.

"Oh, don't tell me that you didn't enjoy yourself. Half the fun of traveling abroad is communicating with the natives."

I agreed reluctantly. "Why don't you tell me something about yourself?"

She shrugged. "Not much to tell."

"Must be something," I said. "You went to America, for one thing."

'Yes." A sad and distant look came into her eyes, as if to think back uncovered old and painful memories. "We lived just outside Vienna. They were happy times for us. We had enough, though we were not rich, like Uncle Fredrik. Uncle Fredrik lived in Germany, near Munich. He was married to my father's sister. My father's family were Jewish, so was Uncle Fredrik. But my mother was Austrian, a Lutheran, so that made me a Mischling, half and half, neither one nor the other. Though that was not a concern before the Nazis came.

Uncle Fredrik's daughter, Ilse, my cousin, came to live with us late in 1935. There had been some trouble with the Nazis in Germany, though I never did know the true reason for her sudden flight. They were good times. I loved my cousin. But she is dead. The Nazis killed her."

"Uncle Fredrik is the one that you have found and won't see you?" I said. She nodded gravely.

"He knows what happened to his daughter. Perhaps it is too painful for him and that is why he won't see you."

"Maybe. But as far as I know, I am his only living relative. You would think, because of that alone, he would want to see me. Anyway, besides that, I owe him so much."

The waitress returned for our order, and Heidi again spoke in rapid German. I had no idea what I was about to eat.

"You owe him?" I questioned, after the waitress had left.

"Yes. He set us up in America. It was his money that gained us entry into the States and set us up when we got there. He had money invested in America, and he opened his bank account for us."

I looked at her, the rings and clothes she wore, the car she drove; she was obviously not hard up so I asked her, "You want to repay him?"

"No." She smiled and shook her head. "He doesn't need anything I can give him. I would just like to meet him, ask him about the others and talk about the old times. I would just like to know that there is someone somewhere who is family. You see, there is no one else."

"If he is well off, perhaps he thinks you want something from him. After all, the war has been over for quite a long time now. You could have looked him up before."

"I know. My fault. I never found the time." She shook her head sadly. "No. Let's be honest. "I never made the time."

"You have no children?"

"No. I wanted them, but it was my husband. But we were busy in other ways. He had a good job with the government and I had my business."

"What sort of business?"

"Hairdressing," she said. "I have several saloons in Ohio and I am thinking of setting up a franchise."

Our meal arrived, a form of pork roast with potato dumplings and gravy, a local speciallity. It was delicious.

To bring the subject back to her story, I said to Heidi, "Why didn't Uncle Fredrik go to the States?"

"He tried. He wanted to take his family. But for some strange reason, they wouldn't grant him an exit visa."

"Who wouldn't?"

"The Nazis. We never found out why. Soon after we arrived in the States, the war started. We never heard from them again."

"Didn't you try to get in touch with them after the war? If, as you say, your uncle set you up, the least you could have done was try to find them and make sure they were alright."

She looked angry for a moment and retorted, "My father did. He returned to Austria soon after the war, but he found no trace of them. Records show that three of them, Fredrik, his wife, Helga and Helmut, his son, all were sent to Dachau concentration camp in 1941; strangely, at about the same time, Ilse was shot while 'attempting to escape'. I knew Ilse, and I don't think she would have tried to escape on her own. It is known that Fredrik escaped, a miracle by all accounts. He was being transported from the camp a few months before the end of the war and he got away. He managed to get through the lines to the Americans. The others all disappeared mysteriously. There is no record of their deaths anywhere."

"Then, could they still be alive somewhere?'

Heidi shook her head slowly. "I don't think so," she said. There are records of them being in Dachau until the time of Uncle Fredrik's escape. After that: nothing. I believe they were killed because of Uncle Fredrik's escape. They were probably taken out into the woods and shot. It was not uncommon for the Nazis to do something like that."

"Then that is why your uncle won't see you. He feels guilty."

"Perhaps" Heidi suddenly reached across the table a grabbed my hand, her eyes looked into mine, as if pleading, imploring me for something. "I have no right to ask you this," she began. "But there was more to our meeting this morning than I led you to believe."

I smiled. "I thought as much."

"No, you don't understand. You didn't see me, but I sat at the table next to yours for supper last night. I overheard your conversation. You are dealing with Mannhausers, and you mentioned Fredrik Stanholt."

"Wait a minute." I could see what was coming. "Fredrik Stanholt – your Uncle Fredrik?"

She nodded.

I shook my head. "No. I cannot help you. My association with Mannhausers is purely business. I have seen your uncle only once and I have never spoken to him. I must be honest with you. I will not jeopardize my business in any way because of your family problems."

Heidi was quiet for a moment; she let go my hand and looked at me bitterly. "I did not want you to jeopardize your business. It was just that, if you did manage to get close to him, I wondered whether you could find out anything for me."

"I'm sorry," I said. "This order is worth millions to my company. Stanholt is a semi-recluse, a difficult man to deal with under the best of circumstances. I cannot afford to complicate things in any way."

"I understand." Her manner became more businesslike. "Tell me, what does he look like?"

"He sat towards the back of the room. But he was tall and thin, with a shock of white curly hair, cut short on the sides. And yes, he wore a patch over his left eye."

"He doesn't have a left eye. He lost it after being beaten by the Nazi Storm Troopers in the mid thirties."

"Then for sure, he is your uncle."

"It certainly sounds like him. He had black curly hair when I knew him, but he certainly cut it like you describe. He was tall, but not that thin. Who knows what happened in that concentration camp. At one time, he acted as a second father to me. I don't understand."

"I probably won't see him again, anyway. I 'm dealing with a man that works for him."

"I am sorry if I embarrassed you," she said.

We finished our meal and I paid the bill. Before leaving the restaurant to continue our day out, I made another quick phone call to the hotel to see if there were any messages. There were none.

We spent the rest of the afternoon pleasantly enough exploring one or two more castles as we made our way slowly back to Munich. We returned to the hotel at six in the evening and I went straight to the desk. This time there was a message from Kruger asking me to call him and giving me his home number.

I suggested to Heidi that we meet for supper. She smiled, pleased that I had asked her, and we agreed to meet in the dining room at seven thirty.

As soon as I reached my room, I picked up the phone and dialed Kruger. He answered the phone.

"McLeod here," I said.

"Oh, Bob, it's Stanholt. He says he would like to see you. Go over the system more thoroughly. Could you go out to his place tomorrow."

"Sure. That's what I'm here for. What time?"

"Ten o'clock in the morning. That all right with you?"

"Fine," I said. "How do I get there?"

"A car will pick you up from your hotel at nine thirty."

I thanked him and put the phone down.

I then decided to call my wife, Sara, in Vancouver, but a quick calculation in my head told me that it was just after three in the morning in that part of the world, and she would not be pleased at being woken.

I lay down on the bed for a while thinking of the days strange events. In no way could I help Heidi. The risks were too high. I owed it to my company and everyone that worked for me to get this contract.

I met Heidi in the dining room exactly at seven thirty, though she had arrived just before me. "Any news?" she asked, as I sat down.

"Yes. It looks as if I shall be seeing your uncle tomorrow. He wants me to go to his house."

"Why?" she asked.

A strange question, I thought, though later I looked back and wondered. "To discuss the system we plan to install for him. What else would he want to see me about?"

"I wish I could come with you."

"That's impossible. You know I would never agree to that. I told you before, I can't be involved."

She sighed and picked up the menu. "Well, let's eat something."

14

We had cocktails, a good meal and a bottle of wine, and I felt in a better mood. We hadn't touched on Heidi's family again, but my mind strayed to my forthcoming meeting with Stanholt.

"I wonder how he managed to build a company like Mannhauser from scratch, with nothing, in such a relatively short time," I said suddenly.

Heidi welcomed the chance to get back on the subject. "He didn't start from nothing. He must have had the box."

"Box?"

"Yes," she said. "A sealed box that Uncle Fredrik brought out of Germany, welded shut, so that only he knew what was inside. He and my father hid it in the chimney breast of our house near Vienna."

"When was this?"

"Just before we went to America."

"How do you know that the box is not still hidden?"

"When my father went to Austria after the war, he went to the house. The box was gone; there was a hole in the brickwork where it had been."

"Well, you can't blame him for trying to preserve what was his," I said.

"I don't blame him for anything," said Heidi. "I would just like to see him, that's all."

I didn't touch on the subject again, as it was obviously dangerous ground between us. We talked of other things. Heidi looked very beautiful, wearing a lovely, off the shoulder, black gown that contrasted her sparkling hair. Her full breasts pushed up from under the top of the gown, displaying her cleavage to full advantage. "You are very lovely," I said, probably because of the amount of wine I had drunk.

She giggled. "Thank you."

"What's so funny?"

"I put this dress on and tried to make myself look nice for you and we have been sitting here for nearly two hours and it is as if you only just noticed."

"Sorry," I smiled. "I told you before, I'm just an introverted computer freak, who's usually writing software or fiddling with the keys of a computer terminal. What do you expect from such a date?"

"You underrate yourself. You are a good looking man."

It was my turn to say thank you. We talked for a while longer, and then Heidi got up from the table. "I think I will go along to my room now," she said. "I have a bottle of wine there. If you would like to come along in about half an hour, we could have a nightcap together."

"That sounds nice," I said automatically.

She smiled, and I watched her leave the dining room and walk to the elevator. She was a striking looking woman. Her room was on the third floor, room 303.

I signed my room number to the bill and set off upstairs, already having second thoughts about going to Heidi's room. If I went there for a nightcap, would I end up sleeping with her? It wasn't that I didn't want to sleep with her; the reverse was true. But I had a lovely wife back home who trusted me, and I, unlike Gilbert, had a conscience.

15

At nine forty five, half an hour after Heidi had left the dining room, I sat in my lonely room wondering what to do. I probably would not sleep very well, for I was worried about my meeting with Stanholt tomorrow; and if I went to Heidi, I would probably sleep alright, though she would try again to involve me with her problems. I moved to the telephone. I would call her and make some excuse. I dialed her room, but though I let it ring for a number of times, there was no answer.

I put down the receiver and headed out into the corridor, my curiosity well and truly up. Now I would have to go and see her. And this excited me, for I knew, if I were to see her, I would probably stay with her.

I took the stairs down to the third floor and walked the corridor until I stood before room 303. I knocked sharply on the door, but I received no reply. I knocked again, but still nothing.

Heidi did not seem the type to play games. If she had invited me to her room, it was unlikely that she would have gone far. And anyway, where was there to go? I tried the door handle but the door was locked. Was it my curiosity or a sixth sense that drove me on? I had seen it done on television; did it really work? I slid a credit card out of my wallet, and pushed it between the door and the frame. I found what I wanted and felt the latch move back. I pushed the door and it opened.

As I entered, I noticed a single lamp burning on the desk illuminating the room. "Heidi," I called. And then I froze in horror, my mouth open and my brain rejecting what my eyes were seeing. The single lamp backlit a macabre tableau. She lay on the bed, staring up at the ceiling, her mouth open and her eyes waxen in startled terror. She had taken off the dress, for she wore only her underclothes. She lay on a blood soaked pillow, with a black hole in her forehead, like a third eye. Just below her left breast, a second hole neatly placed, and from this seeped only a smudge of red.

My legs were jelly. There was no doubt in my mind that she was beyond mortal help. I walked slowly to the telephone, and taking my handkerchief from my pocket, I lifted the handset. "You'd better get the police," I said to the clerk. "Mrs. Mortimer has been shot."

Chapter 2

The full meaning of Hitler's 'New Germany' did not fully dawn on Ilse Stanholt until late in the summer of 1935. To a certain extent she was protected by her father's money. The family lived in a large house in a select residential area on the outskirts of Munich and Ilse attended an expensive private school. All these things helped to insulate her from the happenings in the rest of Germany. Ilse being not yet sixteen, lived at home with her parents and elder brother, Helmut. Her father owned a jewellery business with a chain of small stores across Germany. When Hitler became Chancellor in 1933, it was a worrying time for the Stanholt family, but Ilse's father considered that any political situation could only be temporary. Hitler would not last.

On April the first, 1933, Storm Troopers picketed Stanholt's jewellery shops to comply with Hitler's call for a one-day boycott of Jewish businesses. In May of the following year a mass demonstration was organized calling for the purity of the German race, culminating in the burning of all so called foreign literature. Books written by Jews, Communists and others were burned by the thousand on a huge bonfire in Berlin Square. Although, naturally, these happenings were a worry, they made little difference to Ilse's life. She still attended school; she still had her friends, and she still lived her comfortable life.

When Hitler, in September of the following year, 1935, announced the first three laws for the foundation of the 'New Germany', Ilse like most other Jews became alarmed and afraid. The first proclaimed the swastika as the national symbol of Germany and the flag was changed. The second decreed that only those of pure 'Arian blood' could hold German citizenship. Jews, though German by birth over many generations, were no longer considered Germans. Jews were suddenly without rights or protection in a country that they considered their own. The third, to protect the purity of the race, prohibited any sexual or marital relationship between 'Arians' and Jews.

Ilse had never considered herself anything other than a German. Unlike her grandparents, Ilse's parents did not practice the Jewish faith. They considered themselves as free thinkers, and did not practice any formal religion. Suddenly Ilse and her family were stateless. Her brother, Helmut, wanted to go to America. Many of the family's friends and acquaintances were packing up to leave the country.

"It will not be long," said Fredrik Stanholt. "This Hitler cannot last. The tide of opinion is turning against him. Already there is talk of a coup."

Helmut shrugged. "All the same it might be prudent to leave while we can. We can always come back."

Stanholt was a big man and his face turned scarlet with anger at his son's suggestion. "Give up all that I have worked for? Run and leave everything behind? Run like rabbits? Anyone who speaks like that is not worthy to be called a German." But in truth, Stanholt was not angry with Helmut. He was angry at the turn of events that had led them to this, events that he did not fully understand. Fredrik Stanholt had been an officer in the infantry during World War One; he had fought for his country in the trenches. If anyone had a right to call himself a German, he did.

"No, we will not leave," he said quietly. "Not while I am head of the family. We will see this Hitler in hell first."

Ilse was a pretty girl of medium height with short, dark, wavy hair. Her large brown eyes sparkled when she laughed, which was often. Besides academic subjects, her interests lay in sports and athletics, and by the time she reached fifteen, her figure had blossomed. Her breasts were firm and proud, her hips wide and her waist narrow. In any man's eyes she was beautiful, too beautiful, as it happened, too beautiful for her own good.

To one man she was desirable, desirable to a point where he could think of almost nothing else. This man was her schoolteacher, Hans Becker. Becker at thirty five years old, had been teaching at Ilse's school for four years. Even though Becker was handsome, over six foot tall with slim build, dark hair and pleasant features, he did not get on well with women. He acted awkward and stilted in their company and the only women that he had ever been with were prostitutes. He had watched Ilse grow from a shy, quiet child into a confident young woman. For Becker, she was different from all the other girls in the school; she held a strange, even fatal fascination for him. Whenever he looked up from his desk, or turned from the blackboard, his eyes fell on her first. He dreamt of her. For a schoolteacher, these dreams were dangerous, but they were doubly dangerous for him, because she was a Jew. But the danger had to be faced, for he could not help himself. A man's thoughts cannot be legislated and he wanted her. He wanted her badly. Becker, a member of the Nazi party since 1931, held an important position locally. Because of this position, he knew almost all the Jews in the area. It was his job to know.

Towards the end of 1935 things began to look bleak for the Stanholt's. Even the well-to-do area in which they lived became infected with Goebel's propaganda. People acted differently towards them. People they had known for twenty years dropped them as if they had the plague, crossing the street to avoid speaking to them. Fredrik Stanholt's business went down badly. 'Buy German' the posters proclaimed. And he was forced to display a yellow star in his storefronts to proclaim his ethnic origin. "But I am German," he railed. "I am more German than they." But his cries were to no avail. Hitler, far from being overthrown, had consolidated his position, even to the extent of massacring those he suspected of speaking against him, or having ambition to take his place. Hitler instilled fear into those who served him. He knew only too well the secret of gaining and holding power.

Where the Stanholt's lived there had been few cases of Jews being molested or beaten, but in the city itself, it was almost a daily occurrence, and some had even been killed. One old man had been kicked to death after his store had been broken into and looted by Storm Troopers. But up until the later part of 1935, the Stanholts had suffered no bodily harm, nor any serious financial loss. The school Ilse attended had not been greatly affected, mainly because, though still a minority, the student population comprised a great many Jews. There had been a slow, almost imperceptible, segregation, between the Jews and the others.

On a Tuesday, early in November 1935, Ilse walked to school with her best friend, Ruth Klein. They were engrossed in conversation under the cool sunshine, when Ruth was struck between the shoulder blades by a huge and smelly clod of horse dung.

Startled, they both turned to find five boys from their school following them. The boys laughed and gathered more excreta from the road. The girls ran for their lives, but not before being struck time and again by flying turds. The boys cried, "*Juden*," and gave chase. "Bitches," others of them shouted.

The boys were pleased with there joke as they chased Ilse and Ruth into the school, where the girls were forced to take refuge in the toilets.

Morning classes were missed, as both girls returned home to bath and change. Isle was angry; she knew the names of the boys, and she would have no qualms about getting them into trouble. As soon as posible, she would speak to Herr Becker.

Ilse was unable to see Becker until the end of classes. He taught the last lesson of the day, and she waited patiently until all the other students had left the room. She approached his desk somewhat nervously. "Herr Becker, some boys behaved badly this morning as I walked to school with my friend. I wish to report them."

Becker wondered why she had stayed after the others had left, and this had filled him with a strange excitement. Anxious not to show it, though, he pretended to read some papers. "Oh, did they." He looked up from the desk. "How, exactly?"

"They threw horse dung and called us names. We had to go home and bath and change."

"And what names did they call you, Ilse?"

Ilse noticed the small round badge on his lapel that proclaimed him to be a Nazi, but surely he could not think like the ignorant Storm Troopers. She spoke quietly. "Jew, Bitch, among other things."

A fleeting grin crossed his lips. "It is the way things are, Ilse. You are a Jew; that is the problem. Wait, we will take a few moments to discuss it. " He rose from his chair and walked over to close the classroom door. When he returned he stood close to her, very close and he placed his arm around her shoulder. "It is a pity that one so beautiful as you should have been born a Jew."

Unsure of what was happening, Ilse tried to step backwards, to move away. This could not be the same Herr Becker who taught her at school each day.

Becker tightened his grip. "No, Ilse, don't be frightened. I can help you. I can see that no harm will come to you."

"Please, Herr Becker, I don't need your protection. I just want you to talk to the boys. Tell them not to do it again."

Becker's other arm found her waist and gripping hard, he pulled her towards him, his lips seeking her lips. Ilse turned her head, only to feel his hot breath and the caress of his lips on her neck. She struggled and twisted, and bending her knees in an effort to slip away, her sweater rode up, and his hand found her breast. Ilse pulled her knee up sharply into Becker's groin, knocking the wind out of him and doubling him over in pain. Releasing Ilse, he grasped the desk to stop himself falling. She needed no more than that, and she ran from the classroom.

Becker screamed after her. "You little fool. You need me. You wait and see what happens to you now. You'll come crawling back and beg me for it before I'm through." But Ilse was gone, the classroom door slamming behind her.

Upon arrival at home, Ilse feigned sickness to her mother and went to her room avoiding supper. She needed no company; there were things she must think about. She had better not to tell her parents of Herr Becker's behaviour, or anyone else for that matter. What good would come of it? It was hard enough for the Jews already, and Becker had influence with the Nazis.

The following day Ilse went to school, as if nothing had happened. What else she could do without questions being asked? She brazened it out, as far as Becker was concerned. It wasn't easy for her, sitting in his classroom, listening to the words, but remembering nothing of what he said. She saw him as an animal, tearing at her clothes and forcing himself upon her. Several times she found him looking at her with a strange gleam in his eyes, and a shudder passed through her.

Supper at the Stanholts was usually a late affair, for they preferred to eat together as a family, and Herr Stanholt was never home before seven thirty. On that Wednesday evening, seven thirty came and went, but no sign of Herr Stanholt. At ten o'clock there came an insistent knocking at the front door. Helmut rushed to open it, and within moments he pulled his topcoat from the closet. He shouted, "It's Papa. He's been hurt. I must go to him at once."

Helmut's mother went immediately to the closet. "Hurt? How badly? Where is he?"

"Stay here, Mama. Stay. I will get him. Don't worry. He will be alright." And he ran off down the road behind the young lad who had knocked with the message.

Two hours passed before Helmut returned. Frau Stanholt, far from taking her son's advice, was almost out of her mind with worry. With the help of two friends,

Helmut carried his father's broken body into the living room. Stanholt moaned in agony as he lay on the sofa, his suit ripped and covered in blood. Makeshift bandages were tied around his head.

"Go to Dr. Freedman and bring him here at once," Frau Stanholt instructed Ilse.

"No." Helmut placed his arm around his sister's shoulder. I'll go. It is not safe for Ilse."

Helmut soon returned and the doctor with him. Freedman was Jewish and a longstanding friend of the family. He was medium height with dark, short cut hair with a bristling moustache. His reputation as an excellent doctor was well known throughout Munich.

During the initial examination, the doctor found several broken ribs and some internal injuries, though probably not serious. There were cuts and bruises all over Stanholt's body, though these would heal. Worse, his left eye was badly damaged and was cause for concern.

Later, when Stanholt lay in his bed in a drugged sleep, Freedman addressed the family, "I think he will lose the eye. He should have professional care, really, though I fear to put him in the local hospital. If we could get him across the border to Saltsburg, but no - the journey. He will be better off here. I will have someone come in and dress his wounds and help you look after him."

Thank you, Doctor. I don't know what we would have done without you." Frau Stanholt was still very agitated, her hands moving constantly, clutching and unclutching her fingers.

"I prescribe a brandy for your mother, Helmut. Perhaps it might be a good idea if we all had one." He grinned. "Purely medicinal."

Helmut responded at once, pouring four small glasses of neat cognac.

"Do we know what happened?" asked the doctor, after everyone was seated with a drink.

"The Storm Troopers came," began Helmut. "They waited till Papa was alone in the shop. There were six of them. The smashed everything and looted the shelves. Nobody came to help. The police - they just stood and watched."

The doctor shook his head sadly. "It is the same story everywhere. What is happening to this country? If you are a Jew, it is better to get out."

Ilse spoke up. "Papa won't go."

"Perhaps now he will," said the doctor. "Germany is no place for us."

"Why are you still here?" asked Frau Stanholt.

The doctor grinned. "I have thought about leaving, but you know, I was born here I went to university here. My life is here. This is my country. Why should I allow myself to be driven out?"

To Ilse, the situation seemed hopeless. "That's how Papa feels," she said.

"That is how many of us feel. And anyway, it is better for my people if I stay. Look at tonight. Things like this are happening all the time, and it will get worse."

The following morning Ilse went to school as usual. She was late, but nothing was said. The day went by, but school no longer held any pleasure for her. She put in the time, as she was required to do, but she learned nothing. At the last bell she tidied her desk and was about to leave with the rest of the students when Becker was at her side.

"A moment, Ilse, if you please."

She eyed him warily, and was about to run after the others, but there was a look on his face that she mistook for contrition. She waited, held in suspension, not daring to move but keeping her distance, expecting him to apologise.

"How is your father?"

"My father?" Ilse was taken completely off guard. "He is sick – beaten up by Nazi thugs." And then, with an icy chill, she realized that Becker knew these things already. "He will lose an eye."

Becker looked down at her and said patronizingly, "It is a shame that these things can happen, but it is the times in which we live. Now do you understand why you need protection. You and your whole family are at risk."

"Protection?" Ilse looked down at the floor, no longer able to look Becker in the eye. Her face burned red and she wanted to run from the room, but she had to stay and confirm her worst suspicions. "You? You did this?"

Becker laughed. "My dear little Ilse, if you had been sensible the other evening, your father would be quite well and unharmed now. It is the times we live in. Accept it. There is nothing you can do about it."

Ilse was shocked beyond reason. How could this man that she had always respected be such a monster. Shaking her head in disbelief, she whispered, "How?"

"The Storm Troopers are a weapon to be used and directed. If they do not strike here, they will strike there. Someone must guide them, select the target."

Tears of frustration began to flow down her cheeks. "Why do you hate us so?"

Becker's tone completely changed and he spoke quietly. "Hate you? I don't hate you, Ilse. I want you. I want you more than anything else in the world."

"You cannot have me."

"I will have you, Ilse. Remember your family. I will do what ever it takes, but you will be mine."

Ilse took half a step, as if turning to go. There was nothing more to say.

"Think about it, Ilse. Here is the address of my apartment." He handed her a slip of paper. "Think about it and then come and see me there tomorrow night, say seven o'clock. We will discuss it further."

The following evening came around all too quickly. Ilse had eaten nothing nor slept since her the conversation with her schoolmaster. Her complexion had paled and shadows had appeared under her eyes. The more she thought about her situation, the more she realized she had no choice. If she did not go to Becker, her family would suffer. She went to her father's room and sat with him for a while. He would recover; there was no doubt about that, but the pain still racked his body. Ilse watched as he lay there suffering, and she knew what she must do. At six thirty she slipped on her coat and walked quietly down the stairs. She stood before the front door, when her mother, carrying a tray of cups to the kitchen, entered the passageway and confronted her.

"Where are you going?"

Ilse had not prepared a story for her parents and she quickly stuttered, "I'm going to see Ruth. We have to work on a project for school."

Frou Stanholt, at once suspicious of her daughter's nervous reply, put down her tray on the hall table. Unlike some other parents, the Stanholts had never had trouble with their children and Ilse was thoroughly trustworthy. Why was she lying now?

Frou Stanholt gestured to the parlour. "Come in here, child."

Ilse followed her meekly.

"I saw Ruth's mother today. Ruth has gone to her grandmothers for a while. She has been sick the last few days. Her mother thinks she needs a break."

Ilse was unused to lying, but she could not tell the truth. "I'm sorry, mama. I have to go out. I have to see someone." She turned to walk from the room very close to tears.

"No, Ilse. You don't go anywhere without my permission."

"I have to," cried Ilse, starting to panic.

At that moment, Helmut came into the house. He realized immediately that there was a problem between Ilse and her mother and he stopped to listen.

"At your age, Ilse, you go nowhere without my permission."

Ilse broke down and began to weep. "I have to," she repeated.

Her mother came to her side and put her arm around her. "Now, dear, tell me, who is it that you have to see?"

"I have to see Herr Becker, Mama."

"Your schoolmaster? Why would he want to see you now? Are you failing, child?"

Ilse regained some of her composure. "I don't know. He said he wants to see me."

"Why didn't you tell me in the first place it was your schoolmaster?" her mother said reproachfully. "You didn't have to lie. I suppose you had better go. But tell Herr Becker not to keep you too late. It is not safe for young girls to be out at night."

Ilse made towards the parlour door, only to find her brother standing in the doorway, his fit nineteen-year-old body barring her way.

"Tell us, Ilse, what does he want from you?"

"Get out of the way!" cried Ilse.

"Not until you tell us what he wants from you. Do you think I am stupid? The man is a Nazi, and you are going to his house at night."

Ilse broke down. She could dam her emotions only so much. Sobbing, she ran into her brother's arms. "He will protect us. He has influence and can help us."

As Helmut held his sister, he knew he had guessed right. He had heard of this sort of thing happening to other girls. "Whatever were you thinking of, Ilse. You must not go."

"Of course I must," cried Ilse, pulling away. "God only knows what will happen to the rest of you if I don't."

23

Ilse' mother sat down on the couch. Having watched the interchange between her two children, she could hardly comprehend the meaning of it. "But he is your schoolteacher," was all she could say.

Helmut spoke in a quiet and determined manner. "You will not go to him, Ilse. I would kill him first."

"You don't understand," said Ilse. "It was my fault that Papa got beaten. If I had let Herr Becker have his way, Papa would not have been hurt."

Frou Stanholt, realizing at last some of the burden her daughter carried, went to Ilse and guided her back to the sofa. "Now, child, you had better tell us from the beginning."

When Ilse came to the end of her story, Frou Stanholt forced the decision. There would be no arguing with her. The children would go to her brother. "You will go and stay with Uncle Gunther in Austria. You will go tonight, straight away. Helmut, you will take the car. And Helmut, you, too, will stay there."

"No, Mama. My place is here with you."

"Do as I say. I want nothing to happen to you."

In the end Helmut agreed to stay in Austria for a few weeks, until the incident had been forgotten. He said, "He will be angry tomorrow, but he will soon turn his attention to another."

But Helmut was wrong. Herr Becker could think of no other girl as he thought of Ilse.

. . . . .

Ilse enjoyed Austria. Uncle Gunther's house, though small, was comfortable, and she enjoyed the company of her cousin, Heidi. And Austria was a happy country, not yet infected by the Nazi scourge.

Helmut and Ilse drove through the night to arrive at Uncle Gunther's house, on the outskirts of Vienna, just before dawn. Uncle Gunther accepted them immediately. He needed no explanation, but they told him the story anyway. Upon hearing what had happened, he became extremely worried for his sister and her husband, and with no further thought, he offered them a home, too. But Herr Stanholt's sickness did not allow them to travel and they were not yet ready to move. Helmut stayed for two weeks, enough to fulfil his promise to his mother. Nothing further happened to the Stanholts during that period; they heard no more from Becker, and neither Helmut, nor his mother, told Stanholt the true reason for his daughter's sudden flight.

Ilse' cousin, Heidi, was a year her senior, a pretty girl with a very fair complexion and blond hair. In no time the two were best of friends. Ilse considered going back to school and then on to university in Vienna, but the thought of school made her shudder. She would find a job.

Ilse found a job, in her eyes not much of a job, selling shoes, but the pay was enough to cover her keep and give her a little over to spend. She would frequent the cinema, or go to a play, or sometimes to the local dancehall with Heidi. Both girls, being so attractive, found no shortage of would-be suitors, but they were having too much fun for serious entanglements. One lad came along, a tall and handsome young man from a good Jewish family, and Ilse could not help being attracted to him. His name was Martin Redelmeier, and his family were in the clothing business.

Ilse went out with Martin, occasionally at first, but as time went by, she found herself going out with him more and more. Things would take their natural course, and for two years the relationship between Martin and Ilse grew, both of them coming to know love. The seeds had been planted for what could have been a life time relationship.

Ilse' father, mother and brother fled Germany in the spring of 1937. They arrived as refugees from the Fatherland, and once more Uncle Gunther took them in. Although seeing her parents again pleased Ilse, she knew in her heart that the carefree life she had known as a child had finally gone for good. Uncle Gunther and his wife Erma generously squeezed up and made do, but with so many in the house, it was difficult.

Fedrik Stanholt sold the jewellery business for a mere fraction of its value, but under the Nazi oppression, he was lucky to sell it at all. The amount of money that he smuggled out of Germany, though only a small part of what he had been worth, was enough to keep them comfortable. They would sit it out and wait for things to change for the better.

In 1937 Austria, though in a weak political situation, was still a happy country, but now there were shadows on the horizon. Nazism was rampant and Hitler wanted Austria; he made no secret of it.

In February of 1938, the Stanholt's had been living with Uncle Gunther for almost a year. In that time, Hitler had become even more powerful, and the armed might of Germany had grown to an awesome machine to be feared around the world. German troops were massing close to the Austrian border, and on the 14th of the month, Hitler summoned Kurt Von Schuschnigg, the then Chancellor of Austria, to his mountain retreat at Berchasgarten, in southern Bavaria. Hitler was abrupt to the point of unpleasantness. There would be no discussion; Hitler simply laid down his demands.

Jewish people, the Stanholts among them, watched in horror, if not in outright panic, as, on March the 12th, German soldiers crossed the border into Austria. The Anschluss was complete and Austria had become a mere province of the new Pan-Germanic empire, totally subservient to the master in Berlin.

Immediately the Jews were made to suffer, for again they had no rights and no country. The Stanholts kept a low profile and were fortunate enough to avoid problems with the Nazis. Fredrik Stanholt never worked in Austria, but Helmut manage to find a job as a garage mechanic. Helmut's wages, plus the little that Ilse brought in, helped towards their expenses. One day, shortly after the German occupation, Ilse arrived home to find both her father and Uncle Gunther hard at work repairing the chimneybreast in the parlour.

A large hole had appeared in the brickwork, and broken pieces of brick and dust covered the floor. Prepared mortar waited on a wooden pallet and among the debris, lay a metal box about twelve by twelve by eight inches deep. Ilse had seen the box before when her father brought it from Germany. There were hinges and a latch on the box, but these were now useless, as the box was welded shut. If ever it were to be opened again, it would have to be cut open.

"What on earth are you doing?" Ilse could not hide her naturally curiosity.

Her father looked grave. "We are hiding this box. I will tell you about it when we are finished and when Helmut and Heidi get home."

The two men worked on, while Ilse went into the kitchen to make coffee and help with supper. Uncle Gunther was a good man with his hands, and soon the job took shape. They avoided the use of new bricks, for they needed to disguise the hiding place. Only after the job was completely finished and the mess cleared, did Stanholt summon the children.

"That box contains at least part of your inheritance, some gold and jewels that I managed to squeeze out of the business," he began. "There is also some stocks and bonds, though heaven knows how much they are worth in these troubled times. I cannot estimate the value of the box but it is considerable. Uncle Gunther and I have decided to apply for exit permits, so that we can all travel to the United States, but how much we will be able to take with us is uncertain. If we can get to the States, money should not be a problem. Over the years, I have placed substantial funds in US banks. There will be more than enough to guarantee us entry."

Helmut spoke first. "We should get our applications in for exit permits as quickly as possible. I hear there are thousands of people like us wanting to leave."

Stanholt stared sadly at the repaired chimneybreast. "We shall go and see them tomorrow. They seem to be allowing as many Jews to leave as can afford to go."

"Allowing!" Uncle Gunther interjected. "They are encouraging us. It is nothing less than being kicked out of our own country."

It was Ilse' turn to look at the chimney. "What of the box?"

"We must go and we cannot take the box with us. The house will remain in Uncle Gunther's name, and the box should survive in the chimneybreast if no one knows it is there. Now all of you forget the box. Promise me that you will breath word of its existence to no one."

Ilse had mixed feelings about going to America. The excitement of getting away from the Nazis was tempered by the thought of leaving Martin. That night, as arranged, she met him after supper.

"It is the best thing to do," said Martin, after she had told him. "Many are going."

His words did little to comfort her. "What about you?"

"My father's business is here. If we go to America, we will have nothing. My father will not accept that; he will not start all over again."

"Soon he may have nothing anyway. Look what happened to us in Germany."

Martin held her by the arms and looked her in the eye. "It is better for you to go where I will know that you are safe. My father won't go. He says that Austria is his country and no foreign tyrant will kick him out."

Ilse sighed. "Brave words. I have heard them all before. But what about you, Martin? Suppose I ask my father if you can come with us?"

Martin shook his head. "How can I leave my parents at a time like this?"

Uncontrollable tears ran down the side of Ilse' face and she looked away. Martin pulled her close. At almost twenty, he found his world changing too quickly. "You go to America with your parents, Ilse. One day I shall come for you. Hitler and his Nazis can't last forever."

"If I go to America, I may never see you again."

"You will, Ilse. You will. I promise you."

But it was not a time when promises should be made, for only the Germans were in a position to keep them.

.   .   .   .   .

Both families applied for entry permits into the United States, and at the same time applied to the Germans for exit permits. After that, all they could do was wait. The entry visas came through fairly quickly, as they were more or less a formality. Stanholt had much more money invested in the United States than what was required to assure them of entry. But the exit permits were not granted.

Early in 1939, Uncle Gunther accompanied by Stanholt went again to the Germans. They were required to go to the office of the local Gauleiter. After what seemed an interminable wait, a clerk eventually saw them.

"Your application for exit visas? Why would you want to leave? Has this beautiful country of ours lost its attraction for you?" The clerk grinned menacingly.

Stanholt ignored the clerk's sarcasm. "Others are not having problems. We met the criteria, and we already have our entry visas."

"You think life in America will be so great, do you?" But the clerk began hunting through a filing cabinet for their folders.

"Here they are, pinned together." He pulled two files from the drawer and placed them on the desk. Taking Uncle Gunther's first, he scanned through it. "Everything seems in order," he muttered. He then scanned the second file, taking particular interest in a military memo pinned to the inside cover. "Which of you is Stanholt?" he said.

"Me, is anything wrong?" Stanholt tried to see over the clerk's shoulder.

The clerk slammed the folder shut. "Nothing wrong. You must wait, both of you, until you exit permits are granted. The State has more to do than worry over the whining problems of a couple of Jews."

When the folders were returned to the drawer, they were no longer pinned together, and in two weeks time, Uncle Gunther and his family received their exit permits in the mail.

"We shall wait until yours comes through and then we will all leave together."

'No," said Stanholt. "That would not be clever. Go now while you have the chance. Who can tell what will happen in the future."

"Ours are through. It can only be a matter of days before yours will come."

"Maybe so and maybe not. Anyway, you can go ahead and make a place for us. If you think about it, we will be better off than you. When we go to America, we shall have a place to stay."

Gunther reluctantly agreed. As he shook hands with his brother in law, his eyes looked strained and his face creased into an expression of love and concern.

"Come soon, Fredrik. It is not healthy here. If they do not grant you an exit permit, perhaps there are other ways."

"We will wait, Old Friend. It will not be long now."

Uncle Gunther managed to secure passage for himself and his family on a ship leaving Bremerhaven for New York within three weeks of receiving the exit permits. Accommodation was not the best and they would have to travel steerage, but at least they were on their way to freedom. The Stanholts traveled to Bremerhaven to see them off. As they stood on the dock exposed to the cold February drizzle, cheerful words rang hollow until eventually the conversation died altogether. It was as if they knew that this was indeed a final parting; they would never again be together.

Fredrik Stanholt and his son, Helmut, made many more trips to the local Gaulieter over the next few months, and each time they were told the same. "Be patient. Your turn will come." And each time the clerk read the note pinned to their file, and looked at them with renewed interest. The months slipped around until came September. Hitler's troops marched into Poland, and so began the Second World War. The borders of Austria and Germany closed, and they would remain closed for the duration.

Chapter 3

I returned to my hotel from the police station at close to five in the morning. I had been subjected to an almost constant barrage of questions:

"How well did I know Mrs. Mortimer?"

"What did we talk about?"

"What was she doing in the Federal Republic of West Germany?"

"What was I doing in the Federal Republic of West Germany?"

"Could I think of any reason why someone would want to murder her?"

"What was I doing going to her room at ten o'clock at night?"

"Was I intending to sleep with her?"

The questions went on and then they started all over again. At one time I felt sure that they suspected me of the murder. Finally, a senior officer of the police approached me. "When are you intending to leave Germany, Mr. McLeod?"

"Soon." I looked at my watch. "Not today, but probably tomorrow."

"You'd better check with us before you leave."

A yawning pit seemed to be opening in front of me. I visualized being stuck in Germany for months. "For God's sake, you don't suspect me, do you?"

He smiled, a grim, tight-lipped smile. "No, Mr. McLeod. A professional killed Mrs. Mortimer. He knew exactly what to do and how to do it, a paid assassin and a pricey one at that. We will probably never catch the man who pulled the trigger, but we shall strive to find out who paid him."

"Why do you need me then?"

"You're a material witness. You were the last person to speak to Mrs. Mortimer, and, of course, you found the body."

I wondered fleetingly how I would explain finding the body to my wife, but then I hoped the subject would never come up.

I walked through the silent hotel lobby and the desk clerk nodded to me sleepily as I passed. With my mind completely full of the events that had taken place over the last few hours, I did not give a thought to the elevator. I let myself into the cage and pressed the button for the top floor.

Almost as soon as the car lifted away, I heard, above the noise of clanking cables and tired bearings, a scream, a human scream, loud and clear, as clear as I had ever heard anything in the elevator before, a scream of some poor soul in mortal agony. There was no mistaking what I heard, and I clutched the handle of the inside gate, feeling suddenly unsteady on my legs. The first scream was followed by another, and another, and then a chorus of screams growing fainter as I neared the top of the shaft. By the time I arrived at the fourth floor, I felt sick. I staggered to my room, and then to the bathroom, before emptying the contents of my stomach down the toilet. Afterwards, I sat on the bed until the waves of nausea passed.

I went to bed and must have slept, for I dreamt the same dream again. The sun burned down from a cloudless sky and again I stood before the farmhouse. This time, in spite of the evil presence I could feel radiating from the place, I walked the driveway. I reached the front of the house, but avoided the front door, instead walking on down the side. The wooden side door had four small glass windows set in the top. I tried the handle, but the door didn't budge. Balling my gloved fist, I smashed the window nearest the latch. As I reached in, a bell started ringing. I guessed I had set off an alarm of sorts and pulling my arm from the window, I tried to run. As much as I wanted my legs to work, they were not mine to command. Trapped within my own body, I threshed about wildly and sat up sharply, the telephone ringing in my ear.

I grabbed the instrument. "Hello." I glanced at the clock, barely seven thirty – less than two hours in bed.

"Hallo," Gilbert said cheerfully. "How is it going?"

A thousand answers sprang to my mind, but none of them productive. "Not good." I replied.

"What's up?"

"That blond you fixed me up with was murdered last night." I was probably being unfair, but the way I felt, I didn't care.

The line went quiet. In all the time that we had worked together, I had never known Gilbert lost for words. "You're kidding," he said at last.

"I wish I were. I have spent most of the night in the local police station. Somebody shot her dead in her room."

I went on to outline to Gilbert the events of the previous day, leaving out any connection with Stanholt.

After I had explained as much as I wanted, he turned the subject to the reason we were there. "Anything happening with Mannhauser?"

"I have to see Stanholt at ten this morning. He wants more details of the system."

"Should I be there?"

"You wouldn't get here in time," If I sounded resentful about him being away and leaving me to cope with heaven knows what, then so be it. "No, I don't think so. For some reason he asked specifically for me. Probably wants to go over some of the technical details."

"Where does he live?"

"He lives about thirty kilometres north east of here, a good way past the Mannhauser plant, near a place called Karlsfeld. They are sending a car for me."

"Well, good luck. Let me know," he said and then rang off.

Feeling dreadful, I got out of bed, showered and dressed. I took the stairs down to the lobby and went into breakfast. I grabbed the usual continental breakfast and sat down at a table on my own. I felt sad for Heidi. I hadn't known her very long, and true, she tried to involve me with her problems, but I had enjoyed her company and she had been nice to me. From what she had told me of her life, I could see no reason why she should have been killed. I felt angry. I would very much like to know who was responsible for her death.

I had not told the police, or anyone else for that matter, of her alleged connection with Fredrik Stanholt. We had a contract to secure; we had a real chance of bringing our company into the fortune five hundred and nothing must get in the way of that.

The uniformed chauffer waited for me in the lobby at nine thirty. I felt proud and rather special to be greeted subserviently and then ushered into a large grey Mercedes that was parked at the entrance portico. The journey to the Stanholt estate took almost the half hour, and the final approach was by a quiet road through a forest. We came upon a pair of formidable iron gates, hung from brick pillars. The gates began to open soon after my driver touched a small button on the sun visor. I could see a tall chain link fence crowned with bare electric wires stretching in either direction. A formidable place to break into, or out of, I thought wryly.

The road over the estate wound through the trees for about half a mile, I should think, but the house, a ranch style bungalow of between three and four thousand square feet, was smaller than I imagined. The driveway looped around a fishpond with a fountain in front of the house, and on the step by the front door waited a man wearing a dark suit. As soon as we stopped, he stepped forward and opened the door. "Welcome, Mr. McLeod?" he said.

"Thank you." I held my hand out and he took it.

"Ernst Klauz. I am Mr. Stanholt's personal assistant."

The man stood well over six foot tall with dark grey, short cut hair. His hips were slim and he had a barrel chest. He did not smile and I detected a slight bulge of a shoulder holster under his left armpit. The man was armed.

"Please to meet you." I may have sounded nervous, but I didn't like guns.

"This way, sir." He led me through the house to a large and spacious study, and showed me to an armchair in front of a massive, carved oak desk. "Mr. Stanholt will be with you shortly. Please make yourself comfortable. Can I get you a cup of coffee?"

In spite of my breakfast, my mouth still felt like sandpaper. "Yes. I wouldn't mind. If it is not too much trouble."

"No trouble at all, sir."

He slipped from the room silently, the thick carpeting deadening his footsteps. Having nothing else to do I looked around. A large picture window with a view of the ornamental garden at the back of the house formed almost one complete wall of the room. I could see the driveway stretching back behind the house to a triple garage in the distance. The other walls contained many pictures. They looked expensive, though I am no judge of art. A large grand piano stood in one corner and there were several illuminated fish tanks, one of them set in a stone wall over a fireplace.

"Your coffee, sir." Klaus had returned and I hadn't even heard him enter the room.

"Thank you."

"Mr. Stanholt will be with you momentarily, sir."

He still showed no smile or any indication of warmth and he left the room as silently as before. I pondered him for a moment, huge, light on his feet, cat-like, extremely fit, a curled spring. Under no circumstances would I ever want to tangle with such a man.

I had barely started to sip my coffee when the door opened and Stanholt entered. I recognized him from the demonstration at Mannhauser, tall, and for his age amazingly straight. He wore a light grey suit. His snowy white hair, though cut short at back and sides, grew into a mass of wavy curls on top. His one crystal blue eye moved rapidly, focusing on one thing and then another, missing nothing. The black patch that covered his other eye contrasted sharply with his hair.

"How do you do, Mr. McLeod?" He spoke in perfect English and he held out his hand.

We shook hands. He sat behind the desk and he pulled a folder from the drawer. Inside the folder, among other papers, resided our proposal for the sale of a computer system to Mannhauser.

He went through the proposal for the next hour, quizzing me on every facet of it. His questions showed an uncanny insight, indicating that he had grasped completely what we were doing, and displaying a great depth of knowledge in production systems. But then, from a man that had built such a company as Mannhauser, I could expect nothing less. At last he seemed satisfied.

He looked at me, his one eye seeming to drill into me. "How about another cup of coffee, or a drink, perhaps?"

I stole a quick glance at my watch to find that the time had slipped around to after eleven. "No thanks. I should be getting off. You must have many important things to do."

"As you wish." But he did not seem to be in a hurry to let me go. "How are you finding your stay in Bavaria?"

"A beautiful country," I replied, for want of something to say.

"Are you managing to see some of it?"

"Yes. I spent yesterday on a sightseeing tour." I realized that I had all but forgotten the tour after the incident the previous evening. His questions reminded me sharply of Heidi. "We saw one or two castles, and that place where they put on the passion play."

He leapt upon my statement. "We!" he said. "Is that you and your partner?"

He seemed to be fishing. "No. As a matter of fact, I met a lady in the hotel. She had a car and she offered to take me around."

He smiled broadly. "How nice for you. It is so much better to see places in the company of another, especially a lady. A pretty lady?" he asked.

"Very pretty."

He seemed reluctant to let the subject drop. He grinned knowingly. "Are you seeing this lady again?"

"No." I shrugged. "She is dead, murdered in the hotel last night."

His face appeared stricken and he seemed momentarily lost for words. His surprise showed genuine enough. He shook his head. "How terrible for you. You must tell me what happened."

"I don't want to burden you with my problems. There really isn't much to tell. We had a pleasant day together. I tried to telephone her room last night but she did not reply. I went to investigate and found her lying on the bed, shot to death."

"You must have had an unpleasant time of it last night. The police, they don't suspect you, do they?"

"No, I don't think so. You see, I never met the woman before yesterday, and I know almost nothing about her. I know that she, a recent widow, came from Ohio, in the States. I understood that she had a business over there, and she was here on vacation. That was all I was able to tell them." And that was all I was going to tell him. It seemed safer that way.

He listened intently to every word I said. "What was her name?" he asked.

"Heidi Mortimer." I watched closely for his reaction. He must have known the name, for she had written to him and telephoned him, yet not a flicker of recognition. His acting abilities were beyond question. But his personal affairs were none of my business; I had the contract to worry about.

He stood up, being either satisfied that I had told him everything I knew, or realizing that he would get nothing further out of me. "Thank you for coming, Mr. McLeod. We will let you know our decision regarding your system as soon as possible. I hope the rest of you stay in Bavaria is more pleasant."

After shaking hands again with Stanholt, Klaus appeared in the room as if from nowhere and showed me to the waiting Mercedes.

The red light on my telephone was flashing when I arrived back at my hotel room. I picked up the instrument and dialled the front desk. "Message for me - McLeod?"

"Yes, sir. Mr. Gilbert, room 407 would like you to ring him when you come in."

So Gilbert was back. "Thank you," I said. "I'll call him now."

I dialled Gilbert's room number. "Hi, the wanderer returns."

"I thought I'd better. I can't leave you alone for five minutes. How did it go at Stanholts?"

I did not want to sound over enthusiastic at this point. "Not too bad. He's a hard one to evaluate."

"Well, do we have the contract, or don't we?"

"Honestly, Jim, I don't know. I think there are politics and factors in this that we know nothing about. He promised to let us know soon."

"Ok. I'll buy you lunch and you can tell me all about it."

. . . . .

Gilbert and I met with Rudolph Kruger on the following afternoon, Friday the 15th of January, to further discuss our business proposal. The project for the pilot plant had been approved in principal and we went on to thrash out the details. Within the next couple of days Kruger would select which of the plants would be chosen for this experimental venture. The meeting concluded successfully after about five hours of solid discussion.

As the meeting broke up, I said to Kruger, "We should get back to Canada as soon as possible to start planning the installation."

He agreed, and then said, "There will be no problem with the police, I hope."

I must have looked surprised, for I had mentioned nothing to him about my problems. "I hope not, but I must inform them before I leave the country."

"Herr Stanholt mentioned to me of your difficulties. I am instructed to tell you that anything you need from Mannhauseer, including our extensive legal services, are at your disposal."

"Well, that is very kind of you, but I am sure that won't be necessary. I will book a flight and then tell the police tonight."

We managed to get ourselves on a flight for Vancouver, leaving Frankfurt at 1:00 pm the following afternoon. Just before going to supper with Gilbert, I telephoned the police station.

"Inspector Drexler," I said, as soon as I got through.

Within moments he was on the line. "It's Robert McLeod. I'm booked on a flight to Vancouver tomorrow afternoon. Do you have any problem with that?"

"No, Mr. McLeod. Go ahead. There have been no new developments. Strangely, we can find no reason whatsoever why anyone would want to murder this woman, and yet I am sure the murderer is a paid assassin."

"It wasn't theft?" I knew I was reaching.

"I don't think so. We found a considerable sum of money in her room. Normally a thief would turn the place over pretty thoroughly."

"Well, I hope you get whoever did it."

"You've had no further thoughts on the subject that you would like to share with me, Have you?" he asked.

"No. I have told you all I know." I didn't like lying, but I seemed to be getting better at it.

"Alright then. If we need you for anything specific in the future, I trust you will cooperate with us?"

"Indeed. I will do anything I can."

"*Danke*! Have a good flight."

So that was that. I took a quick shower and dressed to go out to supper. On my way out of the room, the telephone rang. I stepped quickly back inside, and lifted the receiver. "Hallo."

The man spoke with a thick German accent and I had difficulty understanding him. I could not make out his name, but he said he was from the police.

"How can I help you?" I shouted as if this would help him to understand me.

"It ee's a matter of Mrs. Mortimer's body," he said. "We should release it to her family."

"Well, yes," I said, waiting for him to go on.

"We know no one who is her family. You were her friend; do you know if she has any family?"

I paused for a moment. The question struck me as being odd. At last I said, "If I did know of any family, I would have told you before. As far as I know, she comes from Ohio and her husband is dead. She has no children. There must be some family back there, even if it is only on her husband's side."

"Of course. We just thought that she might have mentioned someone to you."

"No, she didn't."

"*Danke*," he said, and then rang off.

On this, our last evening in Munich for a while, Gilbert had found a place where we just had to eat, and after that, a night club that we must not miss. Just to be sociable, I went along with him in spite of the fact that we had a heavy day's travelling coming up. As luck would have it, Gilbert struck up a conversation with one of the young ladies at the night club, and I managed to slip back to the hotel, leaving him there. When I entered my room, I found the red message light again flashing on my telephone. I rang down to the desk and the clerk gave me Inspector Drexler's home number and asked me to call him there.

"Hallo, McLeod," I said, when he answered the phone.

"Are, Mr. McLeod, thank you for calling me. There is some difficulty in contacting relatives of the deceased Mrs. Mortimer."

"I know. Someone has already called me."

"They have. Who was that?"

"I didn't catch his name, but he said he was from your police station."

"That's very strange. I haven't discussed it with anyone else at the station. I am sorry if you are being bothered."

"Not at all," I said.

"I thought, as you were returning to North America, would it be possible for you to make some enquiries for us concerning arrangements for returning the body?"

I laughed suddenly, in spite of the seriousness of the subject. "I am returning to the west coast of Canada. Ohio is close to the east coast of the United States, probably about three thousand miles away. It will be just as difficult for me to find out about anything, as it will be for you. What about the American Consulate? Aren't they responsible for doing that sort of thing?"

"Oh, I see, how stupid of me. I was not thinking. And you are right; we have approached the American Consulate, but these things take so much time."

I suddenly had second thoughts. "It is possible that I may be going to that part of the country. If I do, I'll find out what I can for you."

My statement was not totally spur of the moment. I did have some outstanding business in Toronto, and that could not be more than about six hundred miles from Heidi's home.

"Thank you, Mr. McLeod. That is very kind of you." He paused and then went on thoughtfully, "From the police station? That is very strange. What exactly did he say?"

"He just asked if I knew if Mrs. Mortimer had any living relatives – someone they could release the body to."

"And you replied, of course, that you do not know anybody?"

"Of course," I replied.

"Well, have a good flight, Mr. McLeod. And thank you for your help."

.   .   .   .   .

The Flight from Frankfurt to Vancouver took almost twelve hours including the stopover at Calgary, but I occupied myself making the initial plans for the installation of our system in Mannhauser's pilot plant. The time passed fairly quickly, and by four o'clock local time our plane touched down in Vancouver. My wife, Sara, and my two children, Michael who was ten, and Sherry just three years younger, were there to meet me. Gilbert's wife, Maureen, was also there, a beautiful woman, slim and blond, about twelve years younger than Gilbert. With such a woman waiting for him at home, I always found it incredible that he always looked for new conquests at every opportunity.

After the initial greetings, we said goodbye to the Gilberts and my wife took the wheel of our family car to take us home. I was in no shape to drive after the sixteen hour journey from the hotel in Munich. As soon as we were in the house and the children were occupied in another room with the gifts I had brought them, Sara and I embraced. "It has been a long time," she said quietly.

"Just a week." But even as I spoke, it seemed that far too much had happened for only one week.

"It seemed longer this time. Still, now you are home and we are all together again." I knew she didn't like me being away.

I squeezed her tightly. "I have to go away again."

She released her hold and took a step away from me. "When?"

"It won't be for long. I have to go east for a couple of days."

"Oh, Bob, when?"

"Day after tomorrow – Monday. Get a few things started and then I'll catch the red eye to Toronto."

"Oh, Bob, you need a rest. What is it this time?"

I felt defensive. "Business. I can't run a company without visiting my important clients."

"Couldn't it wait a couple of days and at least give you a chance to get over the jet lag from this trip?"

"No, this time it can't wait."

I suppose I must have spoken sharply, for she did not argue further. "Where exactly do you have to go?" she said.

"Toronto." And then after a short pause, "And Ohio," I added.

"Ohio?" What do you have to go there for?"

I shrugged my shoulders. "Business." Lying to her was a new experience for me and I did not enjoy doing it, but the truth was too complex, and I knew I could never make her understand.

I left Vancouver at eleven o'clock Monday night and I arrived in Toronto at seven o'clock local time on Tuesday morning, barely dawn and bitterly cold. I had forgotten what winter could be like in eastern Canada. Snow covered the ground to a depth of at least four inches. Because I had travelled business class, I had managed to get an hour's sleep on the plane, but I still felt desperately tired. My connector flight to Cleveland did not leave for another three hours, so I went in search of a comfortable seat, where I might rest and maybe doze a little.

Upon arrival in Cleveland, I rented a car and drove out to Barford, about forty miles. I did not enjoy driving in the snow, and by the time I reached the small town, I could feel the strain in my shoulders. I found a small hotel in the business district, not unlike the Marianne in Munich. They put me on the fourth floor – room 405, another coincidence, but the elevator whisked me to the fourth floor in almost total silence; I had nothing to worry about on that score.

I pondered whether to take a rest, nap for a couple of hours, but time was short and I needed to get this business over. I picked up the yellow pages and listed the addresses of all four ladies hair salons in town. One of them had to be Heidi's.

I sensed a feel of quality at Glamorous Occasions and if I had not known this was the right place, having been directed there from the previous salon, I would have guessed. A pleasant and discrete waiting room lay situated just inside the door, and as soon as I entered a young woman in a smart pink uniform came in.

"How can I help you, sir?" She seemed surprised at finding a man in her waiting room.

I hesitated, having not really thought this thing through as I should have. Unusual for me, it had been a spur of the moment decision based on emotions. "I guess I had better speak to whoever is in charge."

"That will be Mrs. Burnley, the manager. If you would wait a moment, I will see if she is available."

I sat down and waited for about five minutes before Mrs. Burnley, a plump woman aged about forty and wearing a pink overall covered with hair clippings, entered the room. She looked harassed, as if I had pulled her from something really important. She looked at me almost angrily and said, "What can I do for you?"

Again I hesitated, and then I stuttered, "I wonder if you could help me. It is about Mrs. Mortimer."

Mrs. Burnley looked sadly down at the carpet. "Poor soul. You know she is dead?"

"Yes. I met her in Germany."

The woman eyed me suspiciously. "You were with her when she was killed?'

"We were staying at the same hotel."

"You'd better come with me." She led me from the waiting room, through the shop and into a private office at the back. Once we were seated facing one another, she began to question me again. "Tell me what you know," she demanded. "We have heard nothing but the sketchiest information from Munich."

"There is not much to tell." And then I went on to tell her all I knew of the facts, leaving out anything to do with Stanholt, of course. After I had finished my story, she looked more relaxed and I think I had gained her trust.

"What do you want to know of Mrs. Mortimer?" she asked at last.

"I need to find her relatives. There must be someone to whom her body can be released. The Munich police are waiting instructions."

You are a long way out of your way for such a routine sort of thing, aren't you?"

"I had business in Toronto, and it didn't seem so far."

She looked at me strangely. "All the same."

"Well, I didn't know Mrs. Mortimer very well but I liked her. I liked her a lot. I just feel the need to do something."

"She was very close to her husband. I never heard her talk of anyone else. His death changed her, of course. She's been sort of lost since then. You should talk to Bennitti, her lawyer; his office is a couple of blocks down the street from here.

At last I felt as though I were getting somewhere. I should have asked about a lawyer in the first place.

She showed me to the front door, and as I turned to take my leave of her, I found her looking at me in that strange way of hers. "Mrs. Mortimer was a nice lady," she said. "And somehow, I think that you must be nice, too."

It was a strange thing to say to someone that you had only just met, but I let it pass. I said goodbye and left her one of my cards, should she ever need to call me for any reason.

Bennitti was younger than I imagined, not more than thirty-five, a short man with black hair and a dark complexion, reaching back to his Italian ancestry. He sat behind his desk holding my card in his hand, when his secretary eventually showed me into his office. He looked at me as if I were intruding and said, "What can I do for you, Mr. McLeod?"

"It is about Mrs. Mortimer," I began. "I am looking for her nearest relative."

He looked down at my card again. "I'm sorry if I should know you, but I am afraid I don't. Perhaps you would tell me who you are and what your interest in Mrs. Mortimer is."

"I realized I would have to explain the whole story over again, and he listened attentively until I had finished.

"Mrs. Mortimer does not have any blood relatives, as far as I know. There is a sister of her husband living in California, I believe. But as far as her burial arrangements are concerned, there is a request in her will that she be buried with her husband here in the local cemetery.

"Perhaps I could give Drexler, in Munich, your name and telephone number, and you could arrange for the release and transportation of the body."

The lawyer seemed please with these arrangements. "That would be very kind of you. Don't worry I will look after everything. I will also arrange the funeral. Will you be attending?"

I shook my head. "I don't think so. I have to be back in Vancouver."

Chapter 4

The beginning of the war made little difference to the Stanholts. The Germans were still very much in control of the situation, but by keeping a low profile, the family managed to stay out of harm's way. Ilse continued with her job at the shoe shop and Helmut stayed with the garage. All hope of emigrating to the USA had gone. In those early days, Austria kept remote from the war, except for the constant movement of troops and supplies. Initially the Germans were victorious on every front; and by June 1940, the French had collapsed and the British were driven back to Dunkirk.

Ilse usually spent two or three evenings a week with Martin, either at his house or at hers. They were to be married one day, when things improved, but for the time being they kept their engagement an open secret. One evening, late in the month of August, Ilse arrived on the Reidlemeyer's doorstep to be greeted by silence when she knocked at the door. Ilse did not understand. Martin knew she was coming, and he would have certainly let her know if he was going out. Besides that, Martin's mother almost never went out; she had been like that since the Germans came. As Ilse walked slowly away contemplating where Martin might be, the front door of the next house on the street opened slightly, and an old woman beckoned from the gap. Thinking that the woman may know of Martin's family, Ilse hurried over to her.

The old woman spoke in a cracked, high-pitched whisper. "They came and took them away."

"Who took them away?"

"Three men in dark raincoats – Gestapo!" The old woman hissed the last word, as if merely to utter the word was a dreadful blasphemy.

"Where did they take them?"

The woman shrugged her shoulders. "Who knows, many are disappearing. Labour camps, they say, but I have heard even worse than that."

Ilse, too, had heard the rumours, but she could not believe them to be true. For sure, there had been atrocities, but this had been going on since 1933. Ilse thanked the old lady and hurried home.

"What shall I do, Papa?" Beside herself with worry, Ilse could think of nothing else. If it had not been for the political situation, she and Martin would have been married.

Stanholt loved his daughter and wanted to help her, but he knew to make enquiries would be dangerous. "What can you do? It is better to do nothing and lie low. Perhaps the reason that they have not bothered us is because they do not know we are here."

"But I must know what has happened to him. He has done no harm to the Germans; why should they take him away?"

Finally Stanholt reluctantly agreed to go with Ilse to Gestapo headquarters and enquire. On the following morning they made their way to number 1 Morzinplatz in downtown Vienna, a majestic building of four stories high with a canopied entranceway supported by a semi circle of columns. In happier times the building had contained the Hotel Metropol, one of the better hotels in Vienna. They stood timidly before the reception desk.

"Redelmier?" A tall soldier, well built and wearing the uniform of a corporal in the SS, bellowed at them. "Are you family?"

Ilse shrank under the soldier's gaze and fingered the edge of the desk nervously. "I am his fiancé. We are to be married."

There were several other men in the lobby, none of them in uniform, but their tall stature, short haircuts and arrogant manner left no doubt as to who they were. Ilse shivered. Whenever she neared these people, the atmosphere seemed cold, as if they were surrounded by intense evil. Two of them were taking an interest in Ilse and her father; it was not often that Jews entered this building willingly.

"The Redelmiers have been taken to a labour camp, where their efforts will be directed to the benefit of the Reich. They will come to no harm."

"They were already working for the Reich." Ilse could not, or would not understand. "Herr Redelmier's factory made uniforms for the soldiers."

"And the factory shall continue to make uniforms, but it has been decided that Herr Redelmiers efforts could be used more appropriately elsewhere."

Close to tears, Ilse said, "What camp have they been sent to? Can I see them?"

"I cannot disclose the camp." The soldier grinned evilly. "But if you are sent there, it is possible that you might see them."

Stanholt took Ilse by the shoulder. "Come," he said. The conversation had turned ugly and he did not like it, also he did not like the way the Gestapo agents were eyeing them. They started back towards the door.

"Wait." One of the agents motioned them to stop. "Let me see your papers."

Stanholt handed over his identity card, while Ilse retrieved hers from her purse.

The agent glanced at them and then said, "Come with me."

They were taken upstairs to the second floor where they were shown into a small room that contained little furniture, other than a desk and a couple of hard chairs. The room still reflected its former grandeur, with thick leather upholstered padding on the doors, which served to make the room virtually sound proof.. The agent disappeared with their papers, and Ilse and her father were left to wait.

"Now what?" said Stanholt, almost beside himself with worry.

Ilse sobbed quietly. "I am sorry, Papa."

Stanholt placed a comforting arm around his daughters' shoulders. "It is not your fault, my dear. Why should you not be worried about your fiancé? It is the Nazis."

They waited in the hot, stuffy room for over three hours, until at last the agent returned. He tossed a buff coloured, manila folder with a yellow star in the corner on the desk. Stanholt recognized it from the times he had been to the Gauleiter's office. The agent sat at the desk and opened the file.

Both Ilse and her father watched the Gestapo agent apprehensively. They saw his eyes focus immediately on the memo pinned to the inside cover. After reading the note, he looked up. "Why is Germany so interested in you?"

Stanholt said, "I don't understand."

"You don't, eh. Well they are." The agent re-read the note. "Interesting. I shall have to find out why."

Stanholt could contain his curiousity no longer. "What does it say?"

"That is no concern of yours." The agents face creased into a frown and he tossed the file on the desk. "For now, you had better go," he snapped.

Ilse could not remember feeling as much relief as when they were finally out of that building and walking home. "What is in the note, Papa?"

Stanholt shook his head. "I have no idea. Except that whatever it says has stopped us going to America."

Ilse never heard of Martin again, or of his family. She missed him terribly at first, but then came the pressing worry for their own survival. More and more Jews were being shipped out to 'Labour Camps'. Rumours of their fate were rife and terrible. Ilse did not believe all the stories she heard, but some of them had to be, at least, partly true.

Unknown to the Stanholt's, late in 1941, Hitler with the enthusiastic help of his subordinates, Himmler and Heidrich, instituted a policy for the 'Final Solution to the Jewish Problem'. At that time Jews were being shipped to labour camps in droves. Trains of box cars, no better than cattle trucks, left Vienna daily, loaded to capacity with helpless Jews, and bound for labour camps in various parts of the German occupied territories.

One afternoon in October 1941, a plain-clothes Gestapo agent presented himself at the Stanholts front door. He carried a dispatch addressed to Herr Stanholt, ordering him and his family to present themselves at the railway station the following morning for trans-shipment to the labour camp at Auswitz. They were to take the minimum of luggage, no more than a small bag between them, as all they would need would be provided.

"So," said Stanholt to the rest of the family after the Gestapo agent had gone. "It has come at last."

Ilse said, "Now we shall find out if the rumours are true."

42

"If only we could have gone to America," cut in Helmut.

His mother, already occupied with the problem of deciding what to take with them, said, "It is no use crying over what might have been."

Stanholt pulled a bottle of Cognac from the cupboard. "Don't know when we will get another chance. Might as well have a drink before we go."

Tears welled in Ilse' eyes. Her father didn't normally drink at all. "Oh Papa," she said.

Her mother, still worrying about what to take, said, "They will give us clothing. Better we pack something to eat and drink. We don't know what the food situation will be like on the train, and it will be a long way."

The following morning they walked to the railway station to find a long line of people such as themselves waiting to be checked in by several soldiers of the Wehrmacht. The line moved slowly, but as they drew nearer the front, they could see a train of loaded box cars standing at the platform beyond. Ilse shivered, and not because of the cold. If this is the way they make us travel, then perhaps the rumours are true. A terrible fear gripped her, for she could not shut these thoughts from her mind.

Stanholt presented all their papers to the soldier clerk, who looked bored as he checked their name against a list pinned to his desk. His finger stopped against one of the names on the list, and a flicker of interest appeared on his sallow face. He looked up at the four of them and said, "Ilse Stanholt?"

"That's me," stammered Ilse, her face quite white.

"Stand over there, all of you." He pointed to an area at the side of his desk. Then picking up a telephone, he spoke rapidly. The Stanholts were unable to make out what he said, except that their name was mentioned more than once. After replacing the instrument, he turned to them. "You will wait," he said Then shutting them from his mind as if they no longer existed, he returned to processing the line.

They stood at the side of the soldier's desk waiting for nearly an hour before another soldier, wearing the smart black uniform and red armband of the Waffen SS, marched up. He spoke first to the soldier clerk, "Is this them?"

The clerk merely nodded.

The soldier turned to them. "Come," he said. And they picked up their few belongings and followed him through the station until they came to an office used by the SS, where an SS officer eventually saw them.

The officer spoke to them sharply, as if they were naughty children. "Your orders have been changed. You are to go to Munich. A train is leaving in half an hour and you are to be on it. At Munich station you will present yourself to the office of the SS. Do you understand?"

Stanholt nodded. "Yes, sir."

"Good." He handed them new travel permits, and then instructed the same soldier who had brought them to the office, to see them board the train.

They were placed aboard the train, and they each had seats, even though the train was filled almost to capacity. When, at last, the train moved out of the station, it slipped past the seemingly endless line of crowded boxcars. The Stanholts stared

43

at them in sick dismay. Ilse pondered on what lucky intervention had prevented her and her family meeting the same fate as the thousands of others. It would not be long before she would find out.

Upon arrival at Munich, they went straight to the station office of the SS, where they were seen by another bored soldier seated behind a desk. After reading their papers, he took them to a waiting room and left them to sit on hard seats for the next four hours.

Helmut, his patience exhausted, his body tired, grumbled, "What are they keeping us for now? They push us around, treat us like animals and then leave us in this God forsaken place for hour after hour. What is the matter with them?"

Still remembering what she had seen in Vienna, Ilse replied, "It is better that we are here than in those boxcars."

Stanholt looked at his daughter fondly. "I only hope you are right, Ilse."

"Why, Papa. Why do you say that?"

"For some reason they have singled us out and returned us here. I can't help but wonder at their reason."

A soldier entered the waiting room. "Ilse Stanholt," he barked.

Ilse got to her feet. "That's me," she said timidly.

"Come with me." He turned on his heel and walked quickly from the room.

Stanholt jumped to his feet. "Where are you taking her?"

The soldier snarled contemptuously over his shoulder. "That is not your concern."

Helmut grabbed his father and pulled him back to the seat, while Ilse followed the soldier, almost running to keep up, as he led her out of the station to a waiting sedan.

"Get in." he motioned toward the back of the car. She did as instructed, and the soldier slipped behind the wheel. The building to which he took her used to be an hotel, but had become temporary accommodation for the SS. After he left her to wait in the lobby, she looked nervously around, trying to hide herself as much as possible within the dark overcoat and under the wide brimmed hat she wore. The hotel had still retained much of the glamour of its previous existence, though grown somewhat tired by the unusual traffic it now received. Men, some in uniform, some in civilian clothes, crowded through the lobby, each hurrying about his own business. A huge chandelier dominated the lobby, and around the walls stood ornately styled furniture of plush red velvet.

This time the soldier returned quickly "Herr Standartenfuhrer will see you now."

She followed the soldier to a room on the fourth floor – Room 405. A tall man in an SS colonel's uniform stood looking out of the window. He did not turn around as the soldier and Ilse entered the room. The soldier clicked his heel, raised his arm in a Nazi salute, turned about face and marched out, closing the door behind him. Only then did the colonel turn round.

Recognition came slowly to Ilse. It had been a long time, and she found difficulty in transposing the schoolteacher of her younger days into the uniform of the German officer standing before her. She gasped. "Herr Becker."

"Herr Standartenfuhrer Becker." The man could not completely retain the grin that struggled to surface on his face. "So, Ilse, after all this time, we meet again."

A combination of fear, uncertainty and surprise left Ilse speechless.

"Take off your hat and coat. Let me see what the years have done to you."

Ilse remained motionless. "I think I had better keep them on."

Becker frowned. "So be it. There's no need to be unfriendly; my offer of protection is still open."

"And my reply will be the same."

"Doesn't it mean anything to you, that after all these years I have never lost touch."

"Why me? What am I to you?" Echoes from the past seemed to be laughing at her as she posed the question she had asked herself so many times before.

"Why you? I can no more answer that than you can. Call it fate." He laughed. "Or perhaps we were something to each other in a previous life. But since the first moment I set eyes on you, Ilse, I have wanted you. Through all these years that want has never diminished. You refused me once, but you cannot refuse me now."

A spark of fire flashed in the Jewish girl's eyes. "You disgusting man. I could never willingly go to you – not if you were the last man on earth."

"You disappoint me, Ilse." Becker sighed. "I would have thought by now that you would have seen enough to at least pretend to be attracted to me. I could be your salvation. Once, I offered you protection from the discomforts of an extreme political system, now I am the only hope you have for life."

"What do you mean?" But even as Ilse asked the question, the rumours she had heard and the awful visions of the boxcars played on her mind, creating a stark backdrop of fear, as if the room in which she stood was an island sanctuary in a world of terror and darkness.

"Whether you want to believe this or not, it doesn't matter to me, but your race is systematically being eliminated. If you return to Austria, you will be sent to a camp where you will be killed."

"They tell us the camps are labour camps, where we will be put to work to aid the war effort. They would not dare to kill us."

"One of the Fuhrer's most cherished desires is to rid the world of Jews. Unfortunately for both of us, Ilse, you are a Jew."

"I have no reason to be anything but proud of my heritage, and I will not become a German officer's harlot."

Becker shook his head, his patience running thin. "If you do not care for yourself, what of your family? Do not forget that they wait even now at that railway station while we argue their fate."

It was the same ploy he used before, and this time there was nowhere to run. Ilse felt the chill wind of defeat. "What of my family?"

"I will extend whatever protection I can towards them. I do not know how much that would be, but I should be able to keep them alive."

Whether Becker spoke the truth or not, he could not be sure. But for him, it was only important that Ilse believe it.

45

"What will happen to them?"

"They will be sent to Dachau. I have connections there and I can see that they are treated well - better than the other prisoners."

"Will I be able to see them."

"No." Becker's tone was hard and definite.

"How will I know they are alright?"

Becker smiled, beginning to taste the sweetness of victory. "You must take my word for it. Ilse, you have nothing to bargain with."

"Herr Becker, I would rather die than go to you. If it were not for my family, I would have you send me back to Austria, whatever the consequences. But you have gone to a great deal of trouble to bring me here. Yes, Herr Becker, I think I do have something to bargain with."

The sweet taste turned bitter in Becker's mouth. "Yes, I have gone to much trouble to bring you here, maybe too much. Only time will tell if it has been worth it. But let me warn you, do not push me too far."

"If I agree to your demands, then I need some positive assurance that you are keeping your word."

It was make or break time, and anyway things could change as time went by. "Alright, Ilse, a letter occasionally is the best I can do."

"If that is really the best you can do, I suppose I have no choice."

Becker sat at his desk, his face a mask of anger and frustration. "You realize this is dangerous for me. I could be shot for what I am doing."

Ilse shook her head. "None of this is my doing."

"Well, take off your hat and coat," shouted Becker.

Ilse jumped, startled by his anger. Then, slipping out of the hat and coat, she hung them up behind the door.

Becker, his eyes alight with lust and desire, told her to turn around.

Ilse had chosen the hat and coat specifically to hide her figure and her looks. It was not wise for a woman of Jewish extraction to advertise her female qualities in those times. And if anything, Ilse had become even more beautiful than Becker remembered.

"You have grown up, Ilse. This is surely a case of the sweet young bud, blossoming into a beautiful rose."

Ilse' dark, shoulder length curls shone above her floral dress. She wore no make-up, giving her the appearance of looking younger, but her figure, her narrow waist, pleasing hips and firm breasts, left no doubt as to her maturity. Becker was pleased with his bargain.

"Sit down," he said.

Ilse did as he asked, wondering what would come next.

"Now listen carefully, because what I am doing is dangerous for both of us. The most important thing for you to remember is that Ilse Stanholt is dead. From this moment on, she is no more. Officially, she will be listed as being shot while trying to escape. Your name is Eve Maynard. Here are some papers with a short history of your life that you must learn quickly and thoroughly." Becker tossed a folder of papers on to the table.

Ilse picked up the folder gingerly. Upon opening it, she found an Identity card carrying a stamped picture of herself, yet another woman's name and birthplace. According to the document, she was a German citizen of indisputable 'Arian' blood.

"How?" she asked in wonder.

Becker looked smug. "Anything can be accomplished if you have the right connections."

"Why is she four years older than me?"

"What difference does it make? It is hard to tell a woman's age that closely."

"But why didn't you make her twenty one?"

"Because that is how old she was."

"Then she is a real woman?"

"Of course. But she is dead, shot, and she will be buried as Ilse Stanholt. Now do you understand."

Ilse did not understand, but she was afraid to ask further. Questions like was Eve Maynard shot to provide Ilse with an alternative identity, or was it just happenstance that provided the body. She looked once more at Becker. Just how far would he go?

"You have no living relatives and you are the mistress of Herr Standartenfuhrer Becker. You live with me on my farm where I raise a few horses, just south of here, near Penzberg. I will take you there later, and you will not leave there for any reason without my express permission. Is that clear?"

"I wish to say goodbye to my parents."

"Impossible."

"But I must."

"If you see your parents again, then you will return with them to Austria. The girl will be buried as Eve Maynard, and you and your parents will be dead within a week. This I promise you."

Ilse turned white. "Then I will never see them again."

"Who knows what the future may hold. Nothing is certain in wartime."

Ilse shrugged her shoulders and looked away from Becker, feeling completely defeated.

"Do you accept my offer?"

Her eyes returned to his, hatred fuelling defiance. "You leave me no choice, but do not forget the letters. Leave me something of my parents."

"I will do my best about the letters, but it will not be easy. Your parents will be informed of your death."

"Then how can they write to me?"

"You have other friends or relatives to whom they could write."

"I have a cousin in America."

"Then I will work something out." Becker's mood changed suddenly and he smiled benevolently. "Now, Ilse, since you are now my mistress, it is time for you to remove your dress."

Ilse gasped involuntarily and glanced towards the door. "Not here. Not like this."

"Why not here? We will not be disturbed, and surely I have waited long enough."

"Please no."

Becker rose up and came around to confront Ilse. Gesturing with his hands, he said, "Stand up."

Ilse meekly obeyed and Becker's fingers opened the buttons on the front of her dress.

"Please, not here."

Placing his arm around her body, inside the dress, Becker pulled her close. "Eve, sweet Eve, I have waited so long." His lips moved across her cheek, searching for her lips. His breath felt hot on her neck and she shuddered. His hand found her breast and she looked up at him, meeting him eye to eye, evacuating all feelings and emotions. It could not be possible for her to be his lover and still have feelings.

As if by prearranged signal, just as his lips found hers, the telephone on his desk sprang to life, startling Becker every bit as much as it startled Ilse. Becker swore an oath and turned and picked it up. The conversation was abrupt and to the point. Becker must report to his superior at once.

"Get dressed. I don't know how long I shall be, but wait here. Do not leave this room for any reason, do you understand?"

Ilse, already buttoning her dress, agreed.

"Study that folder, and if anyone should ask, remember who you are. Eve Maynard, is that clear?"

Before Ilse could answer, Becker had left the room.

Ilse sat at the desk and began to study the contents of the folder again. There were two pages of handwriting outlining a brief history of her life, her identity card, a copy of her birth certificate, and a photograph. The photograph interested her, because it was a recent one and must have been taken in Austria. Picking it up, she turned it over and found some writing on the back: 'Eve Maynard' and there was an address of a horse farm near Penzberg. She could only wonder at the power Becker must wield to have gathered this dossier. Becker did not return for some time and she read the papers through and through again until thoroughly bored. Worried about her parents, she threw the papers back into the folder and tossed the folder on the desk. Unbeknown to her the photograph fell from the folder, fluttered down to the floor and landed, concealed from sight, under the pedestal of the desk. An insignificant event, but fate had taken a hand; an event that would start a chain of discovery, death and judgment some thirty-five years later.

The photograph lay concealed under the desk for three days. The cleaning lady found it as she swept the floor. Most of the staff, those that were not taken into the army, were kept on from the original hotel. But most were not happy. They missed the old times, the pleasant times, when the hotel filled with tourists and businessmen, and there were smiles and tips. Most, like the cleaning lady hated the SS. Particularly, she hated this strutting, arrogant colonel. She would spit on him if she could get away with it. And now she had found a picture of his whore. She took it in her hands and was about to tear it, but hesitated. If she tore it and they found the pieces, there would be questions. There were too many questions already. Better, she decided, to hide it. If there were questions about the missing picture, she could always re-discover it in the future. It took some time before she found the perfect place. A large framed photograph of the Rathaus in Munich, circa 1930, hung on the wall near the door. Taking this picture down, she turned it over and pushed Ilse' photograph securely into the lower left hand corner of the frame forcing it between the frame and the photograph of Munich. Replacing the picture on the wall, she smiled. That'll do him. He will never find it there. In her small way, she felt she had got a little of her own back on the Nazi swine she worked for

Chapter 5

I settled back to a more or less normal routine of work, which at that time was rarely less than fourteen hours a day. I promised my wife a vacation, which we did not take, and I also told her that I would limit my business trips to only those that could not be taken care of by others. I assembled a team of application engineers for Germany, three in all, led by a bright young man named Richard Jennings. We were lucky to get Jennings; he had been sought after by a number of companies, most much bigger than ours, but he liked our product and was anxious to get in at the beginning. Almost three months past before all the contract finalities were through and our lawyers put their stamp of approval on it. Mannhauser's had chosen their plant in Munich to be the pilot plant and Thursday, April the 1st, 1971, April Fools day, saw Jennings and his team board the Lufthansa flight for Germany.

Six weeks later or there abouts, on Monday the 17th of May, I received an urgent phone call from Jennings in Munich. They were in trouble. Apparently, the old guard at Mannhauser's required too much customization of the software. Instead of accepting our methods, they wanted to computerize their way of doing things. It seemed that the political and technical problems were proving too much for Jennings and it would be prudent for me to get out there as soon as possible, otherwise, instead of making us a nice profit this venture could turn into a nightmare.

Immediately I instructed my secretary. "I need a flight through to Munich as soon as possible. Get me on a plane tomorrow, open return, and book me into a hotel room for at least a week. Any hotel down town, but not the Marrianne."

She telephoned the local travel agent and about an hour later she came into my office. "I'm sorry, Mr. McLeod, there are no seats tomorrow or Wednesday. The earliest they can get you away is Thursday afternoon."

"Damn! Have you tried all the airlines?" The question was unnecessary; Helen had been with me some time and she was one of the best.

"There's a big trade conference in Munich. Everything is booked."

"Nothing is getting done. If I don't go over there and sort it out, we have a disaster on our hands."

I regretted putting Jennings in charge. I should have found someone more mature, but then probably, if it hadn't been Jennings, it would have been me. I slumped back in my chair in disgust. "Thursday it will have to be then."

"Did you know Mr. Gilbert is going to Germany tomorrow?"

I sat up. I had forgotten. "Yes, he did say. He is working on something in Frankfurt. I wonder if he could postpone."

"He has two tickets. He is taking Mr. Forest, the new off-shore sales manager with him."

"Oh, no he is not." I grabbed the phone. "Forest can go on Thursday."

The following afternoon, Tuesday, Gilbert and I boarded a Lufthansa 707 bound for Frankfurt. He had the aisle seat, while I had the window. "So tell me about this deal you are working on in Frankfurt," I asked him, when we were settled and the aircraft had reached cruising altitude.

"It's big, Bob. If it comes off, it will be bigger than the Mannhauser deal." He reached into his jacket pocket and fished out a business card. He flashed it to me quickly and I didn't need to read the name; I recognized the logo of one of the largest German auto manufacturers.

"Really?" I was impressed. "You were working on that last time we were over here?"

"Why else do you think I went to Frankfurt?"

"I thought you had a woman tucked away," I admitted.

He laughed. "How could you think such things of me?"

It was my turn to laugh. "I wonder."

"Seriously, while we are on the subject, Bob, when you found that woman's body, what were you doing going to her room at that time of night?" His moustache bristled and his face split into a huge grin.

"Because she didn't answer the telephone."

There was a pause, as if he expected more. "So? Why did you phone her?"

"While we were having supper, she asked me to her room for a night cap. At the time I agreed, but later, after I had thought about it, I decided against it. I telephoned her to cancel out."

Gilbert looked disappointed. "If it had been anyone else telling me that, I wouldn't have believed them. But you, I know. Don't you ever feel like stepping off the pedestal?"

It was a strange question. I hadn't realized that Gilbert thought of me like that. I turned and looked out of the window. The bright blue sky and the field of snow like clouds below us seemed to stretch for infinity. My mind traveled back once more to when I shared that fateful supper with Heidi. "There is no pedestal, Jim. If things had been different, I may have stayed the night. God knows I wanted to."

"She really affected you, didn't she?"

51

I turned back to find Gilbert looking at me with renewed interest.

I left Gilbert in Frankfurt, and I caught the commuter on to Munich. I had left the plane and entered the airport building before I pulled my itinerary from my brief case to find out what hotel Helen had booked me into to. The Marrianne. I could not believe my eyes. I had expressly told her any hotel but that one. For a number of reasons, the elevator not least among them, I did not want to stay there. I hurriedly found a pay phone and started a frantic search for a room in another hotel. The ongoing trade show had every room in the city booked. I was lucky to have reservations at all. I found out later that Helen had contacted Mannhauser, and they had used influence to get me a room, and as I had stayed at the Marrianne before, they thought I would want to stay there again. I look back now and realize that fate had already wrapped its tentacles around me and there was no escape.

I checked in at the somewhat familiar front desk and the clerk gave me my room key – room 405. "No," I said. "You must have something else."

"Sir, the hotel is completely full."

"But I stayed in that room before and I didn't like it."

"All our rooms are similar, sir." He spoke politely, but he obviously thought he was dealing with a crank.

"You are sure you have nothing else?"

"There is a room on the ground floor."

I did not hesitate. "I'll take that one."

"Well sir, it is next to the elevator and rather noisy."

Noisy? What kind of noisy? "Well then, I had better take the one on the fourth floor."

"Good choice, sir. Room 405."

I went up to my room with the bell hop carrying my bag. The elevator creaked and the wires sang, but there were no noises that I could not account for. My imagination worked overtime, for I felt an atmosphere, not an atmosphere of dread or foreboding, but a feeling of something being there, something that I was afraid of and inwardly rejecting, waiting for me, welcoming me back.

The long flight and the lost night's sleep were fast catching up with me and my senses were dull and tired. I ordered room service, and after a quick meal, went to bed. I needed to be at the plant early the next morning.

The farmhouse lay before me just as it had so many times before, the emerald green grass divided into so many irregular rectangles by the white frames of the paddocks, but strangely devoid of horses. I moved on down the driveway as if compelled. I wanted to turn and run, but it was as if my body belonged to another. Only consciousness was mine, trapped like a useless prisoner. I arrived at the back door and passed though it, as I had before, into the dark interior, darker than it should have been, for the sun shone brightly and the drapes were open. The furniture, though in excellent condition, looked to be antique, furniture from a previous era. Upon a table in the corner of the room, stood the wooden cabinet of a radio, the type of radio specified by Hitler and subsidized by his government, so that all the people could listen to his oratory magnificence. On top of the radio, a framed photograph of a tall officer of the SS looked out over the room. I wanted to stop and examine these things, but it was useless. My legs were not mine to command. I passed through another door and then up a staircase.

I had not been afraid of the dark since childhood, but the atmosphere at the top of these stairs, though not completely dark, gave a whole new meaning to being afraid. A multitude of dark shadows jostled in constant motion, and I felt I was being permitted to glimpse a crowded dimension that exists somewhere beyond life itself.

Four doors led from a short landing at the top of the stairs. Two of these doors were closed. With all my heart, I wanted to turn and run, but my legs carried me on down the landing, passed the first closed door, passed the open door of a large bedroom, passed the bathroom, on towards the door that stood ominously waiting for me at the end of the passage. As I approached the door, I resisted with all my will, with every sinew of my body. I didn't want to know whatever dark secrets were in that room. It had nothing to do with me. It was none of my damn business.

I cried out as the curtain that divides reality from nightmare pulled back, and I found myself sitting up in bed, bathed in sweat, my hair standing on end and the telephone ringing in my ear. Automatically I lifted the phone. "Yes," I said.

"Good morning, sir. It is six fifteen." The female voice spoke perfect English.

I lay back in bed for a while, not wanting to get up. I felt hot and flushed and my hands still shook. I had a very full day's work ahead of me and this would not do. The trade show finished at the end of the week and then I would find another place to stay.

That evening I returned to the hotel quite late. There were many details to sort out at Mannhausers. I planned to take supper in my room and then carry on working, but after I had eaten, I felt very tired and could not concentrate to the degree necessary. Jet lag contributed somewhat to the way I felt, but mostly it was my rotten night. I had to do something about it; perhaps I should consult a local doctor.

Instead of working that evening, I decided to go down to the bar for a nightcap. A couple of neat Scotches would help me sleep. I sat down at one of the empty tables and ordered a drink, and had barely taken a sip, when I had company. A short man, about five feet, seven inches tall, quite portly with a mop of red hair that crowned his chubby face came up to my table and asked if he could join me. Without waiting for an affirmative, he sat down. "I heard you speaking English, you American?"

"Canadian," I corrected him. "And you must be English."

He smiled, self-satisfied that I should have guessed his nationality on such short acquaintance. He introduced himself as Charley Smithers. "It's nice to hear a friendly voice. So many Krauts about."

I looked quickly over my shoulder, hoping no one had heard my loud and already slightly drunk friend. "You are in Munich; what do you expect?"

He went on to tell me that he was here for the trade convention and that he owned a successful company that made bathroom fittings. I listened to his conversation with half an ear as I sipped my Scotch. He seemed to be comparing things English with things continental, starting with bathroom fittings and moving up to the characteristics of the people themselves.

He finished his drink and waved loudly for the waiter to bring us another round, pointing with his finger to include me. He was becoming more drunk by the minute. I thanked him for the drink, when it arrived, and he lent towards me as if to impart some personal confidence. "You know something that is always good about Germany?" he hissed.

I shook my head, drawing back a little to avoid his breath.

"The whores." He laughed, his voice carrying across the bar. "You can always rely on getting a good lay in Germany."

I wished fervently that I had stayed in my room, called room service and got on with my work.

"Take the bird I had last night, did she know a thing or two." He gestured and laughed loudly. "Told me she was a psychic, talked to the dead, that kind of stuff. I told her, I don't care who you talk with, darling, as long as you keep moving your ass and don't make too much noise." He bellowed again.

"Psychic?" I said.

He sneered. "Don't know about that. Good lay though. Tammy Findlay, her name; English she was. Funny thing her being English; she must have been trained by the Krauts."

"Where did you meet her?"

He looked at me and grinned sickly. "From the phone book, where else? But don't worry, I've got her number here." He felt in his jacket pocket for his address book, and then he looked at me doubtfully. "She's expensive, you know. You get what you pay for."

He obviously didn't think I could afford her. "I expect I can manage it, as long as she's worth it."

"Oh, she's worth it all right." He had the address book on the table, and taking one of his business cards, he wrote a telephone number on the back. "If she ain't in, leave a message with her maid."

I placed the card in the pocket of my shirt, then bought the man another drink and made my excuses to return to my room. Prostitute or not, I needed to speak to either a psychic or a psychiatrist. I would rather start with a psychic.

.　.　.　.　.

The following evening, Friday, after thinking about it for almost twenty-four hours, I telephoned the number on the back of Charley Smithers card.

A demure voice answered. *"Ja."*

"Is that Tammy?"

"Yes," this time answering in English.

I stammered nervously. "I wonder if you could come around to my hotel room."

She sounded cool and professional. "I am fully booked until Monday. I could come at seven on Monday evening, or after ten."

"After ten will be fine."

"For a first visit, I will need two hundred American dollars."

I had been warned but I didn't expect it to be that expensive. "I see, and how much for the second visit?" I asked the question facetiously.

She paused, wondering if I was playing with her. "It depends," she said at last. "There may not be a second visit."

I finalized the arrangements for her to visit me some time after ten on Monday evening.

I worked through the weekend and by Monday I understood the root causes of the problems with the software installation. I called meetings with various company managers to explain to them what we could do, and what compromises they would have to make in regard to their past system. I seemed to be making progress, though it seemed I would have to customize the software more than I intended to, necessitating me staying in Germany longer than I planned. All the time I thought of Tammy in the back of my mind, and how our meeting would go that evening.

Jennings came into my office just as I was about to leave, and asked me if I would like to go for a drink with him and his team.

"No," I said, more sharply than I intended. "I have work to do."

He looked crestfallen as he left the room and I realize that I must have sounded pompous in the extreme. Still, Jennings performance on the contract to date left a great deal to be desired. It would be some time before I would trust him on a job this big again.

The time by the small clock on my bedside radio said ten past ten, when there came a quiet knock on the door to my hotel room. I walked over and let her in. I didn't know what to expect, but I was pleasantly surprised when I opened the door. The young lady that entered my hotel room did not advertise her trade by her clothes; instead she wore a smart black costume that would not look out of place in any hotel. She was a little taller than I expected, about five foot eight, her platinum blond hair grew shoulder length and matched her pale complexion. When I looked at her, I could understand Charley Smithers' ravings. Her pretty face plus her striking figure made her a very desirable woman.

"Hello, my name is Tammy," she said in a north-country English accent, as soon as I had closed the door.

"Bob," I felt nervous and offered her my hand. "Oh, here you are." I passed her an envelope that I had left on the table.

She opened the envelope and looked inside, her practised eye easily counting the notes. She appeared satisfied and placed the envelope in her purse, and then removed her costume jacket. Things were moving a little too quickly for me, as she began to undo the buttons of her white blouse.

"Hold on a bit," I said, raising my hand.

She looked at me suspiciously. "What do you want?"

I sat down on my chair. "I didn't ask you here for sex. I just wanted to talk to you."

Her suspicions deepened. "You can talk to anyone here in the hotel and you don't have to pay for it. Why me?"

"Somebody told me you were a psychic. Is that true?"

She sat down on the edge of the bed opposite me, the buttons of her blouse still open displaying a thin bra that barely covered her full and well rounded breasts. "I dabble in it. I'm not that good, not like my mum, but I do see things. Is that what you want to talk to me about?"

"I need to talk to somebody," I said. "I need help."

She looked at me condescendingly. "Well, you had better tell me about it."

And so I told her. I told her of the elevator, of Heidi, my dreams of the farmhouse, everything relevant except the connection to Stanholt. I could tell nobody about that. Periodically she asked questions and I did my best to answer them. I ordered a bottle of wine from room service and we each took a drink.

"I suppose we had better take a ride on the lift," she said, doing up the buttons on her blouse.

"Good idea, but I've only ever heard the noises when I am alone." I thought about what I had said. "Am I losing it? Does that make me a crack pot?"

She laughed. "Maybe. We will have to find out."

While waiting for the elevator to rise from the ground floor, we were joined by another couple. We stood at the back of the car, as it began its descent, and Tammy took my hand in hers. As I expected, there was nothing unusual about the ride down. The other couple gave us a puzzled glance as they left the car on the ground floor; they obviously expected us to follow. Instead Tammy pushed the button to take us back to the top floor. She giggled. "They probably think we're going to have sex in the lift."

"I hope not," I said.

The elevator returned to the top floor without anything unusual happening. When the door opened I took a step forward, but Tammy tightened her grip on my hand and said, "Let's try it again."

This time we were alone as the cage descended and I strained every sense to pick up whatever sound or feeling might be there – but nothing, no noise that could not be simply explained away as part of the old machinery. I glanced at Tammy as she stared straight ahead at some point beyond the confines of the elevator. As soon as the car came to rest on the ground floor, she touched the button to send us back again. She remained transfixed in her staring position until the door opened on the fourth floor. This time we returned to my room.

I couldn't keep the tone of resignation from my voice. "Well, that's that. I told you I never hear anything unusual when there is someone else in the car. I suppose I am going crazy." I poured us both another drink from the half empty bottle.

"Oh, I don't think your crazy, except for paying me two hundred dollars to come around and talk."

I handed her a glass. "Did you sense anything at all?"

"It would be impossible to come into this hotel and not sense anything at all. This place is filled with psychic vibrations. Something bad happened here; a lot of people died."

"I suppose a lot of people died when Munich was bombed."

"True, but it is more than that. People were tortured here and died in agony. Nothing else would account for it."

"What am I hearing in the elevator, then?"

Tammy shrugged, thinking back to the recent ride in the elevator. "Who knows? There is a strong presence there, stronger near the bottom. Maybe something happened in the elevator shaft. I think there maybe a spirit form in the elevator shaft trying to contact you."

"Ridiculous!" I said somewhat thoughtlessly. "Why me? I've never been within three thousand miles of this place before this year."

Tammy stood up and turned to find her coat. "You asked."

I realized I had offended her. "I'm sorry. Please don't go."

"I must. It is late and you have had your time."

"Well, what do I do about it then?" I felt frantic, being still no nearer a solution to my problem and being out two hundred dollars to boot.

She started towards the door and then paused. Turning slightly, she said, "Whatever it is that is trying to reach you will go on trying until it succeeds. It will not rest; in cannot rest. You can either leave this place and never come back, or try to find out what it wants."

"How can I find out what it wants?"

"Call me again in two days. I know someone who could help you. I don't know whether she will or not."

After she had left I thought over my options. My first option, leave this place and never come back, sounded good to me, but I decided to give it a few more days. The only explanation I can find for this is that my interest must have been piqued.

The following morning I returned to Mannhauser and began to organize the customisation of the software. Jennings greeted me with a cool attitude, but I expected nothing else. I paid him well for what he did and I could find no excuse for not producing. I organized our people into two teams. I would lead one team of two of us in customizing the software, and Jennings would lead the other for installing the software and training the people. The arrangement seemed satisfactory and still left Jennings more or less running the project. I still needed him; otherwise I would be stuck in Germany for the next few months. Leaving him in charge served to save his face and keep his authority in tact.

I thought of Tammy over the next couple of days. Though she hadn't been much help, I had enjoyed her company, loneliness having quite a lot to do with it. At four o'clock in the afternoon of the second day, I picked up the phone and dialled Tammy's number.

"Bob McLeod, here," I said. "Did you give our discussion anymore thought?"

"Hello, Mr. McLeod. Yes, I have spoken to a friend of mine, a psychic. She is a person I very much respect and she has agreed to see you tomorrow night at eight-thirty in your room at the hotel. Is that time all right with you?"

"Yes. Will you be coming, too?"

I sensed her smile. Her voice softened. "I'd better. Greta's English is not that good."

"Well, perhaps we can all have dinner afterwards," I said quickly, without thinking.

She hesitated. "Perhaps not. I may be pressed for time."

I realised after I had spoken that the evening was probably Tammy's busy part of the day.

I left work early the following evening, much to the surprise of my colleagues. "I have an appointment," I said brusquely, by way of an excuse. I stopped off at a fast food outfit for a burger on my way to the hotel, in lieu of supper.

I was tense, not knowing quite what to expect, as I waited in my hotel room. The hands of my watch told me it was nearly eight forty-five and I had heard nothing from Tammy since our telephone call yesterday afternoon. I had bought a few bottles of wine and liquor from the local store, and I was on the verge of opening one of them to pour myself a drink when there came a quiet tap on the door. I hurried across the room and opened the door.

"Good evening, Bob. This is Greta. Greta Manx."

I had to look down to find Greta. "Hallo," I said. "Won't you come in?"

If I had tried, in my mind, to draw a picture of the opposite to Tammy, I might have come up with Greta. Being very short, probably less than four feet, and slightly on the plump side, she reminded me of a character from Tolkien. I guessed from her grey hair and the condition of her skin that she must be in her high fifties. She peered at me through thick lenses and said something to me in German that I did not catch, her voice sounding like a high-pitched squeak.

"Greta says, 'How do you do?'" said Tammy.

I nodded to the woman and held out my hand. She shook it limply. I was doubtful about the outcome of the evening, particularly if I could not understand a word she said.

For the purpose of our meeting, I had borrowed some wicker armchairs from the hotel and arranged them in a tight circle in the corner of my tiny bedroom. It was dark outside and Greta requested that we turn out all the lights except one small table lamp at the far end of the room. I offered them a drink, but they both declined. We squeezed into the chairs and so tight was it that our knees were almost touching in the centre of the circle. Greta, talking in German through Tammy, instructed us to hold hands. I clasped the soft delicate skin of one of Tammy's beautiful hands to my right, and by contrast, I held the coarse, flabby skin of one of Greta's tiny hands to my left.

Six months ago I would never have believed what I had become involved in now. Then I was secure in my world of computers and cold, clear logic, where two and two made four, and if they didn't, there was something wrong with the hardware or software. Now I was sitting down with these two women and discuss, not only things illogical, but also things that may or may not exist somewhere beyond our understanding.

I was not sure of what to expect as we sat in silence in the corner of the room. Greta had closed her eyes, and Tammy just sat there, staring blankly ahead, hardly moving a muscle. After about five minutes of this I became uncomfortable and started to fidget. Greta did not stir, but Tammy's eyes flashed at me in admonishment. I settled back, saying nothing, and resumed my silent vigil. It was some twenty minutes later before anything happened.

A sudden chill descended on the room, as if we were sitting under an air conditioning vent that had been called to life by a rising thermometer. I shivered involuntarily and Tammy gripped my hand more tightly. Greta stirred in her chair. She twisted her body, rolling her head, her eyes open and her pupils disappearing under her eyelids, showing nothing but the whites of her eyes. She murmured unintelligible phrases, and both Tammy and I strained to listen. The words were totally foreign to me, and even with my limited knowledge of the language, I felt sure it was not German. Tammy more or less confirmed this by looking over to me and shaking her head.

We sat for a further ten minutes. Greta continued to mutter, occasionally becoming quite audible, and at one time actually shouting out like a person might when experiencing a particularly nasty nightmare. As suddenly as it had started, it stopped, and Greta relaxed back in her trance like sleep. The cold chill went off the room and we sat again for another five minutes. Greta stirred again, and in a flick of an eye was fully awake.

At first, she was disturbed, shocked even, as if she had just been a spectator to something really bad, witnessed a grisly road accident, for example. But slowly normality returned as the colour came back to her cheeks.

"Now what about a drink?" I asked. "I need one if you don't."

Tammy turned to Greta and uttered a phrase or two of German and then to me she said, "A gin and tonic for Greta and one for me, too, if you have it." She smiled.

I went over to the tray of bottles resting on top of my chest of drawers. Besides a bottle of red wine and a bottle of sherry, I had laid in a bottle of Scotch and a bottle of gin. There were also a variety of mixes including tonic. I poured both the ladies their gins and I poured myself a generous measure of Scotch.

"Well," I said. "What's the score?"

Tammy took a sip of her gin before replying. "When she communicates with those who have passed on." She saw my look of scepticism. "Talks to the spirits," she said. "For all intents and purposes she is asleep. What she sees and hears is like a dream. When she comes out of it, wakes up, if you like, she can't remember everything that went on. In fact, it is better in some cases that she does not remember. Lack of memory for her can be a safety valve."

I was puzzled. "If she can't remember anything, how does that help me?"

"She will remember enough," said Tammy confidently.

Tammy and Greta began to talk among themselves in German. I could not understand a word they were saying and I sat there sipping on my Scotch, wondering where all this was leading. Suddenly Tammy was speaking in English and I realised she was directing her attention towards me. "It is as we thought. It is a spirit that died here years ago, yet cannot find rest. The spirit will not move upward through the cosmic plain to find re-birth. This spirit, wronged in its last life, will not find rest until this wrong has been brought out into the light."

I listened intently, watching my two companions. Greta talking quietly in German and Tammy giving an instant translation.

"She is asking for help. You are a receptor. You must have psychic qualities, though you may not have explored them before. She communicates on a wavelength that you are easily able to pick up. She needs to rest. She implores you to help her."

"She?" I said, shaking my head.

Tammy returned the question to Greta, who replied immediately in German. "Yes, a young woman in her last life. Her name was either Ilse or Eve; I don't know which. She used one or the other at different times."

"How can I help," I said indignantly. "I'm not even a countryman of hers. I live nearly five thousand miles away."

When Greta was informed of what I had said, she laughed a low cackle, almost witch like. I felt a shiver run down my back. "Beyond the narrow confines of this world," said Tammy, echoing Greta's German, "there are no barriers. Not race, colour, religion, tongue, nor even gender exist within the spirit world. Once we die" – Tammy stumbled. – "Mr. McLeod, we will all be the similar spirit forms."

I looked fleetingly at the pile of computer printouts that I had carelessly laid on the floor just inside the door as I came in from Mannhauser's that evening, as if they were a life belt. I felt myself slipping further from the sane and logical world that I had always known. The barriers that I had so carefully build to protect me from anything that could not be explained by logic and math were slowly crumbling. I felt the skin tighten across my forehead. I was afraid.

"Yes, but what has it got to do with me?" I said.

"She needs help and she is crying out to anyone who will listen. Please help her."

There was silence in the room for a few moments. Both Tammy and Greta were watching me intently, waiting for my response. Unconsciously, I sat playing with my hands. I had always been a sucker for a hard luck case. I knew myself well enough to know that. Stray dogs were a favourite of mine. But this was something else. "How can I help her," I said at last.

"The dreams. She is telling you what to do in the dreams." Tammy continued to paraphrase Greta's German.

"I always wake up in the dream. It never finishes. It is always the same dream." I remembered the strange farmhouse I had seen in my sleep so often.

Greta said something in German and then burst into a renewed cackle of laughter. "Dreams rarely do," said Tammy with a smile. "If a dream comes to a conclusion, then it is said that the dreamer will die in his sleep."

I could find nothing funny in it, but at that point in time my sense of humour had deserted me. "Well, I don't want to die, but how else will I find out what she wants?"

Greta started to speak again, and I listened while Tammy translated. "There are ways to take charge and control your own mind, even while you are asleep." Greta looked hard at me for a moment. "But you may not be capable. I could put you to sleep and then you would dream, but that may be dangerous."

"How dangerous? What do you mean?"

"Too dangerous. I will not interfere." Greta appeared agitated. "The girl will reveal all to you in time."

I was not happy with Greta's conclusions, as I found no pleasure in the girl's attempts at communicating with me. The last thing I wanted was more of these dreams.

Greta was still looking at me, or looking through me, such was her concentration. "You will help her," she said suddenly, through Tammy. "It will cost you greatly, but you will help her. Those who help you in this task may also suffer." I saw her glance sideways at Tammy who was concentrating on the interpretation and did not notice. "I see a future for you, so you will survive, but the road ahead has many twists and turns."

"What's in it for me?" I said, feeling mercenary, and somewhat upset at having all this extra worry thrown on me.

"You will gain very little from it," she said after a moment. "But you will learn of the goodness in the human heart. A valuable lesson, Herr McLeod, for the rest of your life".

"Did she say anything else at all?"

"She said other things, things I didn't understand."

I found the delays frustrating talking to Greta through Tammy. "Tell us everything. What else did she say?"

"She spoke of an image that would help you, an image close at hand, maybe even in this room and she spoke of justice lying under the floor." Greta saw the look on my face. "*Ja*, it makes no sense. Often I hear things from the other side that make no sense. Some of it we must ignore."

We had another round of drinks and by then the hands on my bedside clock said eleven o'clock. I said our goodbyes, and I offered money as they were leaving, but Greta was adamant in her refusal. Finally, I did manage to press a few notes into Tammy's hand.

After the women had left, I poured myself another generous measure of Scotch. I noticed how much the level in the bottle had dropped and I had been the only one drinking it. I had better be careful; otherwise I would be in no shape for work in the morning. Up until now, anyway, I had always been sceptical about life after death. The good side of the coin was that if I wasn't going completely mad, and if what I was getting myself into had any real meaning other than the ramblings of an old psychic and a young prostitute, then maybe there was something more for us after death. What could I do to help this girl, anyway?

61

I pondered a while on what Greta had said: 'An image in this room.' An image could be a photograph or a painting. There were not many pictures in my room, besides the old photograph of the Munich Rathaus, there were only two flower pictures over the bed. The picture of the Rathaus, being an old photograph, could that be what she meant? I went over to it and studied it again. I imagined it had been taken early on a Sunday morning, for there were few people about. And those that were I couldn't make out in any detail. Perhaps a secret was hidden somewhere in the Rathaus, maybe even under the floor. I tapped my shoe on the floor of my hotel room and felt the solid concrete. There would be no digging through that.

Feeling no nearer to solving the problem, I finished my drink and went to bed. I did not dream at all that night. In fact, I slept soundly and awoke feeling more refreshed than I had done in quite a while, in spite of the drink. I went to Mannhauser's in a better mood than I had been in for some time and started to plough through the work. This continued for a week and not only did I get a lot of work done, but I began to think that our little séance had finally laid the ghost. I didn't hear from Tammy again in that time and I began to look forward to my return to Canada.

As I worked, I gained the trust of some of Mannhauser's old guard. I had met similar situations before, where many of the company's old and loyal employees rejected radically new ideas, especially when they were to do with a computer system. To overcome some of this rejection, I involved the more influential of these people in as many of the process decisions as I could. And so, after almost a week, I began to look forward to returning home earlier than I had first thought. By Friday of that week my spirits were heightened to the point that I invited my entire group to supper and an evening at one of the local beer gardens.

The evening was a success. I think we had all been under the strain of a lot of hard work, and there was a general need to blow off steam. Even the barriers that had built up between Jennings and I seemed to erode, and that could only be good for our working relationship. In fact, after he had been drinking quite heavily, he came and took me to one side. "Don't say anything," he said. "But, did you know they are following you?"

"What do you mean?" I said, wondering if he was completely under the influence.

"You haven't noticed," he said, shaking his head. "Mannhauser security follow you to work and they follow you home again. They watch you all the time."

I felt decidedly uncomfortable. Jennings had drunk more than enough and was slurring some of his words, but why would he make up a thing like that? "Are they following anyone else?"

He shook his head. "Don't think so. Just you, I guess, as you are the boss."

Maybe that was it. They were just keeping an eye on their investment. All the same, I did not like it and I would keep my eyes open in future.

Except, for my brief discussion with Jennings, I had enjoyed the evening immensely. By the time I got back to the hotel room, I was more than a little tipsy.

It was late, past midnight, when I returned to the Marrianne, and without ceremony, I threw off my clothes and climbed into bed. I thought of my wife, as I usually did when going to bed miles from home, and then a vision of Tammy appeared in the picture. Guiltily, I pushed Tammy from my mind, but whether I succeeded or not, I will never know, for I was asleep moments after my head hit the pillow.

The farmhouse, as always, stood sparkling in the bright sunlight. Such was the reality of the dream that I could almost feel the warmth of the sun on my face as I walked the long driveway. There was no one about, yet the place looked used, clean, as if under the daily scrutiny of some diligent caretakers. I could see a tractor partially concealed by the barn. From a distance, it looked in fine condition, as if it had just been used to cut hay in the far field, but it was a type that had been long since out of production, probably dated from the early thirties.

As I drew near the house, I became once more aware of the deep dread in the pit of my stomach as if there were dark spirits residing within that neither wanted nor would tolerate my intrusion. I passed into the dim confines of the house. Again it was as if my limbs were not mine to control, but this time my state of mind was such that I ceased to struggle against what ever was happening to me. I walked through the lower part of the house and nothing had changed since the last time. I passed on up the stairs and down the dark landing to stand once more in front of the closed door at the end of the passage. I stretched out my hand to turn the latch. A dreadful fear of what lay beyond the door welled inside me, but this time, instead of aiding this fear and trying to run, I fought against it with everything I had and I pushed the door open.

I was surprised to find that this room was brighter than the rest of the house. The sun streamed in through the window illuminating the plain but pleasant furnishings and decorations. There was a small bed with a light wooden headboard, an equally small dressing table and a chest of drawers. The room seemed light and airy, unaffected by the dinginess of the rest of the house. I closed the door quickly behind me, shutting out the darkness, as if this room was an oasis in a desert of evil.

I don't remember any more. I did not wake up in a sweat of terror. The dream passed, like other dreams pass, and I continued to sleep until late into Saturday morning. In fact, I had risen, had my shower and shaved before I remembered anything about the dream. It came to me while I dressed, and then I remembered it all. I thought, not for the last time, of Greta Manx's words. "The girl will reveal all to you in time." Was this it?

While taking my breakfast in the hotel restaurant, I pondered the problem. I thought again of the photograph of the Munich Rathaus, somehow I felt sure that the picture was part of it. Solving problems was part of my job, and I had trained myself to think outside the problem and look at it from all angles. Perhaps the clue was not in the image itself, but in the very object hanging on the wall.

When I returned to my room, I went straight to the picture and scrutinized it; the glass and the frame were old and dirty but nothing unusual. I took the picture down somewhat nervously, for I thought they may have it alarmed - it could be valuable. But nothing went off, no bells sounded. I turned it over. The paper had browned with age and dirt and cobwebs had collected in the frame. I brushed this off and I noticed that a rectangle of paper in the bottom left hand corner had aged differently from the rest. I picked at it with my fingers and another photograph peeled away.

I sat on the corner of the bed and gazed at her, a pretty girl with a mop of dark curls. She wore a dark coat of the kind worn before the war that gave no clue to her figure or shape. I turned the photograph over and brushed the dirt away. I could see writing on the back of the photograph, but it had become faint over the years and I could not read it. I quickly fetched a small magnifying glass that I kept in my briefcase, and I looked at it through that. Even then I struggled to make sense of it, but at last I read the name, 'Eve Maynard'. Eve? 'Ilse or Eve', Greta had said. I continued working at the writing and eventually deciphered an address near a place called Penzberg named, *Das Sonnig Pferd Bauernhof.* My German was still very poor, but I knew it had something to do with horses. I replaced the Rathaus on the wall, and then sat on my bed, studying Eve Maynard's picture. So I had found it. This was the young lady who was given me all this trouble and now what was I going to do? I had a lot to think about.

Chapter 6

I placed the photograph of Eve Maynard in the inside pocket of my suit jacket, as I didn't want to lose it and I didn't want it to be found by anyone else. I spent the rest of Saturday working at Mannhauser's till quite late in the evening. The following day, Sunday, I took off and explored some of the sights in the city. I bought a few more gifts to take home, and I also purchased a road map of Southern Bavaria. When I arrived back at my hotel room, I scrutinized the map and found Penzberg. It was due south of Munich not far from Oberammergau. Having been thinking about it for two days, now I made the decision. I picked up the phone and dialled Jennings.

He sounded surprised when I told him I would not be in work on Monday, as I felt a little under the weather. I think he thought I was immune from sickness, as it was rare that I had a day off.

Early Monday morning I left the hotel and walked to a local Hertz Rent-A-Car. Being early June, the sun shone down promising a fine day. I rented a small Volkswagen Golf, a small boxy car and nothing like the big Mercedes that I had last ridden in. I followed more or less the same route I had taken with Heidi, but I forked right before I reached Oberammergau. I travelled down a rural road that led eventually to Penzberg, when I saw the farm. I didn't need to decipher the address, or ask anyone where it was; I recognized it instantly, for it was indelibly etched in my memory.

I drove around to the front gates, but they were locked so I parked the car on the grass verge near by. As I walked down the drive, I felt nervous about meeting whoever owned the place and what I would say to them, and curious beyond words to know what secrets lay within, but I felt none of the dark foreboding I had experienced in the dreams. The weather may have had something to do with that, for the sun neared its zenith and the day had developed into a scorcher.

I climbed the two red brick steps to the front door and slammed the large wrought iron knocker. The house rang hollow, my knock echoing back to me. I waited a couple of minutes then tried again. Obviously, no one was home. I walked over the neatly cut lawn and peeked through the front windows. White dustsheets covered the furniture. The owners must be away. Short of breaking in, there was little else I could do.

I decided to walk around the property, and I found the back door with its four small glass panes at the top, just as I had seen in my dream. I walked up to the barn, and sure enough the old tractor stood just inside. It looked old and rusty, but it resembled the model I had seen. The paddocks stood empty but freshly painted. It was obvious the place was no longer used for horses, but someone maintained the place very well. Perhaps, if I went into Penzberg, there might be a town office and I could enquire there. Somebody had to pay the taxes.

As I drove away, I saw a man ploughing a field on the next property. I did not know whether the man would speak English, but it may be worth a try. I stopped the car and called to him from the hedge. He stopped his tractor and ambled over. The lines and creases on his face portrayed his age, coupled with a life spent in the outdoors. We spoke with the hedge between us. He spoke English passably and we managed to communicate.

"I am interested in the property next door. Can you tell me who owns it?"

He looked at me with more than a little curiosity in his clear blue eyes. "You American tourist?"

"No, but close. I am a Canadian and I am here on business."

He nodded. "Nobody has lived there since the war. The house stays empty, but the place is looked after. The grass is always cut and the house is painted when it needs it."

"Have you lived here long?"

"All my life." His face creased into a smile. "This is my home."

"Who was the last person to live there?"

His hand went to the back of his neck as he thought, pushing the light cap that he wore further over his head. "A long time ago. Much has happened since then. A soldier owned the place. He had a few horses. A hobby with him; he made no money at it. A housekeeper lived with him, and he brought home a young bride. He was away at the war, and the women were on their own most of the time."

"What happened to him?"

"It is strange, sort of a mystery. The soldier died towards the end of the war, and the two women simply disappeared."

"What both of them?" I don't know what made me say that, but the further I dug into this puzzle, the more uncanny it became.

"Both of them. Suddenly the place was empty. It stayed like that until well after the war and then was sold for back taxes. Why do you need to know these things?"

Eventually he would get suspicious, the more I questioned him, but I needed the answers. "I like the look of the place and I am thinking of buying an investment property here in Germany." At least I had told the truth with the first part of my statement: I did like the look of the place.

He nodded knowledgably, "You could do worse."

"The authorities never found the women?" I asked, steering him back on the subject.

"Not to my knowledge. At the end of the war things were far from normal. So many missing persons, I doubt two isolated women would get much priority."

"Did you know them at all?"

"Not really. They kept themselves very much to themselves. A very pretty girl with dark curly hair, I think her name was Eve or something like that. The old lady, we called her the dragon, a very severe woman, but she seemed to run the place. The young mistress did as she was told."

"How interesting to learn the local history. Thank you very much." I hoped I wasn't being too patronizing, but he didn't seem to notice.

'You're very welcome," he turned to amble back to his tractor.

"Oh, one more thing," I said. "I suppose the soldier was killed at the front."

The farmer turned back to the hedge. "Some freak accident in Munich. I can't remember the details. Serves him right. I don't think he ever saw the front."

"You didn't like him then?"

'Not really, such an arrogant man in his black and silver uniform, an SS colonel, I believe."

"I see, well, thank you again for your help."

I left the farmer and drove on to Penzberg and went in search of the township offices, which I found without too much trouble. Again, I could communicate with the woman clerk. It still amazed me as to how many people spoke English to some level in a non-English speaking country. I showed her the address of the farm and asked her who owned it. I told her the story about wanting an investment property and she went off to look it up in the files. It wasn't long before she returned.

'Here we are, Herr McLeod." She carried a pink slip of paper, which she laid on the desk and squinted at it through her reading glasses. "Er, Herr Fredrik..."

"Stanholt!" I said.

"Yes, how did you know?"

I shrugged. "I seem to be running into a lot of coincidences lately."

She eyed me suspiciously. "It is strange that you know him."

"Yes," I said, not wanting to elaborate further. "One more thing before I go. Do you know who the previous owner was?"

She thought for a moment. "I remember the property now. It stood empty for a long time before being sold by the township. I will look it up for you."

This time, fifteen minutes passed before she returned; she must have gone back twenty years, at least.

"It was owned by an officer in the Military. His name was Becker. He was killed and there were no relatives."

"Didn't he have a wife?"

Again she looked at me strangely. I could see that my prospective buyer story wasn't going to hold up for much longer. "I don't know about that. There was no other name on the title for the property."

I thanked her and said my good byes, and I told her that I would visit Herr Stanholt and see if he wanted to sell.

I found a small restaurant in Penzberg and bought myself coffee and a sandwich for lunch. So Stanholt owned the farm, and if he found out that I was snooping around his property, I couldn't imagine the consequences. For sure, we could kiss the contract good bye. Playing with fire was new to me, not being a risk taker, but I had to get to the bottom of all this, and I suspected the answer would be found in that farmhouse. On the good side, I felt sure that I had not been followed. I kept a look out, because of the warning from Jennings, but I had seen no vehicle consistently behind me. Therefore, I could assume that no one new where I was. What better time would there be to look in the farmhouse than now?

I returned the way I came, but I did not want to leave the car near the front of the property, where anyone might see it. Instead, I circled round the property using the side roads, which were little more than farm tracks. Just once I did catch a glimpse of a car in my rear view mirror, a Mercedes by the look of it, but I played at being careful and stopped the car to allow anyone following to pass. I saw no more of the car, so I assumed that it had turned off. I reached the top of a hill that overlooked the farmhouse from the back, and I parked the car under some trees and set off to walk across the fields. By keeping to the edge of the farm property, I stayed among the sparse growth of trees and bushes, keeping more or less out of sight until I reached the side of the barn. Unless there were any occupants of the house, I could not be seen from there on in. I walked on past the barn, my heart hammering my ribs as I approached the house. A door slammed behind me and I jumped, my heart almost stopping. Instantly I turned around expecting a confrontation, but no one was there. I began to retrace my steps and the door slammed again. The side door to the barn, hanging on only one hinge, periodically swung with the wind. I breathed a sigh of relief and returned to the job in hand.

I reached the back door and knocked loudly. The sound of my knocking reverberated around the house, but there came no answer. I waited a few seconds and the eerie silence that followed confirmed that no one was home. I scouted around for an implement and I found a rusty tire iron near the barn. Using this, I broke the small glass window nearest the latch, carefully pushed my arm through, I managed to reach the latch.

A musty smell pervaded the interior, a smell of disuse, and the drapes were partially pulled shutting out much of the bright sunlight outside. The furnishings were roughly as I had seen them in my dream, right down to the old radio, but there were no photographs. I climbed the stairs, and as I approached the dark landing, I felt no fear. I made my way down the landing and entered the small bedroom.

Light streamed in through the window, giving the room a light and airy feeling that contrasted to the rest of the house, just as I had seen in the dreams. The room, being very small, contained only a small bed and a chest of drawers. And yet, if there was any clue at all, it had to be in this room. I looked in the chest of drawers, but they were empty. I looked under the bed, but nothing. A picture of a farm scene hung on the wall; I took it down and examined it, but nothing out of the ordinary.

I sat on the small bed completely stumped, my chin in my hands. A rug lay on the floor, an orange rug. It stretched out from under the bed, almost across the room. 'And justice under the floor', Greta's words came back to me. I grasped the rug and scooped it back under the bed. The floorboards were old and well worn, and lay in straight rows, all about uniform length, except for a short connecting board. Kneeling down I examined the short board and could see no nails. I felt in my pocket for a tool and found a couple of Canadian quarters, and pressing the coins down the sides of the board, I managed to prize it up enough to get a grip on it. I pulled the board up and it made a screech of wood against wood. It may have been my hyper imagination, but the sound seemed to reverberate all around the house, even rattling the back door.

I looked into the dark cavity under the floor and I could see nothing but cobwebs and dirt at first, and then I thought I saw a package. I grabbed it and found it to be a cotton material and probably coloured pink at one time but now stained with age and dirt. I brushed it off and unwrapped a book, expensively bound in red leather with a legend impressed in gold leaf on the cover. The covering had done its job, for the book was in perfect condition.

Leaving the floorboard sticking up, I sat on the bed and examined my find. As I turned it over in my hand, I realized I had found a diary, probably a young girl's diary. The pages were filled with neat handwriting and, being in German, I could read none of it. As I sat totally engrossed in the book, an overpowering feeling of being watched came over me. I shivered and the hair stood up on the back of my neck; if there were no ghosts in this house, there were no ghosts anywhere. I looked up sharply to find a man standing in the doorway watching me.

I forgot for the moment that I was the intruder, and I jumped from the bed shouting, "Who the hell are you?"

My sudden move startled him, for he took off down the landing, crashing through the house and out the back door. I followed him, at least as far as the back door and saw him briefly, as he disappeared behind the barn. To chase him further would have been foolhardy. If I caught him, what would I say? It had happened so quickly, that I could remember almost nothing about the man except for his mop of white hair.

As I stood at the back door watching the man disappear, I found that I was still clutching the book securely in my hand. I returned it to its cotton wrapping and then placed it in the inside pocket of my jacket. I went back to the bedroom to tidy up and cover my tracks. Only when I returned to my car did my hands stop shaking and my nerves begin to settle down.

On my drive back to Munich, I tried to piece together what had happened. The man could only be one of two things. Either he was a casual intruder, a burglar, like me, or he had been following me. I thought again of the glimpse I had seen of the Mercedes and there was no doubt in my mind. So Jennings warning had been correct and I was being followed. Who had ordered me to be followed?

It could only be Stanholt, and now he knew that I had broken into his farmhouse. Worse still, he was my biggest and most important client.

I kept a sharp lookout for anything that might be following me, particularly a large Mercedes, but I could see nothing. I made some diversionary moves, turning off the highway and parking in concealed places, but still nothing. In spite of these tactics or because of them, instinct told me it would be unwise to return straight away to my hotel room. I stopped at a gas station on the outskirts of Munich, where a public call box stood on the forecourt.

"Tammy," I said, after reaching her number. "I need to see you urgently."

"It is a bit inconvenient. What is it about?"

"I'll explain when I see you, but it is important."

I could almost hear her thinking. "Alright, I'll come to your room at ten."

"No!"

Tammy was my only ally. On no account must they find out about her. "You must never come there any more. It is too dangerous. Can I come to your place?" Dangerous may have been an overstatement, but maybe not when I thought back to Heidi.

"I don't like having men to my flat. I like to keep my home and my business strictly separate."

I sounded exasperated. "Well, for what ever reason I might come and see you, it will not be for business, your business, reasons."

At last she conceded. "Come here at about ten then, and be discrete."

I don't know what indiscretion I might have committed, but she gave me her address and I said I would be there at ten.

A quick glance at my watch told me that I had four hours to kill. I returned the car to the rental agency, and then found a restaurant, where I indulged in some good German hospitality, including a couple of steins of beer. Time past fairly quickly and I left the restaurant at nine-thirty. I walked to Tammy's apartment and it was a little after ten when I stood outside the apartment portico and rang Tammy's bell. The loudspeaker clicked on and a voice said, "*Ja.*"

The voice puzzled me, for it wasn't Tammy. "It is Bob McLeod. I am here to see Ms. Findlay."

The voice changed to broken English. "Come up." And the lock on the door buzzed open.

Tammy greeted me at the door wearing jeans and a tee shirt. She introduced me to Olga, her maid, who, after a quick, "*Guten tag,*" disappeared into her quarters.

The size of Tammy's apartment surprised me, a spacious living room, a dining room, a very large kitchen, at least two bedrooms, two bathrooms and the maid's quarters that consisted of two rooms and yet another bathroom. Obviously, Tammy was very good at what she did.

"I am sorry to come here if it is inconvenient, but it is important."

She smiled. "Monday's my day off. Sit down and I'll fix you a drink. Scotch, isn't it?"

I sat on the sofa while she went to a hatch that divided the living room from the kitchen and poured a couple of drinks. She gave me my Scotch and she sat down opposite. "Now what is this all about?" she said.

I explained the events of the day in detail and I took the package from my inside pocket containing the book. "Can you translate this for me?" I said, handing it over.

Her eyes went from the book back to me, a look of amazement on her face. "And you have found this book and everything, just from what Greta said?"

"Yes, it took me a week to find the photograph, but after that, everything fell into place."

"All the same," she said, as she took the book from the cotton wrapping.

"Please, tell nobody about the book and disclose its contents only to me. I have a feeling this could be very dangerous."

"You will leave it with me?" She turned the book over and opened it to the first page.

"I would rather you keep it. I don't think it would be safe with me."

"It is a diary," she said simply.

" Yes, I realised that much."

"It is the diary of a girl named Ilse Stanholt."

I caught my breath. "Who?" But the question was superfluous; I heard her quite clearly the first time.

Chapter 7

Eve Maynard became a virtual prisoner of Becker, his plaything to be taken out when he came home and returned to the shelf when he went back to his unit. Her only concession being that she would have been worse off in a concentration camp, but she was a prisoner, never the less, and her wardress, Frou Kinder, never let her get too far from her sight. Frou Kinder was Becker's housekeeper, a large woman in her mid fifties, who wore her greying hair in a fierce bun; she tended to keep herself to herself, speaking only when strictly necessary. When she did speak to Eve, she spoke with a quiet authority, leaving no doubt who was in charge.

There were three bedrooms in the house, Frou Kinder's, the master bedroom and a small box room. Eve shared the master bedroom with Becker, though she only slept in that room when he came home. She preferred the small box room, which, after a while, she looked upon as her own.

Though, in her heart, Eve hated Becker and all he stood for. She knew only too well that if she didn't go along with his wishes it would be the worst for her family. She realized, too, that as time went by, her hold over him would grow, for if it ever became known that she was a Jew, he would be shot. She acquiesced to his sexual demands, and after a while accepted them with a measure of tolerance.

There were compensations for living on a farm in wartime. They ate well, enjoying the best of everything in the way of food. Frou Kinder looked after the housekeeping, while Eve looked after the horses. There were no more than half a dozen animals now, and the young lad who used to look after them now served in a Panzer regiment. The horses provided Eve with companionship and reminded her of happier times in the past. She rode them, and Becker approved as long as she did not leave the property. This she did not do, for she was more afraid to leave her prison than remain in it.

Soon after arriving at the farm, Eve began a diary. She kept it a secret and hid the book under the floor of her bedroom. In it she wrote everything that had happened to her since she was fifteen, when she had run away from Munich all that time ago. She left nothing out, even to the extent of her lovemaking with Becker. She wrote in the diary in the first place to relieve her boredom, but later it became an obsession with her to record everything, for she believed that one day the book would serve as an indictment against the Nazis and bring her captor to justice.

In the early days of their relationship, Becker came home almost every weekend and most nights of the week. But this could not last, for his duties became more pressing as the war continued. Being an intelligent man, he took little notice of the Hype and propaganda put out by Goebels. He had become a Nazi to further his own ends, but things were going badly. The Americans had entered the war, Rommel had been thrown out of North Africa, and now, early in 1943, the Germans were defeated at Stalingrad. Becker began to brood.

Eve noticed the change in him. He came home less frequently, and when he did, his demands on her were almost negligible. Sometimes he would speak of the progress of the war, for he could speak to Eve as he could to no one else.

One evening in the fall of 1943, Eve and Becker were sitting around the fireplace in the parlour, Frou Kinder having gone to her room. He had been discussing the allied advance through Italy with some degree of resignation. "They are coming, Eve. They are coming even as the tide sweeps up the beach when it is on the flow."

Eve struggled to conceal her delight. For her, the allies could not come soon enough, but she knew too well that it was better to keep her feelings to herself. "Perhaps the tide is on the flow now, but surely it will ebb again soon."

Becker smiled wryly. "We are running out of everything, but most of all money. It will not be long before the German people go hungry, you'll see. Whatever Goebels says, the Americans have unlimited resources."

Becker remained quiet for a while and then he turned to Eve and said, "I am having trouble keeping your family safe. My contacts in Dachau are getting greedy. It is all a matter of money, you see."

"You promised." Eve sprang to the defence of her family. "You made a bargain and you must keep it. You must keep them safe."

"I promised only that I would do my best. I pay people to look after them, but I can only pay so much."

Eve looked bewildered. "What are you going to do then?"

"I will keep my promise and do my best, but I cannot comply with their demands for more money."

"You told me that you are soon to be promoted. Surely, then you will have enough power to get them out of there."

Becker laughed. "You overestimate my authority. I could not get your family out of there even if I was Himler himself. Anyway, I wouldn't be surprised if your father had money salted away somewhere. A rich man like him would have made some provision."

The bitterness welled up in Eve. "You Nazis took everything we had. You made us flee from our own country with nothing." Her voice rose up involuntarily.

73

"Shush!" Becker pointed upstairs. "Keep it down; we don't want everyone knowing our business."

"Well, you did," Eve continued in a sharp whisper. "Even our bodies you take and dispose as you please."

But Eve may as well have held her breath, for her remarks made no impression on Becker at all. "We expected to get to America. My father has money there."

Becker laughed again. "I knew you would try. A note in your file with just a hint that your presence may be required in Germany, and not only will they leave you alone, but they won't let you leave the country. So you remain where I could have you when the time was right."

A tear ran down Eve's cheek. "You beast," she said.

Becker stood up and went to the breast pocket of his tunic. He pulled out an envelope and handed it to Eve. "There, I cannot guarantee there will be anymore."

The letter, the third one Eve had received in the two years she had lived with Becker, was written in pencil and addressed to Heidi. Her mother thought she wrote to her niece in America. Eve replied as if she was Heidi, but Becker heavily censored her letters.

The following day Becker left the Munich area and stayed away for a period of two months, leaving Eve to think of the plight of her family. The worry grew inside her coupled with guilt; if she had told Becker of the box, then there would be enough money to keep her family safe. She lost her appetite, eating barely enough for basic nourishment and she became pale and thin. Becker noticed the difference in her immediately when he returned.

"What's the matter with you, child? Are you Ill?" He addressed her as if she were no older than fifteen, as he often did except when he made love to her.

Eve did not reply but went into the kitchen. "What's the matter with her?" he said to Frou Kinder.

"She does not eat, sir. It is almost as if she is willing herself to die."

"She must eat. You must make her."

"I can only do my best, sir." The old lady shrugged and turned to follow Eve.

That evening, as soon as Eve found herself alone with Becker, she broached the question uppermost in her mind. "How are my parents?"

"As far as I know they are as well as can be expected. I have not been in touch with my contacts in Dachau since we last spoke."

"And my brother?"

"As far as I know. To be sure of their safety would be a matter of money, Eve. I told you last time, I can afford no more."

His words did little to comfort her, and she made an excuse as soon as she could to go to bed. What ever her father had put in the box, it would be worthless if she lost her family. Becker would take what was inside, but he would have to pay to keep her family alive, wouldn't he? The Americans were not so far away now. Well, southern Italy was not that far away. If they could survive until the Americans came, then even if Becker took all their money, Uncle Gunther would be able to help them.

She returned downstairs to find Becker still sitting by the fireplace. "There is a box. My father hid it in my Uncle's house in Austria when the Nazis came."

Fire flared in Becker's eyes. "Why did you not tell me this before?"

"I promised my father. If we survive, it will be all we have to live on."

"Better we use it to ensure your family's survival, don't you think, Eve. No good saving it for a future they will not have."

Eve turned away, unable to look him in the eye. "Yes," she whispered.

That night Becker made love to Eve, as he had not done since first they had come together. The thought of what was in the mysterious box had excited him and aroused his passion. Eve could only pray that he would honour their agreement and save her family.

Becker cut short his stay and left the farm early next morning. He did not return for over three months.

Chapter 8

I slept badly the night of my raid on Stanholt's farmhouse, and it wasn't due to any bad dreams. I had returned from Tammy's apartment at about one in the morning, but I did not get to bed until two. Needless to say, I was not at my best when I went into Mannhauser's on Tuesday morning. The day started badly, continued in much the same vein, and by the time I put my jacket on ready to leave, it seemed as if it would have been better if I had not gone in at all. I had been tempted to call Tammy once or twice during the day, but I had resisted. It would be better if I restricted my calls to Tammy, and when I did call her, only from a public call box. Nobody must know of her involvement.

I picked up my briefcase and headed towards the door, when the telephone on my desk rang. I sighed; it seemed that this day was not over yet. "Hallo," I said.

"Oh, hallo, Bob, can you come to my office right away." It was Rudolf Kruger.

"Sure," I said. "Anything wrong?"

"No, nothing at all. Just need a word."

I pondered on the tone of his voice as I put down the phone. It sounded as if he was hiding something.

I went up to the top floor of the building and knocked on his office door. His secretary opened the door and showed me into his spacious inner office without delay. He sat behind his huge desk twiddling with a pencil as I entered. "Oh, there you are, Bob. Thanks for coming at such short notice."

"No problem. You just caught me."

"I heard you were sick yesterday?"

"A little under the weather, and I also had some private business to attend to." I wondered why the question; I didn't have make excuses for not being there to him.

"Better today?"

"A little. Can't say that it has been a great day."

"So how is the job going?"

"Generally speaking, very well. Hopefully, I will be out of your hair soon. The modifications to the software are progressing, and I should soon be able to leave it to my crew."

"Excellent." He sounded pleased but this was not reflected in his eyes. He looked at me searchingly. "Herr Stanholt requests that you go and see him tomorrow morning."

"Oh, what's this about?"

"I guess he needs a first hand progress report."

Progress report on what, but I kept my thoughts to myself. "I had better prepare something."

"I wouldn't bother if I were you. I think he wants to keep it informal."

It was my turn to look searchingly at Kruger. He knew much more than he let on. "Fair enough."

"The car will pick you up at your hotel at nine-thirty in morning."

"Thank you." I could think of nothing else to say.

"Very well." His eyes returned to some papers on his desk, which was obviously a signal for me to leave.

I had a few minutes to spare before my sub-way train left for down town, and I called Tammy from one of the public call boxes on the platform. "I haven't got very far with it yet; I do have work to do, you know." She sounded annoyed that I should call, as if I were pushing too hard.

"I'm curious, just wondering how you were making out. Don't worry about how long it takes; I'll pay you for your time." As soon as I had said it, I realized it was the wrong thing to say.

The line went quiet for a moment and I stood there biting my tongue. She spoke in a quiet bitter tone. "I don't do everything for money. Because of what I do, most men think I can be bought and sold at will. Well, I am an intelligent woman, Mr. McLeod, and there is a part of me that no one can buy."

"I'm sorry. I didn't want you to suffer financially for helping me. That was all I meant."

I must have sounded sincere for she continued. "I can't tell how long it will take to complete the full translation, but the girl was a Jew, and she was being held as a sex slave by a Nazi bastard."

My train was about to leave so I thanked her and put down the phone. I went straight back to my hotel, intending to eat in the hotel restaurant and get to bed early that night. Upon opening the door to my hotel room, my heart missed a beat. My room had been completely turned over. The bed lay stripped, everything emptied out of drawers and closets, and even my suitcases were thrown open and upside down on the floor.

I suppose I panicked and called down to the main desk. If I had thought it through, I shouldn't have done that. My best course would have been to tidy the room up and say nothing, but I was new to this sort of thing. The manager came up and he wanted to call the police. It took all my efforts to dissuade him. I had enough dealings with the police on my last visit. I assured him that nothing was stolen, and indeed, nothing seemed to be missing. The hotel staff had the room tidy in a few minutes, there not being much in the room besides my clothes and a few papers. I knew what they were after, of course, but it didn't really sink in until later, when I sat in the restaurant having my meal.

I had broken into Stanholt's property and stolen a book about Stanholt's daughter. I had been seen in that property; caught in the act, so to speak. My room had been searched, and now Stanholt wanted to see me in the morning. Tomorrow's meeting was definitely one I would rather skip.

After a leisurely breakfast, I returned upstairs and made myself ready for my meeting with Stanholt. I put on a dark business suit and threw a few papers in my briefcase. I had prepared a kind of progress report, though in my heart I knew that whatever else the meeting would be about, that report would be at the very bottom of the agenda. The car arrived exactly at nine-thirty. The Germans, as usual, were the very essence of punctuality. The driver politely ushered me into the back seat of the car, but kept his distance, not saying anything that he didn't have to.

Upon arrival at the house, I was again met by Ernst Klaus and shown into the same room as my previous meeting with Stanholt, though this time there was no offer of coffee. Stanholt came in immediately and sat behind his desk. The sun shone outside, threatening a very warm day, and Stanholt wore a short sleeve golf shirt and no jacket. I regretted my dark suit.

"Good morning, Mr. McLeod. How are you this morning?"

His greeting sounded normal enough and I nodded. "Fine, thank you. And how about you?"

He ignored my interest in his well being and fired the next question. "Your work, how is it progressing?"

"Very well." I opened my briefcase. "I have prepared a short progress report that will give you the finer details. I am hoping to return to Canada within two weeks." I handed him my report, which he cast casually to one side.

"You were expected in the office on Monday and you didn't show up. What happened to you?" I felt as if he was slowly turning the thumbscrews, pouring on the pressure.

"Just a bit off colour, overwork, I think. I needed a break and I took a drive in the country. You don't miss much." For some reason, perhaps to make it seem less like an interrogation, I felt compelled to add the last comment.

He smiled. "I miss far less than you think. Have you made any friends while you have been in Germany?"

"What with working ninety percent of the time, what time has there been for friends?" So he was fishing for Tammy.

"So tell me, Mr. McLeod, where did you go for your ride in the country?"

I could not think how to answer him, and then I decide there was nothing like telling the truth. "I think you already know. Why are you having me followed?"

He was taken back a little, for he obviously expected me to lie. "You are right. I am having my security people keep an eye on you. But that is understandable. You are presently an investment to my company. And look at the trouble you got yourself into last time you were in Germany. Yes, Mr, McLeod, I am looking out for you."

"I see. That's very kind of you, but I think I am big enough to look after myself."

"Maybe." He paused. "Maybe not. Now I ask you again, why did you go where you did on Monday?" He moved his arm across the desk and I noticed the numbers tattooed on the inside of his forearm, clear and unmistakeable evidence of his stay in a concentration camp.

"The farmhouse is a pretty place and I love that part of Germany. Having been past that way a couple of times, I noticed that the farm is deserted. I wondered if it might be for sale. I decided to take a closer look and found the backdoor open, as if it had been broken into. I went inside to look around. I'm thinking of finding the owners and making them an offer."

The look on his face told me he didn't believe a word I said. "You are dancing with me, Mr. McLeod. Dancing with me can be dangerous and, believe me, you are out of your league. How much are you prepared to pay for it?"

He had stumped me for the moment. I had no idea of the price of property in Germany. "I don't know about dancing," I said. "But in Canada such a place would be worth between fifty and seventy thousand dollars. I would have to have it appraised, but I would pay fair market price for it."

"I do not consider myself a fool, Mr. McLeod. I made a fortune in business and the survived a more terrible oppression than you can imagine to make a fortune in business again. Some people believe in coincidence, but I don't. The fact that the horse farm belongs to me is a matter of public record."

"I tried to look suitably surprised, stunned even. "I had no idea," I stuttered. "That's incredible."

He stared at me with that singular steel blue eye of his as if trying to penetrate my consciousness. "I don't know what you are up to, but I should warn you that I am a very private man. People that have tried to interfere in my affairs before have run into a great deal of trouble. You surprise me, for you have more to lose than most by meddling with me."

"I can understand why you're so angry," I said. "I had no idea the farmhouse belonged to you. If I had any notion at all, do you think I would have gone near the place? After all, you are our most important client. Do you think I would have done anything at all to jeopardize our business relationship? My company has a lot of money invested in this project; our growth depends on it." As I spoke, the words had a hollow ring of truth about them.

He laughed, seeming to break the tension. Getting up from behind his desk, he came around and slapped me on the shoulder. "That is the first sensible thing I have heard you say since you came in here." He sat on the corner of his desk, his back ramrod straight, looking down at me with a benevolent smile. "There is a lot of money in this for you and your company. Your software is good, revolutionary even; it would be a pity to cancel the order now. That little hiding place under the floor in the farmhouse, how did you know about it?"

"Hiding place? I suppose it was a hiding place. I walked into the bedroom and the floorboard was sticking up in the air, the hole exposed. I guess the same person who left the back door open had been there before me."

He had put me at my ease a little and the lies rolled off my tongue. As he looked at me now his eyes flared with anger and any semblance of a smile on his lips had vanished.

"You stole something from me, a book, I believe?"

"I didn't steal anything. I found a book, sure, just an old book, a hand written book. I can't make head, nor tail of it, as I can't read a word of German. And I certainly didn't know it belonged to you."

Even as I spoke, I could feel the quicksand moving under me; I just didn't know how far I had sunk in.

"Return it at once, please." He stood up from the corner of the desk and walked towards the door. "The car will take you back to the plant," he said, and he left the room.

As soon as we were on the road and away from the estate, I tried to put my thoughts in order. I had just been through the worst interview I had ever experienced. I always believed that I was essentially an honest man and now I found myself lying and stealing for reasons that I could not understand. What to do now? I had told him of the book so I had to return it. I tapped on the glass partition that separated me from the driver of the Mercedes. He lowered the glass a little and I instructed him to take me to the town centre, instead of going to the plant. He did not like the idea and pretended not to understand, but I insisted and eventually he agreed. He dropped me at St. Peters, a short walk from the Marien Platz.

Once out of the car, I waited until I saw him leave and then I mingled with the crowd. I moved through the front of one beer garden and then out through the rear. Munich is a beautiful city and the tourists were taking advantage of it in great crowds. It suited me, for I could lose myself among their number and I had to be careful. I was sure that Stanholt's people were watching my every move. Eventually, I found a public phone box and called Tammy. As it was before noon, she had not yet left her apartment. "Can I come over and see you now," I asked.

She agreed, and within ten minutes of my phone call, I was sitting in her pleasant living room. "I need the book back," I said. "He knows I took it and he is demanding it back. I have a lot at stake in this."

"You've a lot at stake?" questioned Tammy. "What about that poor girl?"

"The girl's dead; you know that."

"You mean you are wasting my time." Tammy face creased into an angry frown.

"I've got living people's jobs to worry about, future orders riding on my business with Stanholt. This crazy business has gone far enough."

'You should have thought about that before."

"I know. I wasn't thinking straight. Anyway, Stanholt's the girl's father; he's a right to the book."

"You told me you didn't trust him."

"I suppose I don't trust him completely, but I can't explain why. I know he is having me followed, but his reasons may be legitimate. I guess I don't trust him because of the way he treated Heidi, but I only have her side of the story. If she had not been murdered, I would never have been suspicious at all."

"Do you think Stanholt had Heidi killed?"

"No." I shook my head. It seemed inconceivable. "I can't believe that. Why would he?"

Tammy shrugged. "Why indeed?"

"I'm sorry I involved you in this. If you will just give me the book back, we'll forget about the rest of it."

"Forgetting is not always an easy thing to do." Tammy rose up from the chair and went to her credenza and took the book from one of its drawers. "You've given in, haven't you? Capitulated."

I thought back a few hours to my most recent interview with Stanholt. "I don't think I have any choice really. He is the girl's father. The book does rightfully belong to him, whether he knew it was there or not. If I don't go along with him on this, I can kiss goodbye to a million dollars."

"Are you giving him the book because it rightfully belongs to him, or for the million dollars?"

"Both," I said. "The money is important, too."

She handed me the book. "It's not over, you know. It can't be. And you said you would see it through."

I shrugged, spreading my palms upwards in frustration. "I don't know what else to do. I've already risked jail, and nearly thrown away the biggest contract we've ever had. What more would you have me do?"

"I don't know," she said. "All I know is that is that you made a commitment, if not to me, then to the dead girl. You must finish what you started."

I felt trapped. "I need more time to think." Even as I said it, I knew it was a cop out. "But I have to give the book back."

We said a perfunctory goodbye, and she slammed the door behind me as I left the apartment.

With the book tucked in my briefcase, I walked to the subway to get the train to Mannhauser's. I had enough to do without worrying about commitments to dead girls. My reasons for not trusting Stanholt were purely intuition. I had no evidence that he had done anything except have me followed. He was the girl's father and he was entitled to the book. My job was to butt out. Upon arrival at the plant, I wrapped the book in plain paper, gave it to Kruger, who would have the company chauffeur deliver it personally to Stanholt. It was finished. Over. I would forget all about the Stanholt family, finish my work at Mannhauser's, and get back to Sara and the kids.

The stresses of the day had given me a headache and I quit work early for a change. I threw some papers in my briefcase and left the office by five-thirty. The walk to the subway station took no more than a few minutes and when I got there I was surprised to find it so crowded. It was the first time I had been there in the middle of rush hour. I found a spot at the far end of the platform so I could be near the front end of the train.

As the train surged into the station, the crowd eased forward. I was carried with them. There seemed to be pushing from behind somewhere, and I found myself breaking through the front line of commuters. I heard several angry shouts in German and then I felt a God almighty thrust in the small of my back. I was propelled forward. I heard screaming and even as I fell off the edge of the platform, I could see the train rushing towards me.

I have been in situations of acute danger only once or twice in my life, where my mind has entered a threshold beyond fear. The adrenaline is up and the biological clock starts to spin. For a split second everything around me seemed to slow down and I could think with crystal clarity. The rails came rushing up to meet me and I threw myself between them, pressing my body flat to the ground.

Something struck my shoulder blade as the train rushed over me, pressing me down even harder into the dirt. My eyes were tight shut as I lay, my body tense, expecting a deathblow at any moment. The brakes squealed like a cacophony from hell. There were other noises, too, a background of shouts and screams.

I didn't know whether I lost consciousness, or not, but I am sure that I never heard the train stop. I lay there, my cheek in the dirt, blood in my eye and saliva running down my chin, with some lower part of the train pressing on my back. The conductor rail gleamed not more than a few inches from my face. There had been warnings all over the station about six hundred volts, so I dared not move. I could not move, anyway. My body felt as if it had turned to stone. Faces peered through the gaps around the wheels. An official close by shouted at me, but I could not make out a word he said. Eventually a couple of uniformed employees of the railway began to crawl towards me. Obviously the rail had been turned off. They pulled me from under the train as gently as they could, and by the time they brought me up to the platform, an ambulance waited to take me to a hospital in Munich.

"You've been very lucky, Old Chap." I lay on a hospital litter in the emergency department. Most of my clothes had been removed, and the doctor, English by the sound of him, was in the final stages of examining me. He peered at my eye through an ophthalmoscope. "Most people that fall under trains get taken straight to the morgue."

"I suppose they do," I replied, wondering at his bedside manner. Upon my arrival, they had given me an injection for shock, leaving me somewhat unaware of my surroundings.

"You're not badly hurt, a few cuts and a lot of bruising, but I would like to keep you overnight for observation. Shock, you know, and there may be a touch of concussion."

The doctor returned his instruments to a tray at the side of the litter and spoke to a nurse in rapid German and before long they tucked me up in a comfortable bed in a private room.

After picking at what would have normally been an appetising meal, somebody knocked on the door. Without waiting for an answer, the door opened and in walked my old friend from the police, Inspector Drexler. "Well," he began, "you certainly are one for finding trouble. You seem to have strange adventures for a computer expert."

His opening statement was right, of course, but no one was more surprised about that than I. "Good evening, Inspector."

He smiled. "Good evening, Mr. McLeod. How are you feeling?"

I grinned. There was a bandage on my forehead, and a bandage on each knee; this I knew, but beyond that, I had no idea how I looked. "Stiffening up," I said. "But I could be worse."

"You were very lucky. If the train had not been almost stopped, you would have surely been dead. As it was, witnesses say that you were dragged under the train for about five metres."

I had no recollection of this, but it confirmed that I had lost consciousness. "Indeed, I was lucky."

"Tell me, Mr. McLeod, how did it happen?"

I thought back to what, deep down, my mind was trying to shut out. "I fell," I said. "As the train came into the station, the crowd surged forward, and I was carried to the edge of the platform and fell off."

The inspector looked at me with the same look that Stanholt had given me earlier in the day, when I had lied to him, a look somewhere between scepticism and contempt. It was becoming apparent to me that I was not a good liar. But then, in my life up till now, I had not had much practise.

"Since I have been with the police force, many years now, I might add, quite a number of people have fallen in front of our subway trains. But as far as I know, it has always been because of one or two reasons. Those reasons are murder or suicide, Mr. McLeod. Which was it in your case?"

"I told you, I fell," I said weakly.

"How is your work progressing at Mannhausers?"

So he knew about Mannhausers. I didn't remember telling him. "Very well. The project should be finished in about eight weeks. I am hoping to return to Canada in two."

"Then there is no need for you to jump in front if a train because of your work. Is anything else worrying you?"

"I fell, I told you." I felt my frustration rising to the boil.

"I don't think it was suicide," he continued as if he had not heard me. "You are not the type. Also it is obvious you struggled to stay alive. In that case it must have been murder. Is someone trying to murder you?"

"I told you, I fell. Of course no one is trying to murder me. Who would want to and for what reason?"

"That's for you to tell me, Mr. McLeod."

"I can't tell you any more than I know."

"You were lucky this time. Mrs. Mortimer was not so lucky."

"What's Mrs. Mortimer got to do with it?"

He smiled slyly. "If I were to go on a flight of fancy, this is what I might think. Mrs. Mortimer was killed because she knew something. Now the same people are trying to kill you because they think that she told you what she knew. Am I close?"

My mouth opened but no words came out. I shook my head.

"Your room in the hotel was searched yesterday. Why did you not report it to the police?"

"Who told you that?"

"The hotel manager, Mr. McLeod. It is the law. He is obliged to tell us of such things."

"I did not want to tell you, because I did not need the hassle. After the business with Mrs. Mortimer, I did not want to become involved with the police again."

"Have you any idea who would search your room, or what he might be looking for?"

"No," I said. "He might have thought my computer printouts were worth something. I don't know."

"Was anything stolen?"

"No."

"For an intelligent man, you don't seem to know much. Someone is trying to kill you, Mr. McLeod. I would be surprised if you are not in great danger."

"I fell," I said again.

He made ready to leave. "Alright, have it your way. I can't help you if you won't be helped. But remember what I said, next time you may not be so lucky. I will give you a day or two to think about it, and then we will talk again. Good night, Mr. McLeod."

"Good night," I said, as he closed the door behind him.

I looked down at the snow-white linen of the bed sheets. He was right, of course. He had framed in words what I had been dreading to think about. Somebody was trying to kill me. Who? Stanholt?

I threw back the bedcovers and slid my body painfully around until my feet were hanging over the bed. I had not realised how stiff I had become. I clambered unsteadily to my feet. I had difficulty trying to stand and had to cling on to the bed to prevent myself from falling. I felt very shaky indeed, but I managed to shuffle towards the door. When I reached the corridor outside, one of the nurses saw me and a commotion began. I tried to explain that I was only looking for a pen and some paper, but I could not make them understand. Eventually three nurses bustled me back to bed. Within a few minutes of being tucked up again, the English doctor came to my room. I explained to him what I wanted, and after some argument, he agreed that I could write, but for only half an hour. It was then that I started setting everything down. I would place a complete account of everything that had happened to me with a lawyer, only to be opened in the event of my death.

They gave me a stick when I left the hospital on the following day. All my muscles had stiffened and I was still having difficulty walking. My forehead was cut, I had a black eye and bruises all down one side of my face. It looked as if I had been in the ring with a boxing champion. I looked at my ruined suit. And my briefcase had been crushed between the wheels and one side of the platform, my papers scattered from one end of the platform to the other. Fortunately, none of these papers were irreplaceable. I took a cab from the hospital to my hotel, and there I telephoned Mannhauser's and told them that I would be off for the rest of the day.

That day I took the opportunity of completing the journal that I had started on the previous evening. Later, I made an appointment to see a lawyer and left him a sealed envelope with strict instructions of what to do if I met with an untimely end.

That night, after dinner in the hotel restaurant, I entered the elevator to return to my room. The lift-off from the ground floor was accompanied by the usual clank of moving parts and the singing of stretched cables, and then I heard a cry, an awful cry of someone in mortal agony, a lone spirit of the elevator shaft. Fear took hold and I clung to cage. The speed of the car increased as it lifted away from the first floor, and the noise of its machinery grew louder. Yet still I could hear the crying. More than one throat uttering deathly cries now, my lone spirit had been joined by others, but growing fainter as I rose up through the shaft. By the time I reached the fourth floor, I strained to hear any abnormal sound at all. I had not heard anything like the screams in the elevator since the day of the séance. I had thought my ghost well and truly laid, but Tammy was right: It was not over yet.

Partially due to my stiff muscles and partially due to my recent ride in the elevator, I staggered down the corridor to my room, cursing for forgetting to bring my stick. Once in my room, I uncorked a bottle of Scotch and poured myself a stiff drink. I knew now beyond a shadow of doubt that the sounds in the elevator were from a supernatural source, but that knowledge gave me no comfort whatsoever. I sat in my room thinking, and I drank several more generous glasses of Scotch before going to bed. I hoped the drinks would give me the utter and complete rest I needed.

I fell through a dark evil shaft of seemingly infinite depth, not so dark that I could not see, but dark enough to obscure all detail. The concrete walls of the shaft were covered in shadows, human shadows that danced as if projected by fire, and they screamed at me as I fell past. I tried to cry out but no sound would come. My soul a prisoner, trapped inside my falling and useless body. I saw water below me, inky black water from which the shadows seemed to emanate, springing from the wavelets and surging up the wall towards me, their screams growing louder and then diminishing as I fell past them. The water came rushing towards me. I was terrified of water. I had almost drowned once as a child and the fear had stayed with me ever since. I tried once more to scream and at last my body reacted to my brain's command.

I sat up in bed sharply. He time was four-thirty in the morning and every muscle in my body trembled. So much for a good night's rest. At first I was too afraid to lay my head back on the pillow for fear of dreaming again. If I were at home, I would get up and make myself a hot drink, but at four thirty in the Marrianne, there was little chance of getting anything like that. I thought of home and Sara. What time was it in Vancouver? Nine hours difference, so that would make it eight-thirty the previous evening. The kids would have just gone to bed. I would call Sara. I could not worry her with news of my accident, but just to hear her voice. I climbed out of bed and picked up the phone.

85

Chapter 9

The next morning, Friday, I walked into Mannhausers looking like a war hero, or perhaps like someone who had been run over by a train. Although my muscles had loosened a little, they were far from normal. I took my stick just in case I grew tired, and Jennings met me at the door to my office. He looked aghast. "Whatever happened?"

I was in no mood to explain my condition to anyone. "I fell down some steps," I said grumpily.

Jennings must have thought me an incredibly irritable man and the look on his face told me that whatever happened, it served me right, but he said, "Are you fit enough to be working?"

"I'll manage." We went on to discuss the project, and I was pleased and surprised that things were progressing better than I had expected.

I made an appointment to see Kruger later that day, and after I endured more comments on my appearance, of which I was heartily fed-up, we got down to business. I said, "I need to talk to Stanholt."

"You want to make an appointment to see him?"

"I don't need to see him; the telephone will do."

"He keeps his number confidential; I am not allowed to give it out."

"Well, perhaps you could get the number for me and transfer the call to my office," I suggested.

He agreed and proceeded to make the call right away. I made my way back to my own office, and by the time I shut the door, my telephone rang.

"Good morning, Herr Stanholt," I opened.

"Good morning, Mr. McLeod. How are you this morning?"

Wittingly, or unwittingly, he had given me a perfect lead-in. "If I hadn't fallen under a train on my way home from here Tuesday night, I would be better."

He made a sound something between a laugh and a strangled cry. "I beg you pardon?" He was either a superb actor, or genuinely surprised.

"I fell off the platform under a train. Obviously, I should be more careful when riding the subway."

"How dreadful. I am so sorry."

"I know you are looking out for me, so I thought I ought to let you know. I should tell you, too, that it made me think about other things. A lot of strange things have happened to me since I have been in Germany, things I don't fully understand."

"What things?" he cut in.

"You are having me followed. You probably know as much as I do."

"I know that you consorted with a woman who was later found dead. I know that you broke into my property and stole a book that was written by my daughter. And now I know that you have fallen under a train. What else has been happening to you, Mr. McLeod." A note of anger had crept into his voice.

"Plenty," I said quietly. "And being as you are looking out for me, I have written everything down that has happened to me, and everything that has been said to me since I have been in Germany. I have placed this document in the hands of a lawyer. If I should meet an untimely end, this document will be sent to the police. When I leave Germany safely, I will take the document with me and hopefully that will be an end to the matter."

The line went quiet, as he digested what I had told him. "Why are you telling me all this?" His voice portrayed total innocence.

"As I said, because you are looking out for me, you should be aware of all the facts."

"Are you accusing me of something?"

"No, certainly not." I put as much surprise in my voice as my limited acting ability would allow. "All I want to do is continue our business relationship. I want to get this job finished so you will start to benefit from our work. Then perhaps we can install the software in your other plants."

"Then, Mr. McLeod, our aims and goals appear to be the same. I suggest that you get on and finish your work and see to it that you have no more accidents."

He put down the phone and I stood there thinking over what had passed between us. If anything, I was less sure of his involvement than before.

Later that evening, after supper, I sat in the bar reading an English newspaper and sipping an after dinner drink. I saw the hotel manager walk up and say something to the barman. I waved my hand to catch his attention and called him over. "Can I buy you a drink?"

"No, thank you. It is not my custom to drink with clients when I am on duty."

"Indulge me," I said. "You are always on duty and I would like to buy you a drink."

I must have flattered his ego, for he finally agreed and I ordered him a whiskey from the bar. "Why did you tell the police about my room being searched?"

The manager had a very fair complexion and snow-white hair, thinning to the point where his pink scalp showed through in stripes. He coloured a little at my question. "It is the law. If there were more trouble and it came out that I had not reported your room being searched, I could lose my job. I did ask the police to be discrete."

Asking the police to be discrete probably made it worse. "Well, never mind; it is done now. Tell me, how long have you been manager here?"

"Twenty years. It doesn't seem that long, but ever since the hotel reopened in 1951."

"I suppose none of the staff from before the war were re-employed?"

"Only one, to my knowledge, the maintenance man. He grew up as the maintenance man in the old building. Apparently, he knew every inch of the place and they kept him on through the war. He never liked the new building though; he used to say there were too many modern gadgets."

"Does he still work here?"

"No." The manager shook his head. "Not since fifty two."

"Do you remember his name?" I asked, desperate to get some information on this man.

"Hans Balder." A far-away look came into his eyes as he thought back. "I remember his name because of the accident."

"Accident?" I waited for him to go on, but he did not elaborate. "What accident?" I said.

"He was killed in 1952, within a few months of coming back here, a terrible accident. "

Dragging information from this man was like pulling teeth. "Tell me more. What happened?"

The manager looked down at his drink and then back at me. "I've said too much. If things like this get out, it gives the hotel a bad name."

I looked around. "There is no one here but me and I'm not going to blab. And you have aroused my interest."

"I'm sorry. I should not have done that, but I really must say no more."

"Alright." I said, afraid that he would get up and leave. "Tell me something about Hans Balder."

"Ah, Hans." That far-away look returned to his eyes. "An outspoken man and he had no love for the Nazis. He got into trouble towards the end of the war and they fired him. I heard that he was lucky not to have been executed."

"Trouble?" I waved to the barman for a couple more drinks. It was imperative I kept him talking.

"What is your interest in all this, if you don't mind me asking?"

"Historical mainly," I said, not wanting to arouse his suspicions. "I have to have something to take my mind off work occasionally."

"Well, I don't know anything about it other than a high ranking German Officer was killed and Hans was blamed. They said Hans hadn't done something that he should have, and a very important man died."

"You know that much and you don't know the whole story?" I knew the man was holding back.

"There were rumours. I will not be responsible for spreading them. Facts were difficult to get at that time. Things were in a turmoil because of the war."

"If he was negligent, I am surprised you re-employed him."

"I didn't. The owner of this building knew Hans and was very much an anti-Nazi himself."

"Who was the owner?"

At that question he looked distinctly uncomfortable. "He was head of a real estate company. It is a matter of public record." He gathered his drink and looked as if he was about to leave.

"I am interested in what happened here during the transformation period at the end of the war."

"You Canadians wouldn't really know what war is, would you?"

I resented his question and it showed. "I don't know. "I was too young personally, but the Canadians sure as hell did their part in the war."

He realized that he had offended me. "I am sorry. I, too, was not a soldier, but the bombing, you know, that is what I meant."

"Well, I suppose we were lucky enough never to have been bombed at home." While I had him on the defensive, I pushed on with my questions. "Tell me more about Hans Balder? Was he married? Did he have any children?"

"You really are interested in this old stuff, aren't you? His wife was alive when he was killed and he had two children. His son was killed on the Russian front, and there was a daughter, a few years younger than the boy, but I don't know what happened to her."

"Anything else?"

"Nothing." He smiled. "Why don't you tell me something about yourself, Mr. McLeod. I see you leave early in the morning with your briefcase and returning late in the evening. Tell me about your life and what you do."

"Not much to tell," I said. I gave him a brief run down as to who I was, a bit about my company, and about my family. But I could see he was not about to reveal anymore of the history of the building.

.   .   .   .   .

From the progress we were making at Mannhausers, it looked as if I would be free to go home in about a week. Not that I felt any sorrow at the idea of leaving Germany, but I had never been a person to leave things half done. And I knew, beyond a shadow of a doubt, that Tammy had been right. I had capitulated, and the commitments I had made were not realized.

I knew that Stanholt watched my every move, but how closely I could not be sure. I did not want to take any chances. The following day, Saturday, instead of going early to Mannhausers, I waited until about nine o'clock and telephoned Tammy. In spite of all the time I had spent in Germany, I could trust no one except her. The maid answered the telephone and I asked to speak to Tammy and she told me that Tammy was in bed.

"Please tell her I am on the phone. It is Bob McLeod; she will want to speak to me."

"*Ja.*" The maid sounded doubtful.

Tammy was not in the least pleased to be woken up to speak to me. "What on earth do you want at this time of the morning?" she replied to my good morning greeting.

"You were right. I should not have given in like that."

"Are you ringing me at this time of the morning to tell me that?"

"Somebody tried to kill me," I said.

The line went quiet. She did not reply at first, and then, "How? What happened?"

I gave her a brief account and much of her coldness evaporated, and she became concerned, even sympathetic. "What do you want me to do?" she said after I had finished.

"I want you to find me a private detective. I want one that can speak English and can also keep his mouth shut. I wouldn't know where to start looking, and I can't even read the yellow pages."

She laughed. "Actually, I do know someone that might be able to help."

I smiled to myself. Why was I not surprised? "Excellent. But he must be absolutely discrete, and remember, I am being watched."

She told me to stay put for a while and she would try and contact this person. I phoned Jennings and told him I wouldn't be in until later. He did not seem surprised considering the number of bruises on my body. About twenty minutes later Tammy phoned to tell me that a man named Luc would come to my room within in the hour.

Though a Frenchman, Luc Gaudreault was fluent in most European languages and passable in English. He came to my room wearing a dark sports coat, navy blue beret and sporting a thin, curly moustache. He looked French, even to the point of being stereotyped, and I could not help thinking of Inspector Clouseou of the Pink Panther. He slipped silently into the room after I opened the door to his knock and sat on one of my two wicker chairs.

He pulled a cigarette packet from his pocket. "Mind if I smoke?"

"Yes I do," I shot back. The last thing I needed in my room was cigarette smoke.

He shrugged and replaced the cigarette packet in his jacket.

"Would you like a coffee? I can get one from room service."

"No, Monsieur. It would be good if no one knew I was here."

I liked the way he thought; obviously, Tammy had told him some of it. "I am being watched. You know that?"

He nodded.

"I need you to find out a few things for me. Curiosity, you see." He raised his eyebrows at that, but said nothing. "A man worked at this building as maintenance man, before the war, during the war, and for a short time after the war, His name was Hans Balder. The SS used this building, and this man was fired towards the end of the war. He died in an accident here in the hotel in 1952. I want you to find out for me all you can about this man, why he was fired and how he died. I also want to know about his family, are they still alive and where are they."

He stood up. "What you ask seems fairly straightforward. I should have some answers for you by tomorrow." He went on to explain his rates and billing procedures, and then he said, "You do not have to tell me why you want to know these things, but nobody ever uses my services for curiosity."

'Perhaps not,' I said, and then just as he was leaving, "One more thing. I also want to know who owns this building."

After Luc had gone, I sat on my bed wondering if I was wasting my money. Whatever scrapes Hans Balder got himself into were probably nothing to do with my problems. I had just a feeling about him, a hunch if you like. And just lately, since I had been staying at the Marrianne, I began to wonder whether my hunches were truly hunches. I put on the jacket to my light grey suit ready to leave for Mannhausers, my dark suit having been ruined under a train.

That evening Luc telephoned. "I have some information for you. Not all, but I will come around and see you, if you will be there."

I agreed, and within twenty minutes he slipped quietly and discretely into my room. "I know the story of Hans Balder." He pulled a cigarette packet from his pocket, then looked at me and put it back. "There are lots of people that know, but few who are willing to tell. It cost plenty to get people to talk."

"Why should that be?" I asked, knowing I would be the one paying the plenty.

"People that knew things that went on during the war have a habit of meeting with accidents. There are many Nazis that were never caught, in some cases rich and powerful men."

"I see," I thought for a moment, digesting what I had been told. "Is that what happened to Hans Balder?"

"Who knows." He shrugged and seemed reluctant to go on.

"Well, go on, tell me then."

"You are a friend of Tammy's, and that is good, but I would like to have some money before I tell you what I know. You understand, Monsieur?"

I smiled. "Of course. I have an account at the Deutsche Bank here in Munich. Would a cheque be alright; you can cash it in the morning."

"I do not like cheques. They are not good in this business, and it is better that I have no traceable connection with you."

At least a part of his discretion was due to worrying about his own safety – a sobering thought. "Alright, I am a friend of Tammy's and I am good for the money. How about trusting me until the morning?"

"They have made one attempt on your life and a lot can happen in an evening. But I see I have no choice."

I had a few marks in my wallet, but not enough to satisfy his bill. I pulled out what I had. "Here have this on account, just in case."

After a cursory count, he stuffed the money in his pocket. "It is a strange case. It concerns the elevator."

Bingo! Once again my hunches were proving out.

"There is not much to say about his death. Apparently, he had stopped the elevator one night to do some routine maintenance, and fell down the shaft. Later on, they found the elevator in the service mode, locked above the fourth floor doors, and Balder's body at the bottom of the shaft in the basement."

"Wait a minute." I tried to picture what Luc had said. "Would he normally do routine maintenance under the car at the top of the shaft?"

Luc smiled a wintry smile. "It would not seem sensible to you and me, but who knows what went on in his mind at that time. With no evidence of foul play and no witnesses, on the surface it would seem like an accident."

"On the surface," I grunted.

Luc went on. "The incident during the war is more complex. Late in 1945 during the bombing of Munich, the building was hit but not badly. A water main burst flooding the basement, filling it with water. Hans was instructed to shut out the basement from the elevator circuits." Luc shrugged. "Apparently, by adjusting some wires in a box this can be done. After Hans reported to his superiors that he had completed the job, an SS Brigadier with three others went down in the elevator together and were drowned."

"Good God." It still made little sense, but it did concern the elevator. "Wouldn't the fuses have blown, preventing the car from going down that far?"

"I am not an electrician, Monsieur. But in those days, I think, the controls at the bottom of the shaft were all mechanical. When the car descended into the water, then the fuses blew, but this merely trapped the occupants inside, preventing anyone else from bringing the car up. They did not get the bodies out until they had pumped the water from the basement."

"Can you tell me the names of the people in the car?"

"Yes, Monsieur, two of them. I do not know the others. The Brigadier General's name was Becker. A young girl named Eve Maynard was another, his girl friend. The other two were prisoners from Dachau.

I was not surprised, for the loop was beginning to close. "You have done well," I said. "But I would like to know the names of the other dead. No, don't forget Hans Balder's relatives."

"And you will not forget my money, Monsieur."

"Of course not," I said. "And did you find out who owns this building?"

"Yes, it's a realty company."

He went on to give me the name of the company and its principals. I had difficulty hiding my disappointment, for I knew none of them. "I had hoped for a connection. You see, someone who owned the building knew Hans Balder and gave him his job back after the war."

"The building was sold five years ago."

"Oh, who were the previous owners?"

Luc had done his job, and this time he gave me the name of another realty company and its principals. This time I was not disappointed, for I recognised a name: Rudolph Kruger, another link forged in the chain.

Chapter 10

Eve sat down to breakfast to eat a plate of scrambled eggs on toast. Frou Kinder's homemade black bread supplied the toast and the eggs were a product of the few chickens Eve kept in the barn. The overnight chill still hung in the kitchen, as the wood stove had yet to reach its maximum output. The weather outside was cold indeed, for winter had come hard to Bavaria that year. Now, in February 1945, the snow lay evenly over the farm to a depth of two to three inches, creating a Christmas card panorama of the local countryside.

Frou Kinder invariably got up first in the morning, and she re-kindled the stove and had her breakfast before Eve came down. The two women barely greeted one another. All the time they had lived together there was nothing more to their relationship than bare necessity. Neither asked the other for anything more than what was considered duty. Frou Kinder wanted it that way; she did not seem to need friendship of others and she did not seek it. Becker could not have chosen a better gaoler, and, of course, Eve could never talk of her past.

The cold wind suddenly wafted into the kitchen as the back door opened and Becker crossed the threshold. Both women were taken completely by surprise, for Becker came rarely these days and it had been more than three months since his last visit. He smiled, greeting them pleasantly, and dumped a bagful of rations on the kitchen table. "There, Ladies, see what you can do with those."

Eve sprang forward, opened the bag and said, "Oh, how lovely." There were a couple of cans of meat, some butter and some jam. Food was in critical supply in Germany, particularly anything that had to be imported, such as sugar. Eve pulled out a jar of marmalade. "It has been so long since we have had any of this."

"Well, you think yourself lucky, little one. You are better off than most of Germany right now, living on the farm, as you do."

Becker was right, of course. What they didn't grow themselves, they could easily get from their neighbours. "Pity we don't have a cow," Frou Kinder said thoughtfully.

"There is nothing stopping you buying one or two." Becker removed his great coat and threw his hat with its death's head badge on the hook behind the door. Eve hated that hat and its badge and everything it stood for. He stood in the kitchen resplendent in his full uniform tunic and Eve was quick to notice the new insignia. "You have your promotion. Are we supposed to congratulate you?" Eve smiled and seemed genuinely pleased for him, and in a way she was. Even without realizing it, she played a dual role. If he was happy, and he seemed happy now, then so was she. It was better for her, and it was better not to think too much.

"Herr Oberfuhrer Becker." He grinned.

"And so far from being just a schoolmaster in Munich. Congratulations." She bowed her head slightly as she spoke to please him. "What is next for you? How long before you become Reichsfuhrer?"

The last remark upset him and the smile vanished from his lips. "There is but one Reichfuhrer in Germany: Himler; there will never be another."

"Some breakfast, Herr Becker?" Frou Kinder intervened just at the right moment.

"I'll have some eggs." The thought of food returned some of his good humour.

Frou Kinder began to scramble more eggs. "Herr Huber, next door, could find us a cow."

Becker sat to the table. "Good idea. Talk to him after I return to my headquarters."

While Frou Kinder busied herself at the stove, Eve leaned very close to Becker and whispered, "My family, Herr Oberfuhrer, have you heard how they are?"

He smiled at her concern. "Well, I think. I may have news for you later." And then in a normal voice he said, "And now, little one, what plans do you have for today?"

He did seem in good spirits, like some returning benevolent uncle. "I must see to the horses. They need exercise and then I must clean the stable. I planned to do that this morning."

"Excellent. How are the horses?"

"Just the two of them still, but they are keeping well." There had been six when Eve first went to the farm, but three had been sold to reduce costs and one had died of old age.

"Good. I will come out and see them later and maybe tomorrow we will ride. In the mean time, I must not keep you from your important tasks. Do a good job and don't hurry it."

Eve changed into her riding gear in her small back room, and when she left the house to walk down to the stables, Becker was well into his breakfast with Frou Kinder silently watching over him.

Wrapped in her warmest riding clothes, Eve rode the big stallion, Zeus, while leading the mare, Hera. Riding the small boundaries of the farm gave Eve one of her greatest pleasures. She took her time, imagining that she was truly free, even though the cold wind found every tiny piece of exposed skin and pinched it red. Once back at the stables she had to rake out the muck from each stall and spread new straw. And then came the grooming of the horses. She delighted in grooming them, and with Zeus it was almost sensual, watching the ripple of his great muscles under the constant strokes of the brush, and the sheen on his dark coat when she had finished. Hera was smaller and lighter in colour, and as Eve saw Zeus as masculine and powerful, and imagined him like the great god himself, so Hera was wily and intelligent with perhaps a touch of raw cunning; she, too, was aptly named.

Eve felt warm under her riding clothes and her body tingled as if all her muscles had been honed to a point of tiredness. By the time she trudged back through the snow to the house, almost four hours had passed and the scrambled eggs had worn off and leaving her feeling hungry. Becker sat alone in the kitchen reading a newspaper and lunch had not been started. As Eve made her way to her room to change, she said, "Where's Frou Kinder?"

"She left this morning. Her mother is sick and she has returned home."

"That's strange. She didn't say anything."

Becker looked up from his newspaper. "Did she ever say anything?"

"No." But Eve, still puzzled, said, "How did she know her mother was sick. She never received any letters. At least I never saw her get a letter."

"How the hell should I know? She told me she wanted to go and she has gone. It doesn't take two women to look after a small place like this." Becker's agitation lay barely below the surface.

"She should have told me. There are things I should know if I am to run the house."

"You will learn fast enough. Prepare some lunch. Let us see if you can cook."

Eve, feeling bewilderment, quickly went upstairs to change. If Frou Kinder planned to go, surely she would have done some advanced packing. Eve returned to the kitchen and opened a can of condensed soup. The first meal she cooked for Becker would not be exotic.

That afternoon Eve found herself in Frou Kinder's room. Nothing remained of Frou Kinder. It was as if the woman had never been there. The closets and drawers were empty and even the top of the dressing table had been cleared. The bed had been stripped to the bare mattress, and strangely, Eve had not seen the bedclothes in the closet waiting to be washed.

"What are you doing in there?'

Eve turned to find Becker standing in the doorway, his face screwed up in rage. "I just thought the room might need cleaning."

"Get out of there!"

She slipped past Becker. "But there should be some washing that needs doing."

Becker slammed the door. "And stay out."

Becker's benevolent mood of the morning had turned ugly and grew worse as nighttime approached. The reason for this, Eve could not fathom, unless it was due to the progress of the war. It was difficult to get hard news, but there were plenty of rumours. The Russians were advancing in the east and the British and

Americans in the west. It could only be a matter of time now before it all came to an end. Eve would then be free. And her family, if they were alive, they, too, would be free. Eve, again, broached to Becker the subject of her family, but he growled at her and told her nothing. She went to bed in the small room at the back, preferring not to sleep with him, and he did not seem concerned.

The following morning, Becker rose early, put on his old work clothes, and started work in the yard immediately after breakfast. Something Eve had never seen him do before. As Eve washed up the breakfast things, Becker worked in the barn. She saw him through the frosty window and decided to make him coffee; it may help to keep out the cold. The coffee tin was less than half full with the ersatz stuff they sold in the stores. Real coffee was little more than a memory at this stage of the war.

Even though, dressed in her warmest clothes, the wind bit deeply as she went out through the back door. It was cold indeed. Carrying the steaming pot, she hurried to get into the shelter of the barn. As she went through the open barn door, Becker worked in the far corner with his back to her, knee deep in a great hole that he dug at furiously with a spade. On one side of the hole a mound of earth rose gradually, getting ever higher with each spade full, and on the other, a sinister bundle lay wrapped in bedclothes.

As soon as she had passed through the door, Eve blurted, "I've brought you some coffee."

For a second Becker froze, but only for a second. He spun around, the spade poised high in the air. "What the hell are you doing here?" He screamed the words as he jumped from the hole. "You're spying on me." He ran towards Eve, waving the spade like a huge two-handed sword, as if to cut her down.

She backed away and fell over a bale of hay, spilling the scalding coffee down her legs. She screamed, partly from the burns and partly from waiting for Becker to bring down the spade and split her skull. He stood above her, the spade raised to strike her dead, when suddenly, as if a switch had been thrown, he calmed. "Why are you following me about?"

"I thought you might be cold, so I made you some coffee." Eve sat up and rubbed her scalded legs through her trousers. "You made me burn myself." Her eyes began to water.

Becker gently kicked her with his muddy boot. "Get in the house and don't come out unless I say so."

She stood up painfully, gathering the now empty coffee pot and searching to find the lid. "Am I to be a prisoner in the house now?"

"Just do as you are told."

She walked back to the house, and he stood at the entrance of the barn watching her until she disappeared inside and closed the door behind her.

Eve stood at the sink washing some clothes when Becker returned from the barn. He walked into the kitchen carrying a long thin stick, which he threw onto the table. His mood appeared to have deteriorated even further, for he scowled and kicked the door shut behind him. His clothes were covered in mud, and after stripping off his topcoat and boots, he hurled them into the closet under the stairs.

He then stripped off the rest of his clothes and threw them on the floor beside Eve. "Wash those," he said.

She turned to find him standing there completely naked.

"What are you looking at?"

"Nothing," she said automatically, and turned to get back on with her washing. The stove put out considerable heat and warmed the kitchen a degree or two above the comfort level, and Eve wore a thin cotton dress, light pink in colour, for working around the house. Becker took a stride across the room, grabbed the dress at the back of the neck, and wrenched it off. Eve cried out as the dress ripped from top to bottom, leaving her standing in her underclothes.

"You damned Jewish whore, you're getting above yourself."

"What have I done?" she cried, as he threw her against the table, bruising her thighs against the hard wood.

He went for her like an animal, the rage in him exploding as if it had been suppressed for too long. He tore away the rest of her clothes. "You forget." He almost choked on the words. "I own you body and soul. Never do you spy on me."

"I wasn't spying," sobbed Eve, but he didn't hear. He held her with one of his muddy hands at the neck, pushing her flat against the table. Then taking the stick, he beat her. He laid the stick repeatedly across her back, her buttocks and the back of her thighs. Her cries failed to reach him and as he beat her, his penis grew hard and rigid. Suddenly, he threw the stick to one side, having reached a point where the beating could do no more for him, and pushed Eve across the table, angling himself between her thighs and entering her from the rear.

Eve shook with convulsive sobs, her tortured body pressed prone to the table. The pain from the red welts that striped more than half her body paled to insignificance compared to the humiliation of being beaten and raped in this manner. In all the time they had been together he had never treated her so. He grunted and cried out as he reached his orgasm. In eve's memory he had never reached such a climax with her before.

As soon as he was satisfied, he pulled away from her, kicked his clothes towards the sink, and made for the door. "I'll have a bath. Get the washing done and clear the place up."

Eve gathered the remnants of her clothes together and fled to her small back room. Her heart had darkened and any remote feelings that she might haves had for Becker were replaced by an overriding hatred, a hatred that would last until death and even beyond. She lay on her bed for the rest of the afternoon, and in spite of not finishing the washing or clearing up, she heard no more from Becker.

Darkness had fallen by the time she ventured from her room. Dressed in fresh clothes, she went again to the kitchen. Becker had made himself a sandwich for supper and retired to the parlour to read his books and papers. After finishing the washing, she cleaned up and made herself a bowl of soup. Becker entered the room as she sponged the last of the soup from the bowl with a piece of Frou Kinder's dwindling supply of black bread.

Becker looked down at her but she could not meet him in the eye. Her cheeks glowed red with something between rage and humiliation, or perhaps both.

"So, you have showed yourself at last. Don't take it so personally. Every woman deserves a spanking now and again. Some even beg for it."

Tears of self pity welled up in her eyes and all she could say was, "You shouldn't have done that."

"Well, never mind, little one. I have some good news about your parents." The benevolent Becker was back again, the one from yesterday morning.

"My parents?" Eve's eyes were wide open now, wide open and searching Becker's face.

"Yes. If you are a good girl, we will take a ride into Munich tomorrow. And if you are very lucky..." Becker enjoyed spinning the words out as long as he could, while Eve looked on in eager anticipation. "If you are very lucky, you may see your parents."

Eve could barely remain in her seat. The news swept through her body, driving every other feeling and emotion away, except utter happiness and anticipation. Tomorrow, after four years, she would see her parents again. There had been so many times when she became convinced that this could never happen. So happy was she at the news that she didn't think of the complications. For she was no longer Ilse Stanholt, Ilse Stanholt was dead and buried long ago.

"I am going to arrange for you to escape with your parents. I cannot afford to have you and your family around me anymore. You have become an embarrassment to me, and with the allies advancing, it is too dangerous."

Eve heard his words but did not fully comprehend. It sounded wonderful, too good to be true.

"You will follow my instructions implicitly and you will instruct your parents to do the same. Do you understand?"

"Yes," murmured Eve, still in a daze.

As soon as she could reasonably get away, Eve left Becker in the parlour and retired to the small back room. After pulling the journal from the hiding place under the floor, she began to write. She wrote an entry that told of darkness and horror, of beating and of rape, and then she wrote an entry of hope and of the joy of seeing her family again and of the thought of freedom. When she finished, she wrapped the book in the remains of the dress that Becker had torn from her body and placed it under the floor, where it would remain undisturbed for twenty-six years. She would never write in it again.

Chapter 11

As promised, on the following day, the first thing I did was to arrange for Luc to be paid. I drew two thousand marks from my bank account to pay Luc the three hundred I owed him and leave the rest, a considerable sum, with Tammy. I would tell Luc that if anything happened to me, then he must contact Tammy for the money. I felt I knew her well enough to trust her; anyway, there was no one else.

I telephoned the number Luc had given me and was able to reach him before noon. He told me he had good news about Hans Balder's relatives and he would come and see me that evening. He was satisfied to wait for his money until then.

After supper, I returned to my hotel room and waited expectantly for Luc's visit. I felt somewhat helpless at not being able to find these things out for myself, but I knew that Luc would be much quicker and more efficient than I could ever hope to be. He slipped into my room promptly at eight o'clock.

I paid him what I owed him, and explained the arrangements for further payments in case the worst happened. He seemed satisfied.

"Hans Balder's wife is dead. She died shortly after Hans was killed."

"Not good," I said. "What happened to her?"

"I don't know. I guess the loss of her son and then her husband was just too much for her. But I have found where the daughter lives. She is married and has two small boys and lives on the coast near Wilhelmshaven. Her husband works in the docks there."

"Well done. This is better news. How did you find out?"

Luc smiled, a grin that opened his mouth slightly, exposing a row of brown stained teeth. "Secrets of the trade. If I were to tell you, then you would know as much as me."

"I see," I said. "So you won't tell me in spite of the fact that I am paying you."

His attitude softened. "I ask around. People still remember back that far. Old neighbours, co-workers, those sort of people. They talk to me; I do not frighten them like the police."

"Where is Wilhelmshaven?" My geographic knowledge of Germany was not up to much.

"On the North Sea coast, near Holland."

"That far?" My mind delved into the logistics of getting there. "We will have to fly up."

"I do not like aeroplanes, Monsieur."

His comment served to instantly bring me back to the present. "I didn't mean you. I was thinking of someone else."

"Will you be needing me for anything more, Monsieur?"

"Yes, I think so. I will give you a man's name and I want you to find out what you can about him. I know quite a lot already, but there is just a chance you may stumble on something useful. "

"Who is this man?"

"His name is Fredrick Stanholt. He is chairman and chief executive officer for Mannhauser Industries, among other things."

Luc was an intelligent man who lived by his wits. His face creased into a frown and he looked at me hard in the eye. "You think, this is the man who tried to kill you?"

I could almost see the price for Luc's services going up. I shrugged. "Yes. But I don't know why and I can't find a motive."

"He is high profile, this man?"

"Not really. He tends to be a bit of a recluse. I will tell you where he lives, but he has at least one armed bodyguard. I wouldn't make it too obvious that you were enquiring about him, if I were you. And I wouldn't get too close, and, for heavens sake, don't get hurt."

"This job will cost you more," he said.

Surprise surprise. "If you think the job is too dangerous, don do it."

To that, Luc made no comment. He was more concerned with how much he could charge me and get away with it. "Five hundred in advance. How much more, I tell you when I have something."

I counted out the money and then I took out some hotel stationary and scribbled down Stanholt's address. After pocketing the cash, Luc wrote down some information for me. "Helga Loewen," I said, reading his note. The address was a residential district on the outskirts of Wilhelmshaven.

"You will find her there," said Luc. "Her husband works the day shift and she stays home and looks after her boys. The youngest is about one year old."

I wondered whether to phone her and let her know that I was coming, but then I decided against it. I would take her by surprise, before she had time to think.

Customisation of the software at Mannhauser's was almost complete. I was able to leave more and more of the work to Jennings. He was growing with the job and I was quite pleased with the way he was handling things now. Except for a few odds and ends and the final testing of the software modifications, I could go home.

Therefore, if I were to take a day or two off, it would make little difference to the work.

I moved towards the hotel door to let Luc out. I opened the door carefully to make sure the passageway was clear. The man standing behind the door had his arm raised, as if to knock. I was startled to say the least. As soon as I gathered my wits together, I recognized the man as Inspector Drexler, and I had no idea how long he had been standing there.

"How are you, Inspector?" The words blurted out.

It was obvious that Drexler was pleased with the effect his appearance had on me. He smiled. "How are you is more to the point."

"You'd better come in." I opened the door wide. The Inspector entered and Luc, pulling his beret down well over his face, slipped out and headed silently towards the elevator. The Inspector watched him go, taking in everything, missing nothing.

"I'm fine," I said, closing the door. "I am still covered in bruises, but everything is on the mend."

"I say again, you were very lucky."

"How about a drink, Inspector?" I walked over to my narrow selection of bottles that sat on the chest of drawers.

"A Scotch, if you don't mind. Scotch and water. I can't say that I'm on duty. I've done close to twelve hours today and I am on my way home."

It was my turn to smile. "You don't have to justify a drink to me, but I thought, being as we are in Munich, you might ask for a schnapps, or something."

"I noticed your selection. You don't have schnapps."

"Touché," I said.

"I like Scotch, or perhaps a little vodka. Sometimes I drink schnapps."

I was using small talk to play for time. I didn't know what to say to Drexler, except to tell him as little as possible. I handed him the Scotch and water.

"*Danke.* What was your meeting with him about?" He nodded towards the door.

"He's doing a little bit of detective work for me," I said, keeping as near to the truth as possible. "I'm studying the more recent history of the city."

Drexler looked at me with the same contemptuous, sceptical expression he had given me in the hospital. "Mr. McLeod, I have been making a few discrete inquiries about you. In your field, you are a much respected and clever man. You have a pretty wife, two lovely children and a nice home in Vancouver, where you live a model life. You are the envy of most people. You have everything! Then what the hell are you doing mixing with low life like that, and trying to get yourself killed." His voice rose octave by octave until his speech had become a tirade.

I felt angry and embarrassed as I poured myself a large Scotch and sat on the edge of the bed. I realised that I must be getting near to the end of my rope with Drexler. "I assume this is a free country. Every man must do what he must do. I have done nothing wrong, sir. If someone tried to kill me on the subway platform, then I don't know who or why."

For once I had been telling the truth and I could see that he accepted it as such. "That's better," he said. "Perhaps now we can start over. Now tell me again, what is your business with that man?"

I sighed. "He is looking into some historical events for me, particularly events that are concerned with the immediate history of this hotel. I am considering writing a book on the subject."

Drexler looked exasperated. "Do you take me for a complete fool? Look at it from where I stand. You are somehow, however loosely, involved with a murdered woman, an attempt has been made on your life, and now you have employed the services of a dubious individual who lives by his wits among the dregs of Munich. Believe me, that man is well known to the police. I am sure you are in trouble and I want to help you, Mr. McLeod. That is all."

I took another swig of the whiskey. "I appreciate you concern for my welfare, and one day I might be able to give you a clearer picture of what is happening. But at this time, I can tell you nothing more than I already have."

"I see," he said. By that statement, you are at least admitting that something is going on. I will warn you that it is a criminal offence to hide, or not disclose, evidence of a crime to the police. Are you aware of anything we should know of the murder of Mrs. Heidi Mortimer?"

"No, I am not. And I do not believe I am hiding evidence from you. If I should come upon anything that would be of interest to the police, you will be the first to know."

He was not satisfied, but he drank the rest of his drink and made to leave. "I say again, Mr. McLeod, for a clever man you seem to be very foolish. Be careful."

I went over and let him out of the room and he said nothing more, except a curt good evening as he walked off down the hotel corridor.

The inspector's visit, however brief, had upset me. It was inconceivable that I had placed myself in a position where I had to lie to the police. I seemed to be falling into a pit, where the slippery sides were closing in on me and there was no way out. It was probable that even now I could still walk away, no harm done. If I were to walk away, it would leave a great wrong hidden from justice forever. I sat down for a bit and had another drink before I picked up the telephone and called Tammy. She was not in. I should have known. Nine o'clock in the evening was her prime time. I left a message with her maid asking that Tammy call me as soon as she came in.

After having more than my usual couple of drinks, I laid back on the bed to rest my eyes. The next thing I knew the telephone was ringing in my ear and the time was close to midnight. "Hello," I said, sleepily as I fumbled for the phone.

"Hello, Bob. Olga said you called and it was urgent."

"Yes," I said. In-spite of being only half-awake, I was struck by the fact that she had called me by my Christian name. She had never done that before. "Could you manage to take a day or two off, say two at the most," I said quickly.

She paused. "When?" She was obviously puzzled by my request.

"Tomorrow, or the next day."

"Not tomorrow," she said firmly. "Tell me about it. What do you want me to do?"

"I want you to come with me to Wilhelmshaven and act as interpreter. I need to talk to a woman about her father. She may be able to throw some light on the accident that killed Stanholt's daughter."

"I see," said Tammy thoughtfully. "Are you asking me to go away with you?"

She had spoken facetiously, but the truth never the less. "I suppose I have, but you know why. You do want to help me with this thing, don't you?"

She laughed. "Don't get so defensive. I'll cancel my appointments for the day after tomorrow, but I want to get back as soon as I can. This could get expensive."

Tell me about it. I thanked her and put the phone down. I would arrange tickets with Lufthanser first thing in the morning.

．　．　．　．　．

Once more I sat in an aeroplane, but this time, instead of Gilbert, my companion was an attractive woman. Tammy had dressed smartly for the occasion in a dark suit, white blouse and matching pillbox hat. "You do look lovely," I said, when we met, but that was not until we were on the plane and in our seats. I still played the cautious game, if not for my sake, then for Tammy's. We had both gone to the airport separately, and though I saw her several times in the airport building, I made no sign of recognition. The chances were that I was being followed, but it was unlikely that I would be followed onto the plane.

Wilhelmshaven is a typical industrial port city, a busy city with lots of bicycles, probably the influence of neighbouring Holland. The dock area is a mass of cranes, reaching up like a forest around ships that resembled beached whales. We arrived just after noon, and though we had breakfasted on the plane, we decided to have lunch prior to finding the home of the Loewen's.

"What will you do if this woman refuses to talk to you? After all, why should she? She doesn't know you from Adam."

We were seated in a small café and Tammy asked the question just as I bit into a veal sausage. I smiled. "I'll try to use some of my partner's infallible charm. I've worked with him long enough and he sure has a way with the ladies."

She raised her eyes to the ceiling. "This I've got to see."

"If she won't talk," I said, becoming more serious, "we'll have to find someone else who might know something, or perhaps Luc might be able to find something out from her."

"What about Luc?" she asked suddenly. "Is he doing something else for you?"

"Yes," I said, automatically looking over my shoulder to ensure we were not being observed. "I asked him to take a look at Stanholt. You never know, he might find out something I missed."

"A bit dangerous, isn't it?" She frowned worriedly.

I shrugged. "I warned him to be careful." My explanation did nothing to soothe her worried look. "He's charging me extra money."

"My God, men seem to think that money takes care of everything."

I shrugged again. It was a strange comment coming from someone in Tammy's trade, but I let it lie.

The Loewen's lived in a fairly new but modest three bed-roomed house, a house that stood shoulder to shoulder with hundreds of others just like it at the outskirts of the city. As we sat in Frau Helga Loewen's front parlour, I had time to observe the woman more closely. I thought her somewhat overweight and the stresses of bringing up a couple of young children were clearly visible. The youngest hung onto her soiled apron and stared at me suspiciously while the other played with toys in the corner of the room.

Frau Loewen spoke only broken English, so it was left to Tammy to translate. "So it is about my father that you wish to speak. What is it that you want to know?"

"Towards the end of the war, there was an accident in the elevator shaft of the Marrianne Hotel. At that time, your father was blamed. I am interested and I wondered what his side of the story was."

"Why do you wish to know about this? This is old stuff, better forgotten." The woman flushed a little, indicating that she considered my question an intrusion into her privacy.

"Better forgotten for some, maybe. Mysterious happenings took place about that time, especially concerning the German officer that was killed in the elevator. I believe that this accident was a crucial part of something much bigger."

"I am sorry. I do not want my father's name dragged through the mud again. He did not like the Nazis, but he was a proud man. He did not cause the accident."

"Nothing of what we speak here today will be made public without your permission. This I promise you. The last thing I want to do is drag your father's name through the mud. The reverse is true. Maybe I can clear your father of any blame."

After Tammy had repeated more or less what I had said, the woman's attitude softened. "If you promise me those things, I will tell you what I know."

"You have my word," I said solemnly.

The child became restless and pulled violently at the apron, whimpering at the same time. Obviously, he felt that the adults in the room had ignored him long enough. Tammy bent forward and took him in her arms, saying something to his mother at the same time. At first the boy was not sure, but he soon settled under Tammy's gentle handling. "What is it you want to know," asked Frau Loewen.

"Tell me what happened, as far as you can remember."

"My father, he was very upset about it. It was that colonel, or brigadier, he became. My father hated him as much as any of them. My father would say, it was his sort that epitomised the Nazi regime."

"In what way?"

"Arrogant. Strutting. A self styled demi-god. He would never have spoken to a lowly maintenance man, like my father, unless it was to shout at him or tell him to get out. That is why my father found it so strange when the brigadier came to him while he modified the elevator circuits."

"Came to him?"

"Yes. My father had the control box open doing the modifications and the brigadier came and stood by him to watch. He spoke pleasantly, asking my father how it worked. My father was proud of what he did and glad of the opportunity to tell someone about it, even such an officer of the SS.

"So your father explained the workings of the control relays of the elevator circuit to this brigadier. Did your father think that someone touched the box after he had finished modifying it."

"Yes." The answer came without hesitation. The woman was quite definite about it. "It was either the brigadier, or the brigadier had someone else do it."

"Why would the brigadier want to do that?" I asked.

'Suicide," replied the woman. "He wanted to commit suicide."

"Ha," I said. "There are easier ways of committing suicide than that. He could simply have shot himself."

The woman was angered by my scepticism. "If he had shot himself, it would not have looked like an accident and he would not have taken the others with him."

"Why would he want to take the others with him?"

Frau Loewen shrugged her shoulders. "I do not know. Who can tell what went on in the minds of these fiends."

Could Becker have modified the elevator circuits? Probably. No one could accuse him of being short of brains. Why? "Did your father tell the authorities what you have just told me?"

"Of course, Herr McLeod, but they did not believe him. They said he tried to cover for his own inefficiency."

"Who was in charge of the investigation?"

She shrugged. "I can not remember his name. He was an SS major. Another one of them." She paused, deep in thought. "Wait a minute. I do remember his name. Kruger, Rudolph Kruger."

At that point the baby grew restless again, even under Tammy's careful handling and constant attention. After one or two cries and some fairly strenuous struggling, Tammy handed the child back to his mother. There were a few moments before Frau Loewen managed to get the child under control again. "Is there anything else you wish to know, Herr McLeod?" she asked, when she felt able to continue.

"What did your father do after he was let go from the hotel?"

"Odd jobs. Whatever he could find. It was a strange time. He worked helping people with bomb damage. At one time, we thought they might conscript him into the army. Older men than him were being conscripted at that time. After the war finished, he was out of work for a bit and then he started on the re-building program."

"How did he manage to get his old job back at the Marrianne?"

She shook her head. "It was a strange thing, such a coincidence. I was not living at home then, but my mother told me about it. My father was sitting in a beer garden enjoying a drink with one or two of his old friends, talking loudly, I expect, and discussing old times. He was like that when he had a drink. Anyway, later that evening another man tapped him on the shoulder and offered to buy him a drink for old time's sake. Well, my father did not recognise the man at first, but later found out that the man had been a sergeant in the SS and stationed at the Marrianne. My father said he had a strange tattoo on his arm, a skull wearing an SS helmet with a snake twisting through the eye sockets."

The baby started to fidget again and there was a pause while he was re-arranged. I wanted to get as much information as I could, but I realised that we would soon wear out our welcome if we stayed too long. "So this sergeant offered him his job back?" It would seem strange considering the SS had fired him.

"No, not really," she said. "He told my father that the hotel was looking for a maintenance man and he should go there and apply. Well, he did. He went there the next day and they gave him his old job back right away."

"How did the sergeant know about the job?"

"I do not know, Herr McLeod. I don't think my father ever saw the sergeant again. As I said, it was a strange coincidence."

"Yes," I said thoughtfully. The time when I believed in coincidences was passing quickly. "Your father died within a few months of starting back at the Marrianne. An unfortunate accident."

Frau Loewen clutched her child more closely to her bosom and looked away from me, as if the memories of this time were too painful to recall. "Yes," she said. "It was unfortunate. He was a proud man, proud of what he did. He should not have been taken that way."

"What way," I said quickly.

She looked back at me sharply. "An accident at his work. Why? Do you know anything you are not saying, Herr McLeod?"

"I only know what I am told of the whole affair," I said. "But it seems strange that a man who knew his job as well as your father should die in such a bizarre accident. It would seem almost foolish."

"Stranger things have happened in life," she said, getting up from her chair and lifting the baby over her shoulder. She was making it plain that it was time for us to leave. We thanked her and said our hasty goodbyes. We had taken up enough of the woman's time. "If you find out anything that you think I should know, please tell me," she said, as we were leaving.

. . . . .

I pushed my plate away.

"What's the matter, not hungry?"

"No, not really," I said in answer to Tammy's question. We were in the restaurant of a fairly good hotel in downtown Wilhelmshaven. The meal was excellent, but I was in no mood to eat. I took a sip of the wine, a good white, a Weisser Bergunder, or Pinot Blanc, as we know it in Canada. They must save the best for their own.

"You didn't have to get two rooms, you know. What's wrong with being a pair of newly weds for one night?"

So that was what Tammy thought I was worried about – sex! "I can't very well be a newly wed, can I? After all, I've been married for nearly ten years."

"Most of my clients are married men, and none of them seem to worry about it. No one has ever taken me away before without sleeping with me. Don't you find me attractive, or something?"

This was a surprising turn of events. "Tammy, I thought you were in this to help me. Of course I find you attractive. What man wouldn't? But if I were to sleep with you, it wouldn't be right."

"And you never do anything that isn't right?" she said, a measure of contempt creeping into her voice.

"I don't really think that is true, and if it were, it is not something that I would necessarily boast about. But don't you see? We are dealing with something that is beyond normal human experience. Call it madness, or whatever you like, but I have the strangest notion that, if I don't keep myself perfectly clean in all this, I will not live to see the end of it. And, if I do live through it, one day I shall want to tell my wife about it; and when that day comes, I am going to want to tell her the truth."

Tammy reached across the table and took my hand in hers. There was a tear in the corner of her eye. "I'm sorry," she said. "I don't suppose I will ever get the chance, but I would like to tell your wife how lucky she is. Where were all the men like you when I was trying to get serious with a man?"

A shudder ran up my spine at the thought of Tammy ever meeting Sara. They were so different, yet so alike. Sara, with her Scottish Presbyterian background, was also an attractive, headstrong and determined woman. "You've plenty of time," I said. "You are young and very good looking, I may add."

She smiled ironically at this. "Not so much time," she said. "Not in my business." And then her mood brightened and she went on to another tack. "If it is not about having sex with me, what is it that is worrying you? You've hardly spoken a word all evening."

"I've just been thinking about what we learned today."

"We didn't learn much. I thought it was a bit of a waste of time coming all this way, really. You weren't with the woman more than fifteen minutes."

"It was enough. She may not have told us much, but it was another piece of the puzzle, another clue, if you like. It was roughly as I expected."

"Do you know what it all means?"

"I think so. I've looked at everything we know as logically as I can, and no matter how I place the pieces, there is always only one solution."

"Well?" she said.

"I smiled. "I'm not ready to say. It would be a matter of proving it. Pity I had to give the book back."

"Would having the book help?"

"Of course. Besides the book being physical evidence, it contains a day to day account of the crime being committed. We could have scanned it further for more clues."

"I still have the translation."

"What?" I thought she had got no further than just starting on the translation. "Why didn't you tell me?"

"You didn't ask. Anyway, I was mad with you when you took the book. That was wrong. You should not have given it to him, and you knew that."

Women! "I had no choice. I explained that already."

"You can have the translation when we get back to Munich. It's only rough – my scribble. Will it help to prove your theory."

"I expect it will," I said thoughtfully. "The decision I have to make is whether I want to prove it."

That night I lay in my room next door to Tammy's room. I can't say that I slept, for I do not remember sleeping, but I suppose I must have dozed a bit. I could have walked next door at any time in the night, and it would have been all right. But still I resisted, my mind going over and over what I now knew for certain. Fundamentally, I was being asked by a dead girl to sacrifice what amounted to a small fortune in business and financial security. And for what – Justice? There was no such thing as justice; I had been around long enough to know that. Justice in this case could only rock one of the largest corporations in Germany and hurt scores of innocent people. The more I thought about it, the less I wanted to go on. I was beginning to find out new things about myself, things I did not like.

Chapter 12

I arrived at my hotel the following noontime feeling tired and hung over from the journey and the previous night's lack of sleep. Tammy and I alighted from the aircraft at Munich as if we were strangers, she near the front of the line while I waited till almost last. We passed through the airport building without as much as a glance towards one another. We were playing the game and being clever, obviously far too clever. So tired was I that I failed to notice the nod from the hotel clerk to a man sitting on a sofa in the lobby. The man rose and started towards me. Then I noticed him, tall, with a beige raincoat and a dark felt hat. Instinctively I recognised him as trouble and the muscles in my stomach knitted together.

"Mr. McLeod?"

"That's me," I said cautiously.

"You are required to accompany me to the police station." He flashed me a leather wallet that must have contained his warrant card. Strangely, I was, at first, relieved: He was no more than a policeman.

"Are you arresting me?"

"You are needed at the police station for questioning. You are required to see Inspector Drexler."

My old friend Drexler again. "Why the drama? He usually comes to see me."

The policeman spoke in pretty good English, but he had little in the way of a sense of humour. He worried me out of the hotel doorway, giving me barely enough time to leave my bag with the hotel clerk. A police car and uniformed driver waited outside, both of which I had failed to notice upon my arrival at the hotel.

After a ten-minute ride, we came to the police station. They took me to the second floor and pushed me roughly into a sparsely furnished room used only for the purpose of questioning suspects and criminals. Any courtesy previously shown to me had gone. I was angry, and after I had stewed for a couple of minutes, Drexler

109

strode into the room with another policemen at his elbow. "Where have you been?" he demanded.

"What the hell has that got to do with you? And what do you mean by dragging me down here like this?"

Ignoring my outburst, the Inspector went on, his eyes adopting the searching , enquiring quality of a customs officer at a port of entry. "When did you last see Luc Gaudreault?"

I was surprised by the question. "That's easy," I said flippantly, "You were there."

"What was he doing for you?"

"I told you already. I asked him to do some research for a book that I might write in the future. Now please believe me. What else would I want him to do for me?" I felt frustrated. Had they dragged me down here just to talk again about Luc?

"Your friend, Mr. Gaudrealt, was found early this morning in a garbage Dumpster in one of the less desirable parts of Munich. He had been tortured. All his fingers were broken. He was shot through both kneecaps, and then executed by a shot to the back of the head. As far as I know, he last worked for you. Now what is it about this book of yours that makes it so dangerous for anyone that comes in contact with you? Stop lying! Mr. McLeod. What was he really doing for you?"

Luc dead? I should never have given him the assignment. My hands shook and the colour drained from my face. Luc was dead and I had killed him as surely as if I had put the gun to his head myself.

"Well, Mr. McLeod?"

"I looked up, my eyes red and strained. "I guess I need a lawyer," I murmured.

"You don't need a lawyer unless you have anything to hide. Do you have anything to hide, Mr. McLeod? Where have you been?"

"To Willemshaven."

"Willemshaven? What for?"

"Further research for my book." I had no option but to stick to the same story, for if I told the police the truth, they would never believe me, and worse than that, I would meet the same fate as Luc.

"I see," said Drexler, slowly. "And who was it that you went to see in Williamshaven in the course of this research?"

"Helga Loewan." I had no choice but to tell him. He would have most likely found out, anyway. As it was, it gave my writing a book story more credibility.

"What information did this Helga Loewen have that could be useful to your research?"

He was sceptical, but I persisted. "There was a strange case of a hotel maintenance man at the Marianne, who screwed up badly during the war and killed a Nazi officer. He was fired and lucky not to be executed. After the war, he was rehired for the same job, but within a month or two, he died in a freak accident at the hotel. I was just trying to get some background on the story. His daughter is Helga Loewen. Luc found her for me."

This time I had got Drexler stumped. It was a totally new angle for him. Perhaps my book story was not a lie after all. "If what you say is true, this accident will be a matter of police record. Now what were your last instructions to Luc Gaudreault?"

That was a difficult one and I had to think for a moment. I was just about to reply when a uniformed police officer entered the room and spoke to Drexler in rapid German. "Aha!" exclaimed Drexler, looking down at me, "It seems you are one ahead of us, Mr. McLeod. Your lawyer is waiting in the other room. He is demanding to see you."

"My lawyer? He is?" My brain functioned slowly and it was a moment or two before the truth turned my genitals to ice. Not my lawyer – Stanholt's! How had he known so quickly?

The lawyer entered the interrogating room, a big man in his early forties with short cut, wavy blond hair and wearing a light grey suit. He looked at me and nodded as though he knew me, though I had never seen him before. "You are not obliged to say anything, Mr. McLeod, and if you take my advice, you won't." Then turning to Drexler, he said, "I have been instructed by Mannhauser Industries to act for Mr. McLeod in all legal matters while he is in Germany. Has he been arrested, or is he to be charged?"

"No, he is helping us with our enquiries," said Drexler, ever patiently.

"Then are you holding him here against his will?"

"No, of course not," snapped Drexler.

"Then we will leave," said the lawyer, looking down purposefully at me.

I stood up automatically, not wanting to leave, and not wanting to stay. He placed his arm around my shoulder and guided me from the room. We passed through a larger office with desks, or workstations, spaced seemingly haphazardly about. People turned to stare as we passed, and I felt Drexler's eyes burning into my back from the doorway of the interrogation room. The lawyer opened a door and guided me into a corridor that ran the length of the building. We entered the corridor about half way along, and at the far end, two more men were waiting for me. My nerve, such as it was, broke. I twisted around, behind the lawyer, and crashed the full weight of my body into his, slamming him into the wall, just as I had seen the hockey players board their opponents on the television. He grunted, the wind knocked out of him and then he hit the floor. Out of the corner of my eye I saw the two men start towards me at the run. I turned and ran in the opposite direction as fast as my legs could carry me, adrenaline fuelling my rush to escape. I reached the end of the corridor in seconds, turned a corner and I faced another set of stairs. I could hear the crashing of feet behind me and without thinking I threw myself onto the flight going up. I wore fairly soft loafers, deadening the sound of my feet, and they assumed I had taken the down flight. Their confusion opened my lead on them by a few moments, a few precious moments.

I reached the top of the stairs to be confronted by another corridor, the first doors of which were a ladies and men's toilet. I chose the ladies. I crashed through the door, my fingers crossed that it would be empty. My luck held. There were three cubicles, two on one side of the room and one on the other, a couple of sinks and a window over the sinks. The cubicle on its own had a notice on the door and a pool of liquid on the floor, spreading out some two to three feet around it. My German was good enough by then to get the gist of what the notice was about. "Out of Order. Do not use." I rushed over to the sinks and opened the window and looked out. A fire escape stood against the wall about eight feet over from the window, but my heart sank. I was now on the third floor, some thirty feet above the ground. I had no head for heights, and climbing out didn't seem practical. Leaving the window open, I turned to find a hiding place. The damaged cubicle! I leapt back across the room and leaned across the pool of liquid, pulling open the door. Tip toeing through, I entered the cubicle, closing and bolting the door behind me. I stood on the seat, for there was a twelve-inch gap under the door, and then I crouched down to wait.

I didn't have to wait long. In moments I heard feet running in the corridor outside, and the crashing of the door of the men's toilet. It didn't take long to search the men's and then the door of the ladies crashed open. I stopped breathing. I heard him run across to the window. He spent some time looking out, wondering if I had gone that way. I heard him turn and then I heard the slamming of the other cubicle doors. He came to mine. I could hear the rasp of his breath on the other side of the thin partition. He stood back, not wanting to ruin his smart shoes in whatever it was that pooled on the floor. He leaned across and gripped the top of the door. I saw the tension in his knuckles as he pulled, but the bolt held. He stood back beyond the pool and I could almost feel him bending down to look underneath. But from where he was, he could see nothing. My knees were hurting me from my cramped position. I was afraid to breath properly and I was scared to move. At last I heard him retreat to the door. Was he satisfied? I would never know, but suddenly he was gone.

I stayed in my cubicle for the rest of the afternoon, partly because of being too scared to move. The toilet was not heavily used, I figured about four people an hour. I stood up on the seat, looking out through the top of the cubicle, not taking my eyes from the door. As soon as I heard someone at the door, or saw it begin to open, I crouched immediately, and stayed crouched until they left. I feared being discovered by a maintenance man, or a plumber, but I would rather be charged with loitering in a women's toilet than be found dead in a dumpster. I wondered about James Bond. How would he have reacted in these circumstances? He would have cracked all their heads together and been long gone by now. But I was no high-flying secret agent, just a computer programmer, completely out of his depth.

It was getting dark outside when I lowered my stiff limbs from the toilet stool and tip toed through the mess on the floor. They knew I was still in the building; I was sure of that, and I knew them well enough by now to know that they would not give up easily. They would be watching every entrance, so there was no going out the normal way. I went swiftly over to the switch, and turned off the light. Then moving back to the window I again opened it and looked out gingerly. I seemed an awful long way from the ground, but looking down and close to the wall, I saw a concrete spandrel that ran all around the building at floor level of each floor. It jutted from the wall about two inches, maybe enough for a toe hold. If I could get my toes on the spandrel while still holding the window, I might be able to wriggle across to the fire escape. Desperate men take desperate measures. I climbed onto the sinks and worked my way backwards through the window. Clinging to the metal frame, I lowered my legs down the wall, feeling with my toes all the way. I came to a point where I could go no further with any chance of pulling myself back, and still I could feel nothing below my feet. I clung to the sharp metal frame with both hands and let my body go, my toecaps sliding down the brick wall. For one dreadful moment I imagined myself hanging from the window with nothing but thirty feet of air below me, with nothing to do but cry for help or fall, or perhaps both. My toes at last connected with the spandrel. It was better than I expected. I could stand up quite easily by pressing my toes hard against the wall and holding the window frame. With my belly pressed against the wall, I looked toward the fire escape, about eight feet away. The first two feet were easy as I had the window to hold on to. I gathered what little courage I had left to move out further, when the toilet light came on, silhouetting me against the window. Without thinking further, I slithered along the spandrel, one hand flat against the wall, the other still clutching the brick corner at the windowsill, adrenaline pushing me all the way. The window slammed shut, but thankfully she didn't look out, whoever she was. Grazing my face against the rough bricks, I turned to look once more at the fire escape. It was only about four feet away. I could almost jump for it, but I dare not. I wasn't fit and in my heart I knew that I wouldn't make it. Wishing that I had spent my life worrying a little bit more about my physical well being, I began to move along the wall, almost pressing my body into the bricks. Suddenly I was only two feet away. Moving the flat of my hand from the wall, I grabbed hold of the fire escape rail. That was all I needed. I inched my way over, placed my feet on the platform, climbed over the rail and I was safe. I stood there for what seemed an age, letting the evening breeze blow over me, while the sweat ran cold down my back. My body ached and it seemed that all my slowly healing bruises from my run-in with the subway train had been re-activated

The fire escape ended at a platform some six feet above the ground. A substantial privet hedge separated the building from the street, and as I came slowly down the steps, I could make out the felt hat of man standing on the other side. I knew instinctively that he was my enemy. Luckily, a patch of grass deadened the soft thud of my feet hitting the ground as I swung down from the platform. I stood motionless for a moment, not daring to breath, I standing on one side of the hedge and he standing on the other. The building had four sides; the streets bordered two of them. At the back of the building, an alleyway led through to a series of alleyways allowing access to the rear of a number of buildings in the block. Would they be guarding the alleyway? How many men did they have?

My choices were limited, being between the proverbial rock and a hard place. Tucking myself into the hedge and keeping a low profile, I worked my way to the back of the lot, where the alleyway was separated from the building by a six foot high chain link fence. Perhaps my luck was changing and the gods were on my side after all. An empty oil drum stood next to the fence. Keeping as quiet as I could, for though it was quite dark, I was trying to break out of a police station and I did have enemies on both sides of the law. I climbed on top of the oil drum and from this vantage, I could see up and down the alleyway.

The man in the felt hat had moved from near the fire escape to the place where the alleyway entered the street, where he could see two sides of the building, obviously, where he was supposed to be. With him standing there, I could do nothing. I decided to wait in case he moved again. I was getting use to waiting, but my legs still ached from my long stand on the toilet stall. This time I did not have long. The man must have been bored out of his skull, for he started to saunter back towards the fire escape, lighting a cigarette as he went. I stepped on top of the fence and sprang down on the other side with a thump that shook rigid the joints in my legs and thighs, but nothing broke. I darted down the alleyway away from the street, and then down another alleyway parallel to the street. I followed this till it led out to a cross street at the end of the block. I peered gingerly out but could see nothing suspicious, only the approach of a streetcar.

My luck still held and at just the right time, a woman started across a pedestrian crossing, and the streetcar had to slow. I ran out into the street and jumped on. The driver was not pleased, but I threw him a few marks and he said no more. I sat down, daring not to look out, and lowered my head into my hands as the trolley drove on passed the police station.

By then I had gained a considerable knowledge of the geography of Munich. With that and my smattering of German, I was able to get around without too much trouble. The streetcar headed in the general direction of where Tammy lived, and I did not have many choices of where to go. When we were about two or three blocks from Tammy's apartment, I jumped off the streetcar, again not waiting for it to stop and ignoring the driver's crude outburst.

For the next half-hour, I moved in a circular motion, darting in shop doorways, up alleyways and around corners, all the time keeping a close watch around me. At last I decided that if there were any one following me, it would be more than I could do to shake them off. I had to take a chance.

I rang the intercom for Tammy's apartment and the maid answered. "I wish to see Ms. Findley. This is Herr McCloud."

"Ms Findley is out and won't be home until late." Before I had a chance to speak, the intercom clicked off.

Of course, what had I been thinking of? Tammy would be working. I pressed the intercom again. Eventually the maid answered. "This is Ms. Findley's friend, Herr McCloud. I need to come in and wait for her."

"I have strict instructions not to let anyone in while Ms. Findley is out. Now please go away." Again the intercom clicked off.

I had no other choices. I pressed the intercom again. "If you don't go away, I will call the police."

"I am Ms. Findley's friend and I am in trouble. She would want me to come in."

"Your trouble is no concern of mine. I have my instructions."

I must have sounded desperate. "Please, I need to come in. *Bitti.*"

There was a pause, a long pause, and then the intercom clicked off. I was about to turn from the door and go and find a café and try and wait it out, but I knew, if I were on the street for any length of time, they would find me. The door buzzed and the lock clicked back. I pushed and the door opened. A feeling of relief rushed through me. I hadn't realised just how scared I had been.

The maid let me into the apartment and then retired to her own rooms. I desperately needed a drink and I poured myself a large neat gin and collapsed on the couch. I don't remember drinking it but in no time my glass was empty. I got up and poured myself another. I don't know if I drank that one or not, for the next thing I knew I was being shaken. I woke up to find Tammy staring down at me, and looking extremely angry.

"What the hell do you think you're doing by coming here?"

I sat up quickly, squinting at her through half closed eyes and shaking my head to clear my brain. "I didn't have anywhere else to go," I blurted. She was dressed in a black mini skirt, very short at the hem, as was the fashion of the time. Even with all my troubles, I couldn't stop my eyes roving over her long and shapely legs.

"What do you mean?" She frowned suspiciously.

"I got back to the hotel and the police were waiting for me."

The expression on her face asked all the questions.

"Luc's dead," I said.

Even under her make-up, I could see the colour drain from her cheeks. "How?"

"Shot." I said. "Murdered. Tortured. Thrown in a dumpster."

"My God, you'd better tell me about it," she said.

She listened intently while I relayed the story to her, including my adventures in the police station. "Don't blame your Olga," I said at last. "I was desperate; I had to use a lot of persuasion."

"You had no right to come here. Suppose you've been followed."

"I don't think so. I did everything I could to shake off a tail."

"You don't think so!" she said. "You don't know so! These men are professionals."

"If I had stayed on the street, I'd probably be dead by now."

"Before long we may both be dead." She looked hauntingly at the door.

"It's done now," I said. "I'm sorry, very sorry, but I didn't know what else to do." I was sorry for involving her, but I didn't remember asking to be involved, either "Well, the immediate problem is, what to do now?"

"I suppose, as you are here, I'll just have to make the best of it and pray that they still don't know about me. Though, they must know someone is helping you." She offered me a drink, seemingly resigned to the fact that I was there and not about to move very far.

"No thanks," I said. "I had two fairly stiff ones when I arrived."

"What about a hot chocolate?"

"That would be great."

She went into her bedroom and changed out of her working clothes and into a floral housecoat and then I heard her pottering in her kitchen while I remained on the couch pondering my position. Besides being very tired, I knew I was in a state of panic and not really thinking too logically. But for the life of me, I could not imagine what to do next. At last she returned with two steaming mugs. She gave one to me and then sat in the chair opposite. "Why don't you go to Drexler and make a clean breast of the whole thing?"

"Several reasons," I replied. "Firstly, I haven't got a shred of evidence."

"There is the translation," she said, putting down her mug and getting up from the chair.

"Yes, the translation."

"It makes interesting reading." She opened a drawer in a side table and took out two thin exercise books and dropped them on the couch beside me."

I picked up the first one, opened it and scanned a few pages of Tammy's neat handwriting. "This is great," I said, "But it isn't evidence. It is just a copy of what might have been."

"Your interest seems to have waned since Willemshaven."

'Since then I have been grilled in a police station and almost mauled by Stanholt's thugs. I suppose my interest has waned a bit."

"If you read through it, she tells you where a body is buried. It may still be there."

"True," I said. "And after nearly twenty years, it may not."

"Well, you won't find out unless somebody goes out there and does a bit of digging."

At last, the real reason for my hesitation came out, the reason that had held me back all along. "The truth is, Tammy, Mannhauser's owes my company a lot of money and it will be Stanholt's signature on the cheque. If he doesn't pay, we could go bankrupt."

She looked stunned. "How can you think of money at a time like this? How come you start to think about yourself now, especially when you have involved me, and goodness knows how many others? You worry about your good lifestyle and a few dollars, when Luc has just given everything."

She was right, of course, but surely altruism must have its limit. 'We were talking over a million dollars with Mannhauser. It could mean bankruptcy for my company and personal bankruptcy for me. My family would suffer. "I hear what you say, but this means a lot of money and a lot of peoples lives and jobs on the line."

"That may be so, Robert, but don't you think you have gone past that point already."

Tammy had a habit of hitting the nail right on the head. That last statement acted like a bucket of ice water in my face. She was right. There was no going back. I was running for my life.

Sitting there with my head in my hands, the word 'running' echoed through my mind. "I could simply disappear from Germany. Go back to Canada and hope it all blows over."

"Do you think you would be out of Stanholt's reach, if you went home?"

"No. He has companies and agents all over the world."

"Don't you think you had better tell me what it is that you know?"

"If I tell you, then you will know as much as me, you will be as dangerous as me. If they find out you know, they will kill you."

Tammy shuddered and looked over her shoulder at the door once more. "If they know I'm involved, my life won't be worth much, anyway."

Again she was right. We had gone past the point of no return. "If anything happens to me, go straight to Drexler and tell him everything. If there is no secret, they will have no reason to kill you." It was small comfort, but it was all I could offer.

"Understood." Tammy nodded her head. She was a brave girl. "So tell me."

I hesitated. "Here's the theory," I said. It was the first time that I actually put it into words. "That afternoon in 1945 the elevator carried four people to their deaths. The elevator controls were at the top of the building and the flooded basement was supposedly locked out by the circuits. Becker, or his accomplice, interfered with the controls and the occupants of the elevator were drowned like rats. Those people were Ilse Stanholt, her mother and her brother, and I am fairly sure the other man was Fredrik Stanholt."

"That doesn't make sense." Tammy sounded quite indignant. "How could it be Fredrik Stanholt? He's still alive."

"No," I said. "Becker is still alive. He gathered the family together in the hotel, gave them some cock and bull story, dressed the real Fredrik Stanholt in one of his uniforms and sent them to their death in the elevator shaft. Kruger identified the body as Becker. "

"But his eye. How could he have disguised the fact that he hadn't lost his eye for twenty years?"

"He didn't disguise anything. Losing an eye was the price that had to be paid. He knew what he was up against. At that time there was no possibility that Germany would win the war, with the Russians advancing rapidly from the east, and the allies advancing equally rapidly from the west. If caught he would have almost certainly been tried for war crimes and most likely hung. The loss of an eye was a small price to pay and it lent great credence to the argument that he was Fredrik Stanholt."

"What makes you so sure?"

"It's the only reasoning that holds water. Heidi Mortimer was his only living relative who could possibly identify him. He wouldn't see her and she was killed."

"It would have been difficult for him to do all this on his own."

"He has help, all right, his buddies in the SS. The problem is, that help is still with him, still helping him."

"If what you say is true and it all comes out, what will happen to the Mannhauser Corporation?"

"I don't know. Not much. It is a public company, after all."

Tammy was not satisfied. "It was built with stolen money."

"Becker stole the money. The company is sound enough. Becker owes somebody, but whom? As far as we know, Heidi Mortimer was the last living relative. And that is the point that worries me. If he is exposed, it will cause a lot of trouble for a lot of people and nobody will benefit."

117

"If he is not exposed, Becker will benefit," said Tammy.

"Yes. Becker will benefit and justice will not be done." I felt bitter. Deep down, did I really care if Becker got away with it? "Yes, Ilse Stanholt and her family died at his hands, but then, six million other Jews were murdered during the war, what was four more?"

I knew, even as I opened my mouth, that I was wrong. To those four in the elevator it had meant everything. And then I thought of Heidi Mortimer lying dead on the bed. And then I thought of Luc, his broken body found in a dumpster. And then I thought of Sara and the kids, and suppose something like that happened in Vancouver. Tammy was right. I had no choice. "You are right," I said. "But what to do?"

"Well, if you are right about Becker, and he is a war criminal, you might go to the Israeli embassy in Bonn. They are still looking for war criminals. They would certainly listen to you."

Tammy was right again. It wouldn't really matter if they believed the details of the story or not. If it piqued their interest, they may start to look into it. "Good thinking," I said. "How do I get to Bonn?"

"Rent a car in the morning. It is about five hundred kilometers. Go from here to Nuremberg and then straight across from there."

I thought along with her, concentrating totally on my escape and nothing else. I had forgotten that she was in it as deep as me. "I could leave the car in Bonn and fly home from there."

"Yes," she said. "But most probably you will still have to leave from Frankfurt."

"It doesn't matter. I'll get home and let the chips fall where they may." It was the only thing I could think of at the time: To get home and see Sara and the kids again.

Now I had a plan, it felt like a great weight had been lifted off me. At least I had a direction to go in, something to work on.

That night I stayed on Tammy's couch. I didn't seem to sleep at all, though I probably dozed a little. I was up, showered and dressed at five o'clock in the morning, and Tammy was up to see me out. My plan was to leave early, before there were many people about. I was still so naïve; I could not believe that they would be looking for me at five in the morning.

The time had come for Tammy and I to say goodbye. If I made it through to Bonn, I would say my piece to the Israelis, and then get on the first plane out of Germany. I would probably never see her again. We stood at the door of her apartment, she dressed in the same floral housecoat, and I standing in my grey suit, the only clothes I possessed at that moment. "Well, this is it," I said. "I don't know what I would have done without you."

"Oh, Robert." She looked at me sadly, shaking her head. "For a clever man, you do get yourself into an awful lot of trouble."

It seemed to me that I had heard those sentiments expressed before. Drexler! "Listen," I said. "I will phone you every four hours during the day and tell you where I am and how I am doing. If I miss one of those calls, wait two hours and then go to Drexler. Tell him everything you know."

"If you miss one of those calls, you'll probably be in a dumpster," she said.

"That's what I mean. Now I'll call you at nine o'clock, one o'clock and five o'clock. Any change to that schedule can be arranged on the phone."

"Do you think I ought to come with you?"

I thought for a moment. It would be nice to have a companion on such a long trip. "Better not," I said. "I think you would be safer here. I've put you in enough danger already." Oh, how wrong I was. Would it have made any difference if she had come with me? I will never know.

"Well, you take care."

"Of course." I smiled. "You understand what to do if you don't hear from me?"

"Yes," she said, poking her finger on my chest. "And you make sure you call."

I held out my hand. "Well, Tammy, I can't thank you enough."

She took my hand limply, her eyes searching mine, questioning. And then I thought I saw a tear. "Goodbye, Tammy."

She nodded. "Robert."

It was time to go. I took only two steps down the passageway before turning to see her, and then I was back again, in her arms, holding her tightly. "Oh. Tammy."

"Robert, Robert," she repeated. Her face pressed against mine, her tears wetting my cheeks. That was my last memory of Tammy, a memory that I will take to my grave.

It was pitch dark outside and the cool, damp spring air clung to my suit and worked its way through the grey fibres, sending shivers up and down my body. I walked briskly through the streets, making my way across Munich to the same Hertz Rent-a-car I had used before. The car rental did not open till eight o'clock. I found a small café and I went in for coffee and to wait it out.

I sat drinking my strong, black German brew and studying a road map of Germany that Tammy had given me. I would take the Autobahn number A9 to Nuremberg, about one hundred and fifty kilometres and then branch off on number A3 to Bonn, another three hundred and eighty kilometres. About five hundred and thirty kilometres in all, not far by Canadian standards, but I hadn't done much driving in Germany. It was then that I remembered the translation. My hand flew uselessly to the inside pocket of my jacket. I had left it on the couch. I had lain on it all night and it had tucked itself down behind the cushions. Without the translation, my story would sound even less plausible. I sat a moment considering how I could get back to Tammy's apartment without being seen, when a big grey Mercedes pulled up outside the café. The car had dark windows, but two men got out of the front, both dressed in dark trench coats and felt hats. My bowels froze. They were either policemen or Stanholt's men, and policemen didn't drive around in limousines.

They entered the café and while standing at the counter, they spoke in quiet tones to the proprietor. I saw him nod and then he disappeared into the back of the shop. I glanced around to see if there was anyway out, but I was trapped. They walked slowly over two my table. One of them produced an automatic pistol and pointed it squarely at me. The look in his eyes was enough to let me know that if

I should try anything, it would be his pleasure to pull the trigger. I did not know one gun from another at that time, but I have since learned that it was a Walther P38, a Second World War SS officer's side arm. He said nothing but nodded towards the door. The other one took a step to one side to allow me to pass. In the mean time, another man was out of the car and standing on the curb with the car door open.

Chapter 13

After being searched, handcuffed and pushed roughly into the back of the car, I found myself unable to move and sitting between two of Stanholt's bodyguards. I pondered my immediate future. It did not look good. As the car rushed through Munich's early morning streets, I began to protest, but it was useless. They did not speak to me. In fact, they said nothing at all during the whole journey. I was scared, really scared. I remembered the envelope that I had left with the lawyer. Maybe that would save my life. The scenery blurred past the windows, meaning nothing. I could only guess where they were taking me. Then suddenly we turned off the road, though the gates, onto a gravel driveway, and I recognised the Stanholt estate. The car followed the driveway around to the side of the house and stopped near a door, through which they hustled me into the house. We entered on a landing with a short staircase leading up, and a longer staircase leading down. It was there that I saw her, just a fleeting glimpse but I saw her never the less. One second she was staring at me from the top of the short staircase and the next second she was gone. I would have known who it was instinctively, but I recognized her from her photograph – slim, lithe and beautiful with dark curly hair. No one else had seen her; she was there only for me. It could be no one else.

As they pushed me roughly down the staircase to the basement, it gave me some comfort to know she was so near. Maybe in some way she would offer me protection, or was I grasping at straws? They pushed me into a bare, unfinished room, furnished only with one hard wooden chair. The handcuffs were removed, my jacket stripped off, and I was tied securely to the chair, my arms behind my back, my ankles to the legs. The bindings were tight and expertly done. The ropes burned my skin when I tried to move.

Two of my captors disappeared as Stanholt entered the room accompanied by Ernst Klaus. Stanholt, dressed in light grey trousers and a white shirt open at the neck, looked as if he had not been long out of bed. His face had taken on a sickly pallor, his complexion having faded to grey since I had last seen him. He looked older, much older. I wondered for a moment whether I was responsible for his sudden change in health. I hoped so. He stared down at me, seething with rage, his one good eye gleaming and accentuated by the stark black patch over the other.

Klaus was dressed in black shoes, black trousers and a white, sleeveless t-shirt. His arms and chest, as far as I could see them, were covered in a thick crop of black hair, but his head was shaven almost bald. He had a large tattoo on his arm and from where I was tied to the chair, I could not see the pattern properly, but I could only guess. Klaus was the sergeant.

"What the hell do you think you are doing treating me like this," I shouted, trying to muster all the indignation I could.

Stanholt nodded and Klaus took a step forward, swung his giant fist and hit me. My head jack-knifed back over the chair. The blow burst in my ear like an explosion, my cheek burned and I tasted blood in my mouth. Stanholt shook his head. "I gave you every chance. You only had to do your job, keep your nose clean, and make a lot of money. Why? I don't understand."

I looked down at the floor. At that point in time, I don't think I understood either. There was no point in lying to the man now. "You committed a great wrong. A terrible injustice to a young woman and her family."

"What are you thinking of, worrying about what went on so long ago? The world was crazy then. Nothing was real. And you are not even a Jew!"

That last statement lay bare his prejudice. "I suppose, had we been Jews, we wouldn't have got the contract. Is that right, Herr Becker?"

The sergeant stepped forward again and hit me, this time on the other side. For a moment my head lulled. I almost lost consciousness.

Stanholt snarled. "You're in no position to make smart comments. Confine yourself to answering questions. Now tell me, how did you get started on all of this?"

My head swam as I tried to formulate an answer. Eventually I said, "She came to me. She asked for my help."

Stanholt seized upon this. "Who asked you? What's her name?"

"Ilse Stanholt."

I didn't see it coming that time. I saw a blinding flash and my head jerked back.

"You may understand the complexities of computers, but in every other respect, you are a complete fool. What do you take me for? Do you think this is a picnic? Now try again. What made you get started and who's been helping you?"

I could not tell him anything that would implicate Tammy, and as for the rest, he would not believe me anyway. My only option was to remain silent. Klaus hit me a few more times around my face before he started on my already bruised body. In spite of the fact that I was sitting in the chair, he knew exactly how to hurt me. After a time the ongoing pain lapsed me into semi-consciousness.

Stanholt became impatient to leave the room and Klaus paused long enough for me to come back to reality. Pulling an envelope from his back pocket, Stanholt stood in front of my chair. The envelope had been opened, and I recognised the writing and my signature on the front. 'To be opened in the event of my death.'

"It took us a while to find this." He held the envelope so that there was no mistaking what it was. "This is the event of your death, Mr. McLeod. You can either make it easy, or you can die the hard way. It's your call."

With that he marched from the room leaving me in the capable hands of Sergeant Klaus.

They beat me at various times throughout the day. They would work on me for a period, and then they would leave me to recover for a period. I had no idea of the passing of time. I was conscious for most of it, as they were experts at taking me to the edge and bringing me back, but I was not coherent all the time. Once, when I was hit savagely about the body and I found that I was soaking wet. I must have urinated in my trousers without realising it.

I thought of her periodically. The sylph like figure I had seen at the top of the stairs. Surely she had not come to watch me die. Maybe she had. Maybe she was here to take me to the other side. I hurt so badly; it could not be long.

The only natural light in that room came through a small window high up near the ceiling. I had been left alone for some time, longer than usual, when I realised it was getting dark. A whole day had passed in that dreadful place and I was still alive.

The light came on suddenly, a single bulb hanging above the chair and, Stanholt, this time dressed in a business suit, entered the room once more with Klaus. "You stubborn man, Mr. McLeod. For a man who works at a desk all day, you have amazing stamina. But you will tell us everything we want to know before you die. Everybody does."

I could not be sure whether I had told them anything, or not. There were periods when I had not been lucid. I hoped and prayed that I had told them nothing about Tammy. It was dark outside, so she should have gone to Drexler by now. Perhaps they would be here soon. "You won't get away with this. They are coming for you," was all I could say.

"Who are coming for me?"

Klaus hit me hard around the head before punching me in the stomach with as much force as he could muster. I vomited. I had not eaten all day, but what ever was left in my stomach went down the front of my shirt into my lap.

That was the first time I ever heard Stanholt laugh. "Who is coming for me?" he repeated.

"The police. The police will get you in the end," I said, as soon as I could speak.

He smiled, a smile laced with evil. "I have nothing to fear from the police. I have most of them in my pocket" He didn't press the subject any further and nor did I.

"You can sweat it out here for tonight," he said. "Tomorrow you will meet some new people. Like you are an expert in your field, they are experts in theirs. They may strip you and put some wires to your body. That usually works, or they may do your nails, first the fingers and then the toes. I am told the agony is excruciating. You will beg us to kill you. Yes, Mr. McLeod, tomorrow you will die."

They left me then, switching out the light and closing the door as they went. I was alone in the room, albeit still tied securely to the chair. All I had to do was suffer the indescribable hurt and discomfort of being unable to move, and look forward to what they planned for me tomorrow.

The night passed slowly, but in spite of everything, or because of it, I did sleep periodically. I had received no food or drink from them and my tongue had swollen in my parchment-dry mouth. I could still taste and smell the vomit. There was no feeling in my arms, hands or legs. They were right. I was dead already but refusing to lie down. I thought a great deal of Sara and the children, and I longed to be with them. They would miss me, of course, but if I was found in a dumpster, like Luc, then the contract would go through and they would not suffer financially. Gilbert was basically a decent man and he would see to that.

Many times I thought of the phantom girl at the top of the stairs. She must be close by, but where was she? Why didn't she come to me now? She had got me into this. Could she not get me out? My thoughts turned to Tammy. She should have gone to the police by now. Why didn't they come? Then my thoughts turned back to Sara. Oh, my darling Sara, would I never see you again?

Suddenly I sensed her there, in the darkness. I knew she would come; she would come to help me. I woke startled. The dawn light from the window shimmered on her filmy white gown. I wanted to cry out, but a water soaked rag was stuffed in my mouth. I struggled for breath at the same time drawing the water from the rag. She stood in front of me ghost like, a vision, her hand over my mouth. Gradually she took her hand away, and placing one finger to her lips, she gestured for silence. I pushed the rag out of my mouth with my tongue.

The ropes that had tied me lay on the floor beside the chair. I had not heard or seen her untie them. Bending down, she vigorously massaged my legs and ankles. "Remember, if they catch you, you managed to untie the ropes yourself. You have never seen me. You cannot speak of me. Do you understand?"

"Ilse?" I stuttered.

"You do not know my name, nor do you want to. Now do you understand?"

"Yes," I said weakly. "But I need to talk."

"There is no time and you will never see me again. Listen carefully and do exactly as I say. Now please understand."

She sounded desperate, as if it were she and not I that were in this wretched situation. I simply nodded.

"There is a car outside with the keys in the ignition. Be silent. Go quickly, for you haven't much time."

I looked down to my all but useless legs and feet. I had not moved, because I didn't think I would be able to. I wanted help to get to my feet. Holding my arms out, I looked for her but she was gone. I had not heard her go. One second she was there, helping me, the next second she was no longer in the room. My bonds were untied and the door stood open. She had given me a chance. I had been helped from beyond the grave. At that time nothing in the world could have convinced me otherwise.

I knew I had to be quiet and I knew I had to be quick, but movement did not come easily and it was a while before I could get to my feet. My jacket lay on the floor where they had thrown it, my wallet still in the pocket. I tried a few careful but unsteady steps. The pain in my body had abated as adrenaline pumped into my veins. I staggered to the door and looked up to the landing. So many stairs, so far to go. I dragged my broken body up the stairs a few at a time, resting at each interval to catch my breath. The pain of breathing deeply racked my bruised chest, but the need for quiet was paramount. At last, somehow, I crawled onto the landing. The back door was unlocked. My guardian angel had left it waiting for me. Opening the door as carefully and quietly as I could, I moved outside into the cool morning air that caressed my bruised and bleeding body like a bath.

For a moment I stood there in the dawn light unable to grasp my situation. I had been convinced that today I would die, but now there was a chance. Only a chance, for I still had to get away. A car stood in the driveway, just as my angel had said, but more than that, there were two cars, both grey Mercedes, one behind the other about twenty feet apart. I dragged myself to the first and the keys were in the ignition. I opened the driver's door and fell in. My hand went to the key, but I hesitated. As soon as I started the engine, the noise would alert them. They would be after me in seconds in the other car. I had to disable the other Mercedes.

Reluctantly, I got out onto the driveway and shuffled painfully the twenty feet to the other vehicle. Unlike the first, this one was locked and no keys. I tried the door and was about to bend down to see if I could get under the hood, when a movement caught my eye. My luck had run out. I saw a curtain move. I froze, but only for a movement. Shouting and movement came from inside the house. Adrenaline kicked in again and I covered the distance between the two cars in no time at all. I leapt behind the steering wheel, turned the ignition and the car started instantly. I threw the lever into reverse and stamped on the gas pedal, causing the car to leap backwards, spewing gravel from under the wheels. I tried to press my body back into the seat as much as possible to absorb the shock, but in spite of this, my head, back and neck cannoned into the restraints as my car ploughed into the front of the other. The car stalled and they were coming out of the back door at the run. Desperately, I tried in vane to start the engine until I realised the automatic transmission was still in reverse. They were closing on me, but I had the sense to switch the automatic door locks and lock all the doors. I threw the lever into neutral and the car started. I banged it into drive and floored the gas again. The car leapt forward disengaging itself from the wreck behind with an almighty crunch. I hit one of the men who had foolishly got in front of me. His body slid up the hood, hitting the edge of the windscreen, before bouncing onto the grass. Another had grasped the handle to the back door as I took off. His hand became caught and he followed me involuntarily, dragging his feet for twenty meters or more before falling away. I could hear the zap of bullets smacking into the car and several stars appeared in the rear window and one of the side windows. At that moment I was glad to be surrounded by the sturdy body of the Mercedes.

A quick glance in the mirror told me of the state of the other car. The front was stove in, the lights and radiator were gone and it was highly unlikely that it was driveable. I could only wonder what the back of the car I drove looked like. I floored the gas, causing the car to slew from side to side and spit gravel in every direction, as I tore through the estate, the trees and undergrowth flashing past. I turned the last corner and the great gates stood closed at the exit baring my way. Holding my breath in case the gates had been turned off, I pressed the button on the sun visor. The gates began to open. I kept the speed up gauging the distance to the opening gates so that I would pass through when the gap was sufficient. And then the gates began to close. Someone in the house had overridden the car's remote. I pressed down hard on the pedal, for I had no option but to go through regardless. The left hand gate hit the fender and scraped all the way down the side of the car, removing the near side mirror and any projection on that side, including the door trim, but I was through. I hit the brakes as I slewed the car onto the road, and fortunately nothing was coming; I had the road to myself. The good news was that no one was following me yet. If I could just get five minutes start maybe I could get away.

My watch had been removed when I had been bound to the chair and I did not see the going of it. I looked down at the digital clock on the dashboard and the time was just before six in the morning. Traffic was light but would soon get busy. I needed to get through the town and on to the autobahn before the start of the rush. I took a quick look in the mirror and I barely recognised the face that stared back at me - two black eyes, a bruised nose, if not broken, and a fat and bleeding lip. Dried blood crusted on my chin and around my ear. Why had Tammy not gone to the police, as we agreed? Maybe she had. Maybe the police were indeed in Stanholt's pocket. My only option now was to get to Bonn as quickly as possible. I drove as fast as I could without attracting attention, for the last thing I needed was a speeding ticket. I merged onto A9 off Schenkendorfstrasse, leaving me about 150 km north to Nuremberg.

There is no speed limit on the autobahn and I floored the gas peddle and the car leapt forward. Once again I thanked the Lord for Mercedes. With any luck I should be on the outskirts of Nuremberg in about an hour. Then I would turn onto A3 and drive west for another 350 kilometres. I could be in Bonn by lunchtime. My body ached in so many places and my mind felt almost numb. That may have been why I missed the warning until it was almost too late. I had been driving on the autobahn for about twenty minutes when a light on the dashboard caught my eye, an illuminated gas pump. My eyes flashed to the fuel gauge; the needle lay hard pressed on the pin - out of gas! For a moment I could not think straight. The tank had been full when I had left Stanholt's, and then I remembered the shooting. They must have holed the gas tank.

The autobahn arrowed straight over flat, rural countryside, raised on an embankment a few metres above the surrounding fields. There was nothing on the horizon but a few farms and outbuildings. If the car stopped now, it would be seen for miles. I would be picked up in no time, either by Stanholt's men, or the police. As far as I knew, maybe the two were the same. I had to find a place to dump the car out of sight and it had to be soon. The car was running on fumes. As luck would have it, the next exit led down to a rural road, and as I turned off the main road the engine began to miss fire for lack of fuel. The exit curved around and down, and produced a steep bank on either side of the exit ramp, albeit guarded by a low, wooden fence.

I ran the car off the autobahn and stopped near the top of the exit. Placing the lever in neutral, I got out with the door open and pushed the car down the slope while holding the steering wheel. With the wheels turning, I steered the car off the exit road and towards the embankment. The car went through the fence as if it wasn't there and plunged over the embankment hitting the ground and rolling over on its roof some twenty feet below. The wreck could quite probably be seen from the rural road, but not from the autobahn. All I needed was time, time enough to get away.

I stood on the exit road, thankful that traffic was light. I had two choices. One, I could start walking. It would be a long walk and the chances were that I would be picked up within the hour. Two, I could thumb a lift. It seemed a no brainer, so I walked back towards the autobahn. I had barely got back to the grass verge at the side of the road, when I saw a car moving fast in the distance. I was ready to run forward with my thumb in the air, when what must have been instinct sounded off warning bells in my brain. As the car drew closer and materialised I saw that it was a Mercedes, almost identical to the one I had just disposed of. I threw myself flat on the grass, hardly daring to breath. The car flashed past and I could see three men in it, dressed in beige top-coats and brown felt hats. Stanholt's men! They had been that close behind me.

Time wore on and the number of vehicles on the road began to increase. I sat on the grass verge, thumbing as the various cars and trucks flashed past, my chances of getting a lift diminishing with every passing minute. I was on the brink of giving up my quest for a lift and starting to walk, when a small and rather shabby truck came into view. It was brown in colour with a flapping canvas covering at the back and going a little slower than most of the traffic, perhaps getting close to the minimum speed limit. Hope springs eternal and I raised my thumb once more. As the truck went past I saw the driver looking at me. I raised myself from the grass as I watched the truck continue down the road. I could almost feel the driver's indecision. Suddenly, about one hundred yards further on, the truck slowed and pulled over and I was on my feet and running as fast as my bruised body would carry me.

I reached the truck and the driver, looking out of the window, said something in German that I guessed to be asking where I was going.

"Nuremberg," I said.

He nodded towards the door.

I opened the door, climbed up on the step and slid into the seat beside him. "Thank you," I said in English. And then quickly, "*Danke.*"

He looked at me, I think surprised that I wasn't German.

"American?" he said, as he pulled the truck back on to the road.

"No, Canadian," I replied.

His face split into a broad grin. "Ah, I have a brother who lives in Canada," he said in passable English.

It seemed to me that almost everybody I met in Europe had, if not a relative, then at least a friend living in Canada. At times like this it could be very useful. "Where abouts," I asked, hoping he wouldn't ask me if I knew him.

"He lives just outside Winnipeg in Manitoba. Have you ever been there?"

"Indeed I have," I said. "It can be very cold."

He agreed and told me that he had visited there on a number of occasions but only in the summer. "I have heard much about the winter," he said.

"Your face," he said. "What happened?"

"I'm on my way to Bonn. I had a car accident," I lied.

"You look as if you should be in hospital. When did this happen?"

"This morning. Early. But I have urgent business in Bonn."

Thankfully, he didn't pursue the subject, and now the immediate stress had eased, I began to feel sick again. I sank back into the corner of the cab, my head resting as best I could on the hard metal. Sitting back in the corner served two purposes. One, I could rest a little, and two; I was more or less out of sight from any passing vehicles.

Suddenly, we were approaching a roadside service centre. My driver looked briefly in my direction. "How about a coffee?" He said. And then he added, before I could reply. "You look as if you need it."

My mouth was bone dry and I was in desperate need of something to drink. But, even as I was about to say no, the truck was off the highway and on the exit ramp. "Fine," I said. "That will be nice."

The service centre consisted of a large tarmac stand with gas pumps in the front and a restaurant further back and behind the restaurant a huge parking area accommodating many large trans-continental trucks. My driver headed towards the restaurant where there were a few cars parked just in front of it, one of them a large grey Mercedes. Whether it was a Stanholt car, or not, I will never know. I slammed my hand down on the metal dash. "Don't stop! Please drive on."

I startled my driver badly and he looked at me to see my battered face reflecting pure terror. He sighed and then I heard the engine noise pick up. He steered the truck away from the restaurant and towards the entry ramp. Within moments we were back on the autobahn. He looked squarely at me. "You will tell me about it, please."

I owed the man an explanation and it should be the truth. If I told him the whole truth, would he believe me? Probably not. My driver's age, I guessed, would be in his late forties. He had a dark complexion, thinning hair and a face that was glazed blue with the beginnings of a heavy beard. He was certainly old enough to have been in the forces during the war. "Were you ever in the army?" I asked.

"The Weremacht." He shrugged. "A corporal. Mainly on the Russian front, other places as well."

"Then you know of the SS?"

"Bastards!" He almost spat the word. "Politicians and policemen dressed up as soldiers."

"Would it surprise you to know that some of them are still operating today? Some of them escaped justice and are still living by the same standards and morals as they did during the war. Protecting themselves and there interest at the expense of anyone who might get in their way."

He did not seem surprised. "They did this to you?" He gestured towards my bruised face.

"Yes," I said. "Not a car accident. I'm sorry about that."

"How did you, a Canadian, get mixed up with them?"

"It is a bit of a long story."

"We have almost another hour before Nuremberg," he said.

Now we had come to the bit where I couldn't tell him the whole truth, but I decided to tell him as much as possible. I desperately needed a friend. I started more or less at the beginning, missing out the bits of my visions and nightmares, and just telling him that I learned of Becker's activities through a young woman who knew the story.

He listened intently to my story, shaking his head and nodding periodically. "They did some very bad things," was all he really said when I finished my narrative, and then he said. "Why you? Why did you get involved? You could have just ignored it."

"I don't really know. I didn't intend to get involved, at least not to this extent. It just kind of happened."

We were about fifteen kilometres south of Nuremberg, when he pulled the truck of the autobahn and onto another road. By this time I really did not know where I was. "I take you somewhere," he said. "You get cleaned up. We have good meal. No SS."

We traveled down the road for about three kilometres and we came to a small town. He seemed to know the town very well and we pulled into a side street and he parked the truck. "This way," he said. And I followed him across the street. We went into a small café, but not by the front door. Instead, we went in through the back and stayed in the kitchen. It was not long before a woman came in from the shop. "Kurt!" she exclaimed, and ran over and kissed him lightly on the cheek.

"Hanna," he said, placing his arms around her shoulders. Then he turned to me. "My sister, Hanna."

"How do you do," I said nervously. "My name is Bob McLeod."

"He is a Canadian," said my driver.

She turned to me. She wore an apron as she had been working in the café and her straggly blond hair hung down to her shoulders. She was probably younger than Kurt, but not much. On reflection, I think she must have been quite beautiful when younger, but the bloom had definitely gone from the rose. Upon seeing me properly, her hand sprang to her mouth. "Oh, Mr. McLeod, what have you done?"

There was no point in lying now. "I was beaten up," I said. I'm trying to get to Bonn."

Kurt spoke to her then in rapid German that I could not follow. She nodded and then she gestured for me to go with her. I followed her out into a small bath-

129

room where she bade me sit down on the toilet stool. She pulled a first aid box out from under the sink and began to tend my wounds. She cleaned and bathed my face. She put bits of plaster here and there and some drops in my eyes. After she had finished, I felt somewhat better, but nothing but time would heal my body. She was kind and Kurt was kind. It was then that I remembered Greta's words, and not for the last time. "You will learn the goodness of the human heart."

I joined Kurt back in the kitchen, where we had a good meal of roast pork and dumplings, washed down with lots of coffee. After the meal, all I needed was sleep, but there was no time for that. Kurt disappeared into the restaurant and came back with a newspaper under his arm. He settled back in his chair to read, while Hanna fussed about clearing the table. My German was still not good enough to enjoy a newspaper. Kurt turned straight to the sports pages. That seemed to be all he was interested in, and I found myself staring at the open front page. I must have turned white, my body rooted to the spot, for my own picture, my passport picture, stared back at me. There was also a picture of Tammy.

Hanna saw me first. "Mr. McLeod, What is it?" And then she saw the picture, too.

"Kurt!" she exclaimed.

Seeing the looks on our faces, Kurt sprang from the chair. He placed the newspaper on the table, looking hard at the picture and then at me, and then back to the picture again. "It is you," he said.

"What's happened?" I still did not know the context of the story.

Kurt read the headline. "High class call girl murdered. Canadian businessman wanted for questioning."

In that small kitchen I felt them shrink back from me, as my mind grappled with the thought that Tammy was dead. Although it had been only thirty hours, it seemed a long, harrowing time since I left Tammy's flat with little or no sleep. I stared at the floor unable to move. Involuntarily, tears welled in my eyes. I looked up at my host and hostess and shook my head. "She was my friend."

Neither of them spoke for a while, and then Kurt said, "Whether we believe you or not, things are different now. You are a wanted man."

"I killed her," I said. "I killed her as surely as if I pulled the trigger myself. It seems to me that anyone who tries to help me is killed." I looked at them and they were both staring at me, Hanna's face portraying a look of horror. "I have to tell you that you are both in great danger. The best thing for you to do is to turn me in."

Hanna spoke first. "Suppose we call the police. If you are innocent, nothing can happen to you."

"Nothing can happen to me? I wish I could believe that. The men who did this will have set me up."

"What will you do if we don't call the police?"

"I must get to Bonn as soon as possible."

Hanna looked puzzled. "Why is it so important that you get to Bonn?" .

I sighed. "It was Tammy's idea. If I can get to the Israeli Embassy, they will understand. They might be sympathetic to my story. I will never make the police understand."

My mind was torn between my own immediate future, and grieving for Tammy. In the mean time Kurt and Hanna were speaking together in rapid German. They appeared to be arguing. In the end they seemed to come to some sort of agreement and Hanna had become their spokesperson.

"Are you married, Mr. McLeod?"

I was surprised by the question. "Yes. I have a wife and two children in Vancouver."

"This woman, Tammy, she was a prostitute, was she not?"

I began to see where this conversation was leading. "Yes, I believe she was."

"Then what is a married man, like you, doing to know such a person?"

I had to think for a moment. This was difficult, as I had not told them about Illse. I looked Hanna straight in the eye. "She helped me when I needed help. I never slept with her, nor have I ever been unfaithful to my wife."

I could never have lied convincingly to Hanna, and now I thanked God that I had obeyed my instincts and did not have to.

She looked hard at me for a second and then nodded her head. Turning to her brother, they once more spoke together in rapid German. At one time I saw Kurt point to a paragraph in the newspaper, but his conversation was beyond my understanding. My mind travelled back to Tammy. She had not gone to the police because she had been killed. Why had I gone back to her after the incident in the police station. I should have steered well clear. If I had been smarter, I would have got out of Munich then. I may have got away with it. At least I would have been no worse off and Tammy would be alive. I blamed myself squarely for Tammy's death, a blame that I would carry with me for many years to come.

Hanna's voice interrupted my thoughts. "We will not call the police, Mr. McLeod. We will help you, but only as far as Nuremberg."

I breathed a sigh of relief. "Thank-you," I said. I shook my head. "But why? I am a total stranger to you, even a foreigner. You might be risking your life."

"We believe you." Hanna spoke softly, her eyes filled with compassion. "We trust you and you are in trouble."

At this Kurt spoke up. "You told me that you might as well have pulled the trigger. They didn't use a gun; they slit her throat."

I felt the colour drain from my face at Kurt's harsh and insensitive words. What had they done to her before they killed her. My mind could only speculate.

Chapter 14

Kurt dropped me at an intersection about three blocks from Nuremberg railway station. I watched the dilapidated old truck pull away from the curb as he went about to make his delivery and I realized that I knew almost nothing about him, neither his address, nor even his surname. How, if I survived the next few days, would I ever be able to thank him? I wore a dark raincoat, a flat working man's cap and a pair of dark sun glasses, all provided by Hanna - her husband's, I believe. It was the best we could come up with for a disguise, but the sunglasses were a bit out of place as the weather had turned dark, cloudy and overcast with a strong hint of rain to come. All the same, I decided, it was better to keep them on. How Hanna would explain the loss of the clothes to her husband, I could only guess.

The Mercedes must have been found by now. I had dumped it just after six in the morning and even above the noise of the passing traffic, I heard a distant clock strike four in the afternoon. If they had found the car, then they would guess I was heading for Nuremberg. It would be almost certain that they would be watching the airport, as well as the bus and railway stations. With little choice, I decide on the train and I would hope that my flimsy disguise would hold up.

The streets were becoming crowded with the start of the rush hour and I blended in with the crowd as best I could. There were a number of uniformed police-man at the entrance to the railway station watching the people as they bustled to and fro. I placed myself between two or three local commuters and hurried through the entrance, keeping my head down and feeling the man's scrutiny boring through my weak camouflage. I was over the first hurdle only to come upon the second. A man, a big man, leant against a column pretending to read a news-paper. He wore the customary brown felt hat and instinct told me he was one of Stanholt's men. And then I saw another, a second man sitting on a wooden bench, seemingly, idly watching passers by.

I arrived at the ticket kiosk and at first asked for a first class ticket to Bonn and then changed my mind. Second class would be better; I needed the crowds. Even as I paid the man for the ticket, I twisted my head to see behind me, and then a number of things happened at once. The man from the wooden bench was on his feet and walking rapidly towards me and another man, a younger man with dark hair and dressed in dark clothes, headed purposely towards me from the station entrance. I was trapped.

Without retrieving my change, I grabbed the ticket from the startled clerk and ran. I hadn't come this far to be caught now. Without glancing around, I raced down to the platform in blind panic, pushing my way through the crowd, ignoring the shouted obscenities behind me. I had to get away. I pushed onto the platform, flashing my ticket at the ticket inspector, not knowing the destination of the train standing at the platform. At the first open door. I leapt onto the train. Only then did I take the time to look back. Both Stanholt's men seemed to be arguing with a couple of well-built soldiers at the platform gate. They must have run into them and the soldiers had not taken kindly to being pushed around. Of the young man with the dark hair, I could see nothing.

I made my way down the train along the corridor walking from carriage to carriage, pretending to look for a seat. People stared at me, I suppose because of my dark glasses and bruised face. But their stares gave me no comfort, for I must have stood out from the crowd like a coloured man at a White Supremacists convention. One thing was sure. If I tried to get to Bonn by conventional methods, I would be caught. As far as I could see, my only chance was to try and thumb it again and hope for another Kurt. When I reached the last exit at the front of the train, I got off.

There were still plenty of people milling about. They must have been waiting for another train to pull in on the other side of the platform. There was only one way off the platform and that was though the gate, past Stanholt's men, and I could not go that way. Trying to make myself invisible, I moved on down the platform, looking at the big diesel engine with interest, pretending to inspect it. When I reached the front, I paused and looked behind. Nobody seemed to be taking any interest in me; maybe I was invisible. There were two tracks separating my platform from the end platform, and across those tracks a wicket gate used by the station staff to handle baggage and freight stood open. I jumped down in front of the big engine. My legs went to jelly as for a moment I experienced deja vue. All too recently I had been here before: under the wheels of a train. I hopped across the tracks, scrambled up onto the other platform and scurried through the wicket gate. I was in a large room surrounded by shelves filled with packages. Two porters were sorting through the packages as I burst in. Startled by my appearance, one of the porters shouted something at me in guttural German. I waved my ticket and told him that I would be back in a minute. There was a door to the street leading from the room, and without further argument, I raced through it.

I found myself in a side street, which was used specifically for delivering goods and freight to the station. The road led from the front of the station to a rail yard that contained many tracks loaded with various rail cars. I had escaped yet again, or had I. Looking left towards the main road, there stood, with his back to me, the young man with the dark hair. Who was he? Not Stanholt's man; I was sure of that. A plain-clothes policeman then. My only chance was through the goods yard. Turning right, I ran as fast as I could, keeping my body tucked into the station wall. I ran among the rail cars, ducking and weaving through the maze like passages. I never looked back and I did not know if my pursuer had seen me or not. After what seemed an age but was probably only a few minutes, I rested by the open door of a rail car feeling winded and all in. Looking around, I could see nothing of my pursuer. Surely I had lost him in that wild chase over the tracks. I would lie low for a while and make my escape when it was dark. I turned to clamber into the black interior of the rail car, when I felt the hard steel of a gun pressing into my back.

"Do not move."

The voice spoke in English but heavily accented. I froze, my hands still grasping the side of the doorway. His hand swiftly and expertly checked me for a weapon. He seemed satisfied. "Mr. McLeod, I believe. You've led us a merry dance."

He relaxed the pressure of the gun and I turned around slowly to face him. He was young, less than thirty, I would think, with dark complexion to match his dark hair. He wore a black leather bomber jacket, dark trousers and black running shoes. He looked extremely fit. "Who are you?" I said.

He smiled. His lips were thin and mean. "Who do you think I am?"

"The police?"

He raised his eyebrows. "Yes, Mr. Mcleod. Something like that."

His answer had me all the more puzzled, but I was convinced that he was some sort of policemen. "I didn't kill her, you know. She was my friend."

"Didn't you?" he said, his brown eyes searching mine. "Isn't that what they all say?"

"I suppose I need a lawyer."

"There will be plenty of time for lawyers later. But for the moment we have to get out of here and be quick about it. You will give me no trouble or you will be shot."

He placed his arm around my waist, the gun pressing into my side yet concealed by my own raincoat. "Move with me and be careful. I would hate the gun to go off. There would be so much paper work if that happens."

We walked back through the rail cars to the side street and stopped at the edge of the road. He waved his arm at someone or something I couldn't see. Within moments a small black Citreon skidded to a halt in front of us.

"Get in," he said, opening the back door. I did as I was told and he got in beside me. After all my efforts, I was caught, but by who, I did not know.

.   .   .   .   .

This car was very different from the car in which I had last been taken for a ride. I was squeezed in the back along with my captor, with barely enough room for my knees. There were four in the car, including the two of us in the back seat. The driver was another young man, tall and slim, by the look of him, dressed in a dark raincoat. The occupant of the front passenger seat was a woman, though I had not seen her face. She wore a beige coat with a headscarf that covered most of her head.

I felt more dejected than afraid. I was caught. I was sure my captors were not Stanholts people; therefore, my life was probably not in immediate danger. I would have to find a good lawyer and maybe I would have to stand trial. What sort of evidence had Stanholt rigged against me? Would the truth come out? I could prove almost nothing of what I knew.

Suddenly the car slewed hard around the corner to a cacophony of screaming tires.

"What's the hurry?" I gasped, the wind momentarily knocked from me.

My captor looked towards me, a mild grin on his lips as if he was enjoying all of this; he nodded with his head out of the back window. I twisted round in the tight confines of the back seat. The grey Mercedes was so close; I could clearly see the fierce look of total concentration on the driver's face. Worse than that, the man sitting next to him held a gun out of the window, and even with my limited knowledge of the subject, I recognized it as an Uzi. And then the back window exploded in front of me.

I hunched down in the seat and tried clear my mind of all thoughts. I knew that if I thought about anything at all, I would panic. The car weaved from side to side as more bullets thudded into the back. If I had not been crammed in so tightly, I would have been thrown all over the place. We rushed through a red light and with a bone-shaking jar, struck another car. Dropping into a lower gear, our driver sped away, but not before I heard the crash as the Mercedes hit the same car. Involuntarily, I took a quick look over the seat out of what used to be the back window to see the Mercedes rushing towards us, and a battered Volkswagen sitting on the sidewalk, steam coming from the radiator. Another burst of gunfire and then I knew without doubt he was aiming at me.

I had no idea where we were, for I knew nothing of Nuremburg. We raced through narrow back streets, far too narrow for the kind of speed we were going. The powerful Mercedes pulled out to pass us, when our driver took a sudden right. We only just made it around and I am sure the near side wheels left the ground. Glancing back, I saw the Mercedes following us, two wheels well off the ground, bouncing over the curb. I prayed silently that he would roll, but somehow the driver bought the car back under control and he roared down after us again.

Before long the Mercedes caught up with us again and pulled out to pass. I saw a third man in the back seat; he also had an Uzi. He waited until the Mercedes would be along side and then he was going to let me have it. I looked at the flimsy door of the Citroen. How many bullets would that stop? About a hundred metres further along, the street split into a Y, one fork leading to the left the other fork leading to the right. The Mercedes pulled along side of us. Any moment he would open fire. The engine in the Citroen screamed. Our driver aligned the car to take the right hand fork, forcing the Mercedes further to the right. Bullets started to pour into the side of the car. I felt a sharp pain as something nicked my leg. At what seemed like the last moment, our driver flung the car to the left, and after bouncing over the corner of a curb, we careered on down the left fork. My first thought was that we had got away. We would be safe, at least temporarily. Glancing back once more, I saw the Mercedes following us around. Already on two wheels, he hit the curb hard and stuck a hydrant, sheering it off at the base, and then he rolled, the car spinning around on its side, water spraying everywhere from a huge fountain in the street. It crossed my mind that this was the third of Stanholt's cars to be ruined that day; a strange thought to have at that particular time.

The car settled down to what seemed to be a slow, but normal speed. We cut down various streets, constantly turning, twisting and doubling back, to avoid being found again. I could only imagine what the Citroen looked like from the outside. Sweat ran down my face, in spite of the gale being drawn into the car from the open back. I looked at my captor. He seemed un-phased by the whole affair; in fact, he was grinning. My leg hurt and I looked down to see my trousers torn and soaked in blood. I touched the wound gingerly and found that a bullet had caught my leg and had passed through. Fortunately it must have been well near spent after coming through the car door.

My thoughts returned to my immediate worries. Where were they taking me? If they were the police, then, after the recent car chase, they would know the sort of people we were dealing with. But they were not the police, so who where they?

Having been in Germany for some time, I was used to the sound of the language and after a while, I shut it from my mind. It was the case as I sat in the back of the car while the couple in the front conversed together. I heard them speaking and I ignored the sound, while I pondered my own fate. After a while the sound of their voices began to filter through. They were not speaking German. I listened intently. I recognized the language, if not the words.

"Hebrew!"

The girl in the front seat spun around. "You speak Hebrew?"

I hadn't realized I had spoken aloud, but at that moment in time, my world revolved over and over. My hand gripped the door to make sure it was real. Was I in a dream, or worse, was I dead? The face of the girl beneath the scarf was the face of my guardian angel. "Ilse," I said.

She frowned, glanced toward my captor and said, "Why does he keep calling me Ilse?"

"Her name is not Ilse," he turned to me. "And you will never know her name."

"She saved my life."

He raised his eyebrows. "More than once."

Again I was completely out of my depth. I began to wonder if I knew anything at all. The girl in the front seat was obviously not a phantom, and she had just as obviously saved my life in the house, but she looked so like the girl in the photograph. I had to accept that, for there was nothing else I could do about it, so I said; "She will always be Ilse to me."

He nodded. "So be it."

Now it was clear to me that these people could only be only from one organization. "I know who you are now. It all makes sense."

"Then you had better keep it to yourself. You should have discovered by now, some things are better not to know."

"I was on my way to see you. I was trying to get to you." `

"We know."

"How could you know?"

"It is our business to know."

I was with the MOSAD, the Israeli Intelligence Service; there could be no doubt about it. Now I knew, in spite of everything, it was going to be all right. I think that is the first time I began to think there was a good chance that I would get out of this alive. I began to look forward to the future. I would see my family again.

Maybe it was the after effects of what I had just been through, but the worry of my situation seemed to leave me. I spent the rest of the journey in the car in a kind of euphoria caused by a sense of overwhelming relief. So much so that for a while I took no interest in where they were taking me. We had come out of the city and were travelling once more on the Autobahn. I had assumed they were taking me to Bonn, when I realized that we were travelling south. The last place I wanted to go was Munich. My euphoria disappeared in a flash and once more I was afraid.

"Where are you taking me?"

My captor, who had been in conversation with the two in front, turned to me, a look of irritation on his face. "You will find out in good time."

"Why are you taking me back to Munich?"

"Munich?" he said. And then he turned to the others and said something in Hebrew and they all laughed.

I could do nothing but sit back in the seat and worry. They were young people, strong and intelligent. Even though I was only thirty-seven, beside them, I was an old man.

The car sped along the autobahn at high speed, a speed I would not have believed it capable. Above the wind noise coming through the opening behind me, I heard the sound of a police siren. It could have been for anything, but somehow I knew it was for us. We were not home yet. The next exit came rushing up and our driver took the ramp with no slackening of speed. Even as the car tore down the side road, all heads except the driver were looking out of the non-existent back window. The police siren continued on the Autobahn towards Munich.

"Close," said my captor. It was the first time he had opened a conversation with me.

"So where are you taking me?" I said. "Surely it won't hurt if I know."

"Nearly there," he said.

We were nearly there. The car suddenly slewed rapidly and turned off the road and into what looked like an aero club, a small field with a runway. There were a number of small aeroplanes tied down near a club house, a few gliders parked nearby, and at the end of the runway, a twin engined machine with its propellers turning, as if waiting to take off, but the door was open. The car continued across the bumpy grass towards the plane. We stopped near the open door, and my captor leapt out, urging me to follow him and be quick about it. I did as I was told and slid across the seat and limped out. My captor slammed the car door, and the car roared away across the field again, back towards the exit. I looked towards the car momentarily wistfully as my guardian angel left me and I would probably never see her again.

With no time for thinking such thoughts, my captor hustled me up the two steps into the body of the plane. A woman standing at the entrance slammed the door shut as soon as we were inside.

"Strap yourself in," said my captor, already clipping his belt in his lap

As soon as the door shut the engines roared, the plane turned fully onto the runway, and we were racing over the rough grass. Suddenly the wheels left the ground and I looked out of the window to see the field falling away beneath us. Then I saw the flashing blue lights. Two police cars, one behind the other, entered the field through the same entrance we had used just moments ago. It had been that close.

"We shall be in Bonn in less than an hour."

He sat facing me and I looked up at him. "Thank you," I said. Without him, I would never have left Nuremberg alive.

The lady hostess brought us both a coffee. I grabbed mine like a man who had spent a week in the desert without water. The last time I had any sustenance at all was with Kurt and Hanna at lunch. It was now well into evening. Not a long time, really, but it seemed like a lifetime.

Within minutes she was back with a first aid kit. She bade me put my leg up on the seat and she went to work cleaning the wound. It struck me as she worked that cleaning a gunshot wound was an everyday occurrence for her. I could not help but wonder who these people were and why they did what they did. She cleaned my wound, applied some antiseptic cream, and bound it with a bandage. Tears began to run down my cheek. I don't know why I cried, or for who; it had just been a very long couple of days.

Chapter 15

"So, Gentlemen," I said, "That's about everything. Your people flew me to Bonn and here I am."

Levin continued to look at me with those hard blue eyes of his. It was some moments before he spoke. "Why?"

"What do you mean, why?" I said.

"Why did you get involved? You are a businessman. Your business is installing software and making money. Why risk all that for something that has nothing to do with you. And you, not even a Jew."

He had made a deliberate attempt to provoke me, but I was too tired to see it. All I felt was a blind fury at his tone and his questions.. "Of course it has something to do with me," I shouted. "The man is an evil murderer and he has to be brought to justice." Perhaps now, in my anger, I had answered the question that had been plaguing me for so long. "I have to live with myself and I have to live with my fellow man. Maybe I am not such a good businessman. Maybe, I don't want to be. But you ask same questions as Stanholt. How different are you from him?"

Levin smiled and raised his hand. "Calm down, Mr. McLeod. Take it easy. We need to know these things."

The man in the rumpled navy blue suit rose slowly from his chair in the corner of the room and handed Levin a small piece of paper. He then walked over to the door, held the doorknob but then paused, waiting for Levin to ask me another question. Levin read from the paper. "What do you think your chances are of completing your work with Mannhauser now, and further, getting paid for what you have already done?"

My outburst had subsided. "No chance," I said without hesitation. I think I knew this even before my discussion with Tammy in her flat. "I expect they have closed us down already."

"You must have put a lot of money into this. Will you survive financially?"

"Probably not personally, but our product is good. Someone else will pick it up and run with it."

"Someone who will not throw it away, like you did?"

Levin was baiting me. Now I was sure of it. I did not dignify his question with an answer. I was tired and it was getting late. I heard the door close and I looked up to find the man in the blue suit had left the room.

"Did you know that Becker is dead?"

"Becker? Dead?" What is he talking about? "How? When? What do you mean?"

"Becker died of a massive heart attack this morning, just after five am."

"He couldn't have done. That was about the time I left his house."

"Exactly," said Levin.

This took a bit of thinking about. If Stanholt were dead, that could make quite a difference to me. In spite of this, It seemed as if he had escaped and I said, "Then he has escaped justice after all,"

Levin raised his eyebrows before he spoke. "In the strictest sense of the word he has. He will never have to face a court of law, but he is dead, never the less."

I was struck by an overwhelming sadness, not for Becker, but for all those who had died because of him. "Then it has all been for nothing."

"Not really." Levin shook his head. "We have this." From the top drawer of his desk, he pulled a red covered book: Ilse's diary, as well as the two exercise books containing Tammy's rough translation.

"How on earth did you get those?" I couldn't believe my eyes.

"Your friend sent the translations to us."

"Tammy? But she couldn't have. She was murdered."

Levin put his hand to his forehead and frowned in concentration. "We have pieced it together like this," he said. "Ms. Findlay must have found the books soon after you left her flat yesterday morning."

Was it only yesterday morning? It seemed like weeks ago.

"She realized that the books would add credibility to your story so she parcelled them together and had her maid take them into town to courier them to us. When the maid returned to the flat, she discovered her employer's body."

"So as soon as the maid left with the books, Stanholt's men came. They must have been waiting outside."

"We think that likely."

"And I suppose, that is how you people knew about me, but Tammy didn't have the original diary; Stanholt did."

"Yes," said Levin. "We have been suspicious of that organization for some time. We did not know all of it, by a long way." He pointed to the books on his desk. "As you know, our operative penetrated Stanholt's organization. She sent us the original diary this morning. Apparently, she found it in Stanholt's safe."

"Your operative? My guardian angel, you mean. And penetrated, that's a funny word for it. She looked exactly like her." I pointed at the book on his desk.

"I guess that's why she was successful. Stanholt likes girls that look like that. Everybody has a weakness."

I shook my head. "In Heaven's name, what would make a young woman, like her, do such a job?"

"As a young child, she survived Auschwitz, but all her family were killed. She has her reasons, Mr. McLeod."

I suddenly felt ashamed of the thoughts that had crossed my mind and I realized, once more, that I knew almost nothing. I shook my head. "I am so sorry,' I said.

"Now that you know, Becker is dead, I will ask you again: What are your chances in completing the Mannhauser job?"

"I don't know. Better," I said. "But Kruger is still there, and he is as much a part of it as Stanholt."

Levin looked at his watch. "Suppose I said that Kruger is well on his way to Tel Aviv by now."

I laughed impulsively. "What would he want to go to Tel Aviv for?"

It was Levin's turn to smile. "I don't think he did want to go, really. We popped him and Ernst Klaus into the diplomatic bag and shipped them out this afternoon. They will stand trial for Crimes Against Humanity. A trial is more than they gave their victims."

"Wonderful," was all that I could think of to say.

"And now," said Levin, "What about you?"

"Me? I don't know. I am desperately tired. I'm filthy. I need a bath and a good night's sleep and then, I suppose, I will have to face the police."

"As far as we know, the police have no real evidence against you. They want you for questioning, sure enough, but other than that, they have nothing, certainly nothing of which to extradite you with."

"Extradite?"

"I believe that it would be in our interest that you do not talk to the police. We do not want them to get that much of an inkling into the extent of our operations in Germany. Therefore, I propose that we rob you of your bath and your night's sleep and pop you, too, into the diplomatic bag and ship you to Tel Aviv."

"Tel Aviv? You aren't going to make me stand trial, are you?"

Levin laughed at this, and I suppose, on reflection, it was a silly thing to say, but I was desperately tired at the time and I was having trouble thinking straight.

"Of course not," said Levin. "You will be taken straight from the airport to a hotel in downtown Tel Aviv. There you will be left in peace until you are rested and reasonably fit again. Then you may make your way home to Vancouver by any route that you may choose. However, I should avoid changing planes at Frankfurt, if I were you."

"So be it," I said. "Thank you."

Levin looked at me for a long moment with those powerful blue eyes, and then he said, "No, Mr. McLeod. Thank you."

He arose from the desk and it was my cue to leave. "There is a plane at midnight, in an hour and a half, and there is a limousine downstairs waiting to take you to the airport. You have nothing more to worry about."

He opened the door to let me out of his office. "I hope one day you will tell us how you really found the book. I should be most interested. Ghosts in the elevator, that's a good one!"

Epilogue

Colonel Levin was as good as his word. They almost carried me into the hotel room in Tel Aviv, for I was completely exhausted. I undressed and got into bed and that was the last I knew of anything for the next ten hours. When I awoke, late afternoon of the following day, my grey suit had gone and new clothes were laid out for me. I got out of bed, showered and dressed. The clothes were a perfect fit. Upon the dresser lay my wallet and a new passport. I picked up the passport and it looked exactly like the one I had left in the safe at the Marianne. There were no stamps in it, except for an official entry stamp into Israel. I picked up the wallet and everything was as I had left it with the addition of a raft of Shekels, Israeli currency. I counted them quickly to find them enough to see me through my stay in Israel. I was hungry, very hungry, but my next task was to telephone Sara. Oh, how was I ever going to explain all this to her?

After an hour on the phone with Sara, I phoned Gilbert. It seemed that ripples had gone through Mannhauser with the news of Stanholt's death and of Kruger's disappearance, but it was a public company and neither of these two events should affect our relationship with them. It seemed that, in spite of everything, we would not lose by my actions. Gilbert was more than a little curious as to what I was doing in Tel Aviv, but I did not enlighten him. He came to the conclusion that I had been working too hard and probably had some sort of breakdown.

There were a number of ways I could fly home, but there was something else I had to do. I chose to fly to Toronto via Amsterdam, and then I would fly to Vancouver from there. As soon as I arrived in Toronto, I boarded a flight for Cleveland, Ohio. Like before, I rented a car from Cleveland airport and drove out to Barford. Nothing had changed, of course, except now the snow had gone and the countryside had turned green and warm. It really had not been long since I was there before, although it seemed a long time. I drove past the hairdressers and stopped outside a florist shop and picked up a dozen yellow roses. I found the cemetery without too much problem, but it took me quite a while to find the grave. The stone was fairly new, but already the words 'Albert Mortimer' had weathered. Underneath had been added '& his beloved wife Heidi' and this looked very recent. It was a simple grave and I knelt down and placed the roses in the centre. "There," I said aloud. "I did my best. I am so sorry it could not have been more."

At that very moment the wind sprang up and some trees and bushes nearby swayed as the draught passed through, rustling the summer leaves and making a sound remarkably like the whispering of a female voice. She seemed to say, "*Danke.*"

No, it could not be. My imagination was getting the better of me. I stood up and turned towards the cemetery gate. I needed to get home to Sara and the kids, and get on with the rest of my life.

The End.